Hawthorn

PRIDEFUL MAGICK COLLECTION
BOOK FOUR

TENTH ANNIVERSARY EDITION

HOLLOW RYAN

This is a work of fiction. The characters, incidents, and dialogues are products of the author's imagination and are not to be construed as real. Any resemblance to actual events or persons, living or dead, is entirely coincidental.

Hawthorn

Second Edition

Copyright © 2017 by Hollow Ryan

The moral right of the author has been asserted.

Published by Hollow Ryan

Ebook ISBN: 978-1-968729-10-3
Trade Paperback ISBN: 978-1-968729-09-7
Hardcover ISBN: 978-1-968729-11-0

Cover elements courtesy of:
Vintage Damask by DarkMoon_Art via Pixabay.com
Realistic Smoke Fog by Hakan Kaçar via Vecteezy.com
Hawthorn by _Alicja_ via Pixabay.com

Cover Design by Christiana Nehmsmann
Interior Design by Christiana Nehmsmann

Designer's Note: of course the horny book is the longest one

Books By Hollow Ryan

Prideful Magick Collection

Ivy

Oleander

Valerian

Hawthorn

Avens

Demon Kin

Demon Kin: The Queen

Demon Kin: The Lovers

TABLE OF CONTENTS

For Aurora
Not all happy endings are what we expect them to be, but they are what we make them.

Chapter One

FIRST IMPRESSIONS

Fixing things and starting over had become second nature. Even so, I wasn't sure I'd learned enough to fix this.

"This is why I wasn't allowed to see him before closing," I remarked, my nose wrinkling at the ugly green house.

My mom grinned at me in that way that declared she was entirely unrepentant about her decision. I almost couldn't keep a straight face, knowing she was where I got that from.

"He'll take us all year and drain all of our reserves, you know."

"We know," she answered, unperturbed. "But he'll be grand when he's finished."

I fought the smile as best I could, shaking my

head at her optimism. Releasing a sigh, I said, "The first thing I'm going to need is a privacy fence for that backyard."

"You can see it already, can't you?"

Looking back at the house, my eyes grazed over the 'before' image and were rewarded with an 'after' a second later. Nodding to my mom, I said, "Yeah, I can see it."

"Then you know it'll all work out."

"It always does."

It was our new family motto. An exchange that rose from the ashes of my sixteenth year and the five months I spent in a coma. Whenever things seemed difficult or we stretched ourselves too thin, all three of us thought back to our darkest days and knew that we could overcome anything after having lived through them.

"Want to see the inside?" Mom asked, breaking into my reverie.

"Do I have to?"

"Unless you want to spend the night on the curb."

My eyes lowered to the sidewalk before shooting back to the house. Twisting my features into a considering expression, I pretended to debate my choices. Mom chuckled before grabbing hold of my wrist to pull me up the walk. As soon as she realized what she was doing, she dropped my hand like she'd been burned. Again.

Hurt shot through me and I worked to keep it off of my face. Her reaction was to be expected. A mere two years ago, I'd made sure the threat held. It would take her more time than that to fall back into old habits.

Not that we would ever get back to what we were. The time of my perfect and easy relationship with my parents was long gone. Buried beneath a sea of bodies, omissions, and betrayals. It was impossible for the three of us to reconcile the old wounds. But we could move past them.

Forcing a smile and chipper tone, I linked my arm through my mother's and gestured toward the crumbling heap before us. "Come on, Mom. Show me the rest of this palace that you and Dad stole."

The itch to transform the drab clay color into a burnt orange was almost overwhelming as I stared at the four walls of my attic bedroom. It didn't help that I could see clearly the growing brown spot that indicated where the roof had been leaking. If I used just a little bit of magick–

I shut the thought off right then and there. No more magick. At least for a while. When I could put the mundane back in balance with the magick, then I could reopen that door. Until then, it was normal living for me.

At least it was getting easier. When I'd first cut off my magick, it had been almost impossible to ignore the pulsing inside of me that begged to be used. After a year, however, the barest flutter drifted over my skin as the magick acknowledged my desire, but respected my restraint.

With a sigh, I turned to my desk and added 'check for mold' to my to-do list. Then I plugged in the alarm clock and set the time on it before climbing into bed. One more first night in a new house. Then would come my first day in a new town. Following that was my first day in a new school. After experiencing the same set of firsts several times before this, I was no longer emotional about them.

Except this time. Because this time was the last set of firsts I would have. This would be the last time I lived under my parents' roof. The last new thing we shared. After this, I was going back to everything that was familiar and haunting.

For the first time, the rest of my life didn't seem so far away.

My expectations for Grant didn't exist. As with my past schools, I never felt the need to integrate into the small societies I passed through. Being in a town for only a few months at a time, it meant I was able to go unnoticed. I enjoyed every scrap of anonymity that was available to me. Especially since I knew it would not last much longer.

The first day of school brought with it the usual excitement, and I was engulfed in that chaos as soon as I walked through the door. At the same time, it was as if the building radiated a certain expectation, and even though I'd gone mundane, I could have sworn there was magick embedded in its bricks.

I was still in a kind of confused daze while consulting the papers sent to my house after I was registered. One page contained my schedule, another a map, and a third my locker information. None of which proved to be much help.

When I felt the girl approaching, I had no idea she meant to actually engage with me until she said, "No offense, but you look like a lost puppy. Let me help you."

Looking up at her, I was surprised by how pretty her brown eyes were. "Um…"

"Can I see?" she asked, ignoring my discomfort. Knowing it couldn't hurt, I passed her the paper with my locker information on it. She raised her eyes to mine again and smiled. "Mine's not too far off. I'll show you."

She didn't even wait for a response, instead turning and melting into the crowd. I had no choice but to roll my eyes and follow after her. Thankfully, we didn't have far to go from the front door as she led me down a few hallways. We entered a corridor with a wall of windows on the left, looking out at the courtyard, with lockers covering the wall on the right. At once, the girl stopped and spun around to face me, sending her skirt flaring out around her.

"Here we are," she announced with a wide smile.

"Thanks…"

"Oh, yeah, name, right," she laughed. "I'm Delaire, but you can call me Del."

I grinned. "Alexandria. I prefer Alex." For strangers, at least.

"It's nice to meet you, Alex. And sorry about the 'lost puppy' comment. You just..."

"Looked like a lost puppy. I got it," I said with a grin. "It's okay. I'm kind of used to it at this point."

One eyebrow rose and I had to admire how artful her expression was. "Move around a lot?" she asked, leaning against the lockers as I entered the combination on mine.

"You could say that. Three houses in the past year, not counting my dad's military moves prior to then."

"Oh? That sounds intriguing."

More than she knew, though I wasn't about to tell her that. Instead, I emptied my bag of the binders I'd set up for my classes and stacked them on the too-small shelf at the top of the locker. Then I shrugged out of my jacket and hung it up inside.

When I returned my attention to Delaire, her teak eyes were running up my body in silent contemplation. The moment she realized I'd noticed, she grinned and said, "You don't care much for first impressions, do you?"

I shrugged. "They don't matter much if you don't intend to impress anyone."

She bowed her head in acknowledgement. "Fair enough. I still find myself doing the whole dress-up bit for my first day, though. Makes me feel powerful and alluring." I laughed as she ended the description with a dramatic pose.

"I think I'm going more for the 'forgettable and unnoticed' vibe."

An eyebrow arched upward. "I don't think that's going to work."

Before I could ask, the doors at the end of the corridor burst open. A magick breeze pushed through the corridor, almost physically moving students out of the way. I raised my eyebrows at the dramatic display before my eyes narrowed in on four women standing on the other side of the threshold.

They strode into the school, each abreast of another. The first was a statuesque beauty with flashing green eyes and long, brown hair. Beside her was a golden blonde whose expression radiated a haughty disdain for others. A redhead followed them, though there was enough brown in her hair to warrant the label of 'auburn.' At last, however, entered a true marvel. White hair and icy blue eyes were the defining markers of the youngest girl, which somehow seemed to negate the fact that she was almost as pretty as the three that came before.

If it were only that they were beautiful and dramatic, I might not have taken notice of them. But that wasn't all. With each step that they took, a pulse of magick reached me. Fresh and thriving from the eldest. Scorching and intense. Contemplative and aloof. Cold and isolated. Together, they were a force to be reckoned with, and I had to believe it was a rare thing for them to be separated.

"We call them the Season Sisters."

As if Delaire's words were a trigger, their eyes latched onto me. At once, their magick surged forward, seeking what they knew I kept buried. Something that was eager to respond.

I could feel it pulsing inside of me. A beacon that was bursting through my ribcage with each rapid beat of my heart. The magick fluttered through my veins, awakening every cell of my body as it tried to combat the intrusion. Their intent was to identify other witches, and my magick was eager to exploit just how useful a vessel I was.

As casually as I could manage, I raised my hand to the locket around my neck. Habit forced the magick out of me and poured it into the gears that caused the little clock to keep time. It was something I'd done so often in the past year that I almost couldn't feel what Morgan or her eldest daughter, Freyja, had added to it in the past.

Their magick spiked with the depletion of mine and their curiosity permeated the hallway. Four sets of eyes were locked on me as they each seemed to debate whether or not introducing themselves was something they wished to endure. In the end, the eldest sister squared her shoulders and turned away.

Another pulse of magick shot out from the second girl and I caught my breath as my magick once more leapt to the surface. This time, I let it linger. Just long enough to help me take stock of my surroundings. My mouth fell open.

"There are over thirty witches in this school,"

I murmured. Then I let my eyes meet Delaire's. "Why so many?"

She gave me an almost weary smile as she announced, "Because you are in the heart of Crone's Crescent territory. And you just met their princess."

Chapter Two

LAWLESS

Delaire seemed surprised when my first and immediate reaction wasn't to bombard her with questions. In truth, I was trying to keep a handle on my curiosity. There were so many thoughts flying through my head, I couldn't fathom which question to ask first. With so many witches in such close proximity, I wanted to know everything I could about them. Not that we had time to satisfy my curiosity; the bell rang a split second after Del named the Season Sisters as Spring, Summer, Autumn, and Winter Solas.

Walking into my history classroom, I was surprised to find that I was the first one there. For which I was grateful, since it meant that I could take up my customary seat in the back corner, farthest from the door. Ever since my stint in a juvenile detention center, I was more than a little paranoid. The more I could avoid having anyone at my back, the better.

Soon after, the second bell rang and a flood of people were ushered into the classroom by a short woman with frizzy brown hair piled atop her head. Light brown eyes were magnified in her round face by thick glasses that perched on a tiny nose. With a commanding look over her students, she then turned from us to begin writing on the board.

Ms. Dixon was her name, and her first two rules of the class consisted of being on time and no talking. Both of which were violated within the first two minutes.

I'd just begun to wonder why the three seats around me remained empty when the door flew wide and four people strode into the classroom. Summer was the only one I recognized, and her eyes widened in the same second that she registered me. For a second, she wouldn't move. Then the male witch holding her hand began to pull her toward the empty seats. Behind them, another male glanced my way and headed for the only other empty seat in the class. He wasn't going to compete with the man that followed after.

From the moment he entered, I could feel it. A rush of power pushed ahead of him into the room, announcing his presence in a way that belied the necessity of an introduction. It was a forceful, churning kind of energy. A blast of heat hit me, identifying him as a fire element almost without equal.

The moment my eyes met his, the air deadened. An electrical charge gathered near me, pushing back at his flames with sparks of lightning. Goosebumps abounded along my skin as the hair on the back of my neck stood on end. Unbidden magick sang through my blood, and was answered by something equally as lawless inside of him.

Our eyes remained locked, keeping us prisoner for several endless, agonizing, breathless seconds. I almost gasped aloud when I felt his fire dive into me. It raced through my veins, turning the blood into magma. Radiating out from my heart, I felt it travel every inch of my body before it surged into my brain. Pure terror overwhelmed me. My eyes snapped shut and I wrenched my face away toward the windows. All the while my breath came in ragged, shallow gasps.

My breath hitched when I realized that I could still feel him. Every breath. Every step. Even the trail of fire and lightning battling over my skin as his gaze traveled over me.

The minute he sat down in the seat beside me, I forced myself to turn my face to the front and take a deep breath. Pressing the locket into my chest, it was more difficult than I expected to coax the magick into the heirloom. With his magick still drifting through the room like a thick billow of smoke, my magick was doing all it could to prove that it was dominant. My will was stronger, however, and it soon flowed into the locket as I let out the breath I was holding.

His eyes were still trained on the side of my face when I felt his magick begin to shape and hone itself. My eyes snapped open as my body became more attuned to the invisible threads. Like a serpent, it slithered toward the front of the classroom, layering itself around our teacher. The second the tendrils of his magick delved into her body, my mouth dropped.

I kept my eyes locked on Ms. Dixon as his

magick worked through her mind. Normally, when it came to coercion, it was easiest to slide an idea or insinuation into a person's active thoughts and then leave them to react. What he was doing was a bit more complex than that. He was performing a rapid manipulation that formed actual thoughts and ideas while making it seem like it originated without outside influence.

I was appalled. Appalled and slightly impressed. And even more suspicious.

Before I could react, Ms. Dixon turned away from the class and went to her desk. Without looking at us, she announced, "I will be taking attendance now, and will be assigning seats as I do so. You all better like where you're sitting now, because that's your home for the rest of the semester."

My lips parted in true and utter amazement. He'd performed a convoluted manipulation spell ... so that our seats would be assigned. The logic behind that was astounding. Then his eyes raised to the corners of mine, seeking a connection, and I knew that this was why. For the rest of the semester, I would be forced to sit beside him and endure the unwanted attention. Unless I did something about it. It was both a challenge and an insurance policy.

Ms. Dixon then proceeded to rattle off our names, marking them on her chart as each student responded. My teeth gritted together as she read my full name aloud and I was forced to respond to it. Once she called off Summer Solas, her eyes raised one last time and landed on the man beside me.

"And Grey Walker. It appears we have everyone. Now, let's get started with an outline of what we're going to cover this semester and move right into the fun stuff."

It was not fun for me. Not for a single bloody second, because I couldn't concentrate on anything she had to say while he ignored her in favor of staring at me. Perhaps what really disconcerted me, however, was his ability to focus on other things.

Even though his eyes continued to travel over my body, leaving a trail of electric fire in their wake, his magick was far from docile. As before, he honed it and sent it traveling through the school, taking part of his mind with it. It was so forceful and powerful that it was easy for me to track it through the building, but being unfamiliar with the school, I had no idea who or what it was targeting. I was more than a little unsettled when it burst apart and spread throughout several locations, with at least three spells being laid at once.

Every ounce of restraint I possessed went into forcing myself not to look at him. To not ask him what the hell he was doing. Or demand to know exactly what was going on. Instead, I kept my eyes busy on everything else in the classroom except for him.

I felt like a coward. The moment our eyes had met in that doorway, something had happened. An odd chemistry was forming between us with each passing second, and I couldn't understand the cause for it. Grey was a stranger to me, and I had no reason to care about him. Nor did I have a desire to know him. Deep down, part of me had already classified him as a threat, despite my lack of reasoning for it. He was a problem that I needed to be resolved, and soon.

When the bell rang, I shot up out of my chair and darted for the door. The whole time, I swear

I could hear the air crackle with static. Once I was out of his line of sight, the entire right side of my face felt like an ice pack was being held to it. Without the strange sensation that his eyes wrought, it felt like I'd broken a fever.

Shaking it off, I made a brief stop at my locker before I headed toward the other side of the school. It was with a profound sense of calm that I entered my second hour class.

Only to have it vanish the moment I walked through the door.

It wasn't one of *those* moments. The world didn't vanish the moment my eyes met his. My heart didn't jump in excitement and I didn't catch my breath. There were no butterflies antagonizing my stomach, and I didn't get lost in the depths of his ash-colored eyes. It was not one of those moments.

It was much better.

Electricity hung heavy in the air, waiting for some catalyst to transform it into lightning. His energy was a warm embrace of vibrant flames that danced around the edges of the room.

Where the two elements met, they clashed with snaps and cracks before a suffocating silence fell around us.

I felt alive. Wired. Adrenaline shot through my blood and my hair practically stood on end. Every nerve ending in my body was awake and aware in a way they hadn't been for years. It reminded me of a time when I rejoiced in my magick. When it did not define me, but was defined by me.

Even with the frantic pace of my heart and the strange longing that grew stronger every second that I looked in his eyes, I felt at ease. I was literally in my element, and I had not felt so powerful in ages.

When I looked away, I knew I would be angry at myself. I would wonder what had gotten into me and I would ask a thousand fruitless questions as I tried to build up my barriers against him. All because I knew, in this moment, that none existed between us. Which was how I knew that I was having the exact same effect on him. And I did not regret it.

Maybe thirty seconds passed where we stood across a room and stared at each other. Whatever adrenaline I harbored, I knew was also pulsing through him. The quick, shallow breaths I was forced to take, he mirrored. It would be that way until one of us looked away.

It had to be me.

He was too curious. Too intrigued by what was happening between us. I could see it in his eyes that he would not stop. That he did not want to. And he saw no reason to deny himself this pleasure.

It was that arrogance that caused me to close my eyes.

The air hissed and crackled when I stepped farther into the room. Our energies surged around us, each movement promising to be more volatile than the last. When my eyes opened, I could see sparks flashing in my peripheral vision. I tried to keep my attention on them as I made my way to the back corner where he was waiting.

His belongings were on the desk beside mine, making me think I'd taken up his normal spot. Not that he appeared to mind. Instead, he stood between the two, leaning against his with his arms crossed over his chest.

Grey's eyes traveled over me as I set my own

belongings on my desk. I paused behind my chair, gripping the back of it while keeping my eyes averted. There was no way I was going to attempt to sit when that meant getting within inches of him. And he knew it.

When the bell rang, he didn't move. Not for several long, anxious seconds. Because it made me anxious. Because I was on edge. And because I was afraid in a way he was not.

Whatever bond we shared, it terrified me.

Chapter Three

HIJACKED

I couldn't forget for a single second how close we were. When he finally moved, I was quick to sit, but there was nowhere near enough space between us. There was also too much.

The desire was undeniable. It was something that was triggered when our eyes first met, and it hadn't diminished for a single second since. Feeling his gaze trace my skin, some malignant part of my imagination decided to wonder what it would feel like if it were his hands. I couldn't shut that thought down fast enough.

I was so lost in my head, I almost didn't notice Mr. Watts introducing himself at the front of the room. He seemed friendly enough, talking with a few students about their summers and answering questions about his own activities. In the end, I couldn't have been more grateful when he called the class to order and Grey's gaze darted to the front of the room.

After the brief introduction to himself and the class, Mr. Watts decided to give us a warning. My stomach knotted as he announced, "Now, you all know this is an elective course and Creative Writing is nothing more than an easy grade for most of you. I'm here to tell you … well, it kind of is. Not to say I'll be grading you on a curve, but bad writing is failing and good writing is passing and mediocre needs improvement. That's how this works.

"It also isn't going to be just my problem. If your writing is going to make someone's eyes bleed, then I'm not going to suffer alone. Now everyone look to the person sitting beside you. This is your critique partner for the rest of the semester. Every time you are required to turn something in to me, they're going to read it first. And it will be your job to use the skills learned in this class to critique their work before they embarrass themselves by handing it in to me. Also, if you miss days, this is also the person you're going to for your missed assignments. So, you better hope they take good notes and pay attention. Knowing this, I'll give you the next ten minutes to become acquainted."

In that moment, I felt like I had a suspicion confirmed. This was likely another thing Grey had manipulated in order to make us dependent on one another. Which pissed me off in ways he had never wanted to discover.

Leaning back in my chair, I sighed and closed my eyes. That's when I felt a gentle, almost teasing sensation flutter through the air between us. My eyes snapped open and shot to his without thought. The surprise I felt was tangible. Which was how his triumph felt the moment our eyes met. A second after the surge, I tore my eyes from his and glared at my desk.

This was worse than I thought. It wasn't just the way my skin felt when he looked at me or the intense reaction of our eyes meeting. Nor was it all about the strange attraction that pulled at us. No, now this had to involve our emotions. Things that were supposed to be safe and private were now on display for a stranger to examine as they wished. I'd never felt so violated in my life.

He felt that. I knew it the moment he identified the fury and horror that burst out of me. Surprise filled him in a degree almost as strong as my disgust. It made me even angrier that he couldn't see it as I did. That he didn't want to see it as something more than a curious occurrence.

Grey's eyes left me and I felt him try to pull back on his emotions to hide them from me. And if this was straight empathy we were dealing with, he would have succeeded. But it wasn't.

Whatever existed between us was a magick of a sort that we couldn't control. We couldn't connect to it or manipulate it. More or less, it felt like a net laced with chemistry and hormones had been thrown around us, and there was no way out. No way to sever the ties or ignore their existence.

When he realized it, another shift occurred. The surprise melted away and a complacency entered into the link. I almost snorted at feeling its false edges. There was too much smugness skittering around it for it to be true. Even in his emotions, this man was trying to manipulate me.

All of a sudden, he leaned forward a little and announced, "Grey Walker."

I almost didn't answer, except that he already knew my name from our first period. Best to give him a name he was allowed to call me by. "Alex."

For a few moments, we said nothing at all. Even though there were whole paragraphs of speculation and conversation that we could have traded, we didn't say a word. I was grateful for the silence. When I decided to break down and dissect this whole mess, I didn't want him around. Already he was proving to be a great distraction.

When he looked at me, it wasn't as if my entire face flared with the mixture of heat and lightning. It was more specific than that. Which was how I knew when his eyes traveled over the hair that fell down my back, or when they trailed over my shoulder up to my neck. The hair on the back of my neck prickled as his gaze drifted along my jaw, glanced at my ear, and shot to my lips. There, they lingered. Yet, it was my eyes he was most interested in.

Even in the link, there was an anticipation lingering there. Almost a hunger for our eyes to meet again. To form that incredible bond that caused us both to feel powerful and alive.

What was worse was knowing that it did not all come from him.

When his eyes began to trace the edges of mine again, the longing flared. A heat rushed through me and my lungs cried out as my breath caught. My pulse raced, eager for me to do the unthinkable. Everything urged me to give in and enjoy the sensation.

I curled my hands into fists and closed my eyes instead.

"You are a stubborn one," Grey murmured. His tone wasn't mocking so much as amused. There was something else in it, too, which I wouldn't have been able to identify without the link. Yet, I could sense the same intrigue lacing through the other emotions, though he tried to temper it.

For one brief moment, I tried to control my emotions, and it felt so wrong to do it. There had been times and situations in my life where I had to learn to take a step back and work out some of my issues, but never before had there been an audience for it. Even when Morgan was teaching me, I knew that she could shut off her empathy the same way I could. She wouldn't be attached to me as I tried to work through whatever was happening.

Grey was attached. Waiting. Experiencing everything I was experiencing. In a way, it was humiliating. I had an excellent poker face when I had this much inner turmoil going on, and it was wasted on everyone but the one person I needed it for.

Gathering together what little composure I could manage, I turned toward him and raised my eyes to his lips. Staring at them, I felt a little irritation at not being able to meet his eyes, since that was how I was raised.

"I don't think I can be any more clear, Grey Walker, when I ask you to please leave me alone."

He raised an eyebrow at me and his lips quirked into a smirk. "Ask. Then I will answer."

I knew the answer. It was written in the way his eyes kept darting over mine, urging them to raise a little higher. The dare flooded through the link, and I could almost feel his own adrenaline spike. No, I didn't need to ask the question, but I wanted it on the imaginary record in my head.

"Will you please leave me alone?" I almost

made it sound genuine.

"No." He was too pleased with his reply. "Not because I wish to infuriate you, but because I don't believe I should. Everything happens for a reason, right?"

"Doesn't make it a good reason," I grumbled. Once more, I leaned back and closed my eyes.

Grey had just opened his mouth to say more when Mr. Watts recalled our attention. Our ten minutes were up and my relief drowned the link. Once again, Grey's curiosity spiked, but even he could not ignore our teacher any longer. Not that either of us had a hope of paying attention.

He would never be able to understand. I think even he knew that. My reaction to all of this wasn't something he would ever have expected, while his reaction also surprised me. It just went to show how different our realities were.

Despite myself, I was curious about that. Considering how many witches were roaming the school, I was sure Grey had to be part of the same coven. Which meant he'd grown up with them. He had been raised amongst a community of people able to do what he could. The idea was as foreign as it was intriguing to me.

The class went by quickly after that. None of my attention was in the room, and all of it edged around Grey and this predicament we were in. I hoped that it was just a reaction of our magick. Other than Morgan, I had never encountered a being as filled with power as myself. Yet, the power gap between Grey and I wasn't too great. Something my magick was having a riot with.

Our real dilemma was if this didn't settle. If it was an actual bond, then it was far more frightening. Bonds were formed for reasons, and I couldn't think of a single one that required me to be attached to a stranger.

When the class ended, I leapt from my chair as I had before. Darting around my classmates, I was one of the first people out the door. Taking the route that Delaire had outlined on my map, I proceeded to my third period class. Relief flooded me when I entered the room and found no sign of Grey Walker. It transformed to acute horror when I realized I knew exactly where he was, because I could still feel him.

Some portion of my brain had been hijacked and pieces of Grey Walker had been placed inside of my head. It was a kind of sacrilege I didn't think could exist. My stomach twisted and I did my best to get through the day with the knowledge that this was something more than magick that needed to settle. In the space of an hour, my worst fear had been realized.

Chapter Four

PRINCE

When I exited my fourth period class, I was gratified to find Delaire exiting the room across the hall. It felt natural to fall into step beside her as we headed back toward our lockers. For a moment, I thought we'd have a gentle silence continue with us. My mistake.

"So, how is it going?"

For a split-second, I debated whether or not to ask. But I figured it'd probably be common knowledge in a short time, so I bit the bullet. "What's the deal with Grey Walker?"

Her brows shot up her forehead and her lips parted. "You've already caught the eye of the prince?"

It was my turn to raise my eyebrows. "Prince?"

"Hold on. You'll need a visual before I can explain this," she insisted.

As soon as we entered the cafeteria, I knew what she meant. The room was divided, with the coven witches taking up a significant corner, and everyone else giving them a wide berth. In the center, appearing to hold court, sat Spring Solas and Grey Walker.

It was the first time I noticed how guarded Grey was. He smiled and laughed as though he were in his element, but I could feel the strain along our bond. And though he sat beside Spring, neither spoke to one another. That didn't stop her from sneaking glances at him that he managed to ignore.

The second I entered, his eyes shot to me and I barely avoided meeting his gaze. His smile grew a little wider, and his curiosity flared. A moment later, he went back to his conversation as though nothing in particular was going on. When Spring's eyes cut to me, I understood why.

"They're coven royalty," I murmured, trying not to be obvious in my staring.

"That they are. From what I've heard, Grey is currently the most powerful witch in all of

Crone's Crescent. It's the reason he's the prince."

"And Spring? It can't be about power for her. She doesn't even compare."

It was true. His magick filled the room like a cloud of smoke. Everything beneath it was suffocated by his presence. Hers, on the other hand, was weak. A candle flame beside a wildfire. Yet, she was far from cowed by him. Out of all of the coven members, Spring was the only one that forced her magick up to meet his. Not in defiance, but an attempted show of solidarity. To prove to the coven witches that her place was beside him.

Delaire shrugged. "No idea. Though it has to be something keeping her on top. They're not shy about dragging someone down who they feel is unworthy."

For a minute, I was surprised that Delaire didn't have more information for me. At the same time, I could see a clear division in the coven's corner of the cafeteria that kept any and all others far from them. With as detached as they kept themselves, I was kind of surprised by how much she did know of them.

"Ah, there they are," Delaire murmured,

looking at something over my shoulder.

Turning, I spotted two girls joining the end of the lunch line. One was short and voluptuous with brown skin and ebony hair kept in two braids. The other was closer to my height with pale, freckled features and brown hair that bore a strong red tint. She also had *his* eyes.

"Come on. You don't mind if a few people jump ahead of us, right?" Delaire asked, already stepping out of the line and heading back to where her friends were. I tried not to appear too reluctant as I followed her.

"Hey," Delaire said, a wide smile appearing on her face as she wrapped an arm around the short woman. Turning to me, she announced, "Alex, this is Catori, the platonic love of my life. And this is Faye."

Standing close to her, it impressed me to feel the magick she harbored in her. While she was young, it was still enough to equal Spring. After her Ascension, it wouldn't be too far below what Grey could hold. Which made sense, since they were obviously related.

"I'm Alex."

"Nice to meet you," Catori said with a smile.

Faye's head tilted to the side as she scanned me from head to toe. A grin pulled slowly at her lips until it spread across much of her face. Without looking away from me, she told her friends, "She could give Grey a run for his money. If she ever let it loose."

It wasn't until right then that I realized how much magick was filling me. How much had been filling me since second period. At once, I was ashamed of myself. Being around so many witches, I'd been too distracted to adhere to my penance. And too defensive not to keep some of it active within me. Until I was able to balance the magickal and mundane, however, I had to let it go. Grabbing hold of the locket, I siphoned everything I had gathered into it. At once, half of the magick in the room disappeared.

Faye's jaw dropped at the same time that thirty witches turned to look at me. I kept my eyes straight ahead, refusing to follow the thread of sensation that would lead to Grey Walker. At the same time, I caught Delaire's raised eyebrow and Catori's confused expression from the corner of my eye.

"Okay witch-meter, what just happened?"

Catori asked, poking Faye in the side.

Shaking her head, the girl cracked another smile. "Does it feel easier to breathe in here to you?"

Delaire and Catori exchanged glances. "As a matter of fact..."

"I told you. She puts Grey to shame. Why do you put it in the locket?" Faye asked, addressing me for the first time.

I shrugged, unwilling to divulge that answer to a stranger. "Seemed like the best place for it, considering the circumstances."

Faye said nothing in reply to that, though her grin got larger. Then Delaire distracted us by moving through the lunch line. When we had all paid for our food, I was more than a little surprised when we fell into step behind the young witch. And she led us straight toward the coven corner.

"Relax," Delaire hissed, "we're not walking into a lion's den. And we're staying on the outskirts."

I snorted. "At this point, no one is allowed to tell me to relax."

As a point, I swept my eyes over the corner

where almost thirty people ducked their heads so as not to appear to have been staring. Only two sets of eyes didn't flinch out of the way of mine. Spring met my gaze with a cool expression, but I passed over her in a dismissive manner. I couldn't pass over Grey.

I was lucky we reached the table before that happened. My body froze for several heartbeats as the atmosphere around us grew dead. The crackle of static filled my ears and a heat wave rolled through the room in an instant. When I felt the first flickers of longing snake through me, I dropped my eyes back to the tray I'd set on the table.

My body was shaking as I sat down slowly, pushing the tray a little away from me. If that was what I had to look forward to every time I was in a room with him, I wouldn't be able to function. While he had been distracted, it had been easy to avoid his gaze. Then I'd gained his undivided attention and my willpower went to hell.

"Alex? You feeling okay?" Catori asked.

I shook my head, unwilling to answer. Pulling my tray back to me, I pushed the food around with my fork. All the while, my new acquaintances watched me while the other witches kept stealing glances. The only one who didn't stare was Grey, but I could feel his curiosity hanging thick in the air.

"You don't have to feel threatened by them," Faye murmured.

The statement was so shocking, I began to laugh. Raising my eyes to hers, I marveled at how normal it was to be looking into eyes like his and not feel that overwhelming connection. Shaking it off, I asked, "Is that what you think? That they intimidate me?"

She shrugged. "That's what it looks like." Her voice was nonchalant, but I could see that she was watching me in a way that indicated she was studying my every nuance.

Again, I shook my head. "I haven't given them that power over me. Nor will I." Then I pointed with my chin to where Grey sat. "You can tell him that for me. That whatever threats I face, they come from within. Not from him."

Faye stiffened, her spine straightening as I studied her. At the same time, Cat and Del looked at her with inquisitive expressions. Whatever she was tasked with doing, they didn't seem to know of it, but they weren't surprised. After a few seconds, I watched as Faye forced herself to relax inch by inch.

"Well," she remarked offhand, "I guess espionage is not one of my future career choices. How did you know?"

I wasn't going to tell her that it was Grey who gave her away. That it was because he was doing his best to ignore me that made me suspicious. When he didn't attempt to eavesdrop on the conversation, I also had to wonder what was stopping him. In the end, there was but one reason I knew that whatever I said to her would be relayed back to him.

"You have his eyes."

Faye raised her eyebrows, her head tilting unconsciously like she was going to look back at him. Instead, she kept her gaze on mine. For a second, she debated how to answer. All while Cat and Del watched us as if we were their favorite drama.

"Cousins," she said at last.

I nodded, though I was leaning toward siblings. Amidst the curiosity, a fierce protectiveness also filtered through the air, courtesy of Grey. Which was my hint that something about Faye might make her a target. From someone other than myself.

My gaze traveled over the other witches, catching some of them staring at me with mixed expressions of awe and fear. Others, however, weren't looking at me, but the freckled girl across from me. Their features were twisted with hostility and suspicion.

"And your loyalties are to him. Not them." My voice deadpanned. Because I'd seen those looks before, and I knew why the coven witches bore them. "You're a solitary."

The first flash of genuine surprise flitted over Faye's face before she was able to school her features once more. At last, in an exaggerated nonchalance, she said, "Solitary or not, I am a wealth of knowledge. Would you like to learn some of what I know?"

I was sorely tempted to take her up on that offer. There were so many questions I had. About the coven. Her life. Family. Existence. Though I would have loved nothing more than to sit her down for a full-blown interrogation, part of me knew that it wouldn't come without a price. Already it was more than I could contemplate.

"One day, Faye, I may take you up on that offer. But not while you're reporting to him. Tell him that the question stands, and I hope he changes his answer."

Chapter Five

INSATIABLE

"She likes you."

A fist squeezed my heart and I bit back a groan as Grey fell into the seat beside me. Since I had a surplus of credits already, I'd been given a back-to-back study block following lunch. The first half of it, I'd been alone. Then I'd felt him coming and I did what I could to prepare myself. I still wasn't ready.

Taking a breath, I stared at my desk as I remarked, "Should I be flattered by that?"

From the corner of my eye, I saw him give a single nod. "Yes. Trust does not come easy to her."

"Nor to me. Especially when someone is sent to spy on me." The censure was thick in my voice, but what really bothered me was that some portion of the atmosphere surrounding us also became infused with it.

Grey shot me a wide grin. "She volunteered."

I shook my head, trying to hide my own smile. Part of me could swear, if it was just a normal interaction, I could continue the banter with nothing but light amusement. At this point, I was kind of used to guys hitting on me during my first few days. Sometimes it would take them a whole month before they caught on that I wasn't interested. But it had always been an interesting experience in one way or another. With Grey, it could have been the same.

Except that it wasn't.

My smile faded of its own accord as I settled myself into the conclusion that not speaking to him was the best course of action. The less we had to do with one another, the better off we would both be. His curiosity would fade over time, and I would get to move on with my life as if this connection didn't exist. I carefully steered my thoughts well away from the desire that often reared its ugly head. That was something I'd have to learn to live with as well.

Grey knew when I decided not to reply. A

moment later, I caught my breath as he leaned toward me, holding the back of my chair with one hand, and leaning on the desk with the other. When his face was an inch away from mine, he murmured, "I don't like this any more than you do, you know."

My teeth gritted together and I forced myself to take a long, slow breath. "It doesn't *feel* like it."

"You doubt me because I don't worry about it like you do. You shouldn't worry, either. Nothing ever lasts with me."

Too late. Though his voice was mocking and suggestive, he couldn't hide the stab of bitterness he felt. That sharp spike of rage was all too familiar.

I was glad when he buried it. Of everything that could make me consider speaking with him, that familiar pain and anger would have been it. With it set aside, we could both ignore its existence. Which meant we did not need to bring it up ever again.

"If I could avoid any beginning with you, I'd be ecstatic. The sooner the end is in sight, the happier I will be. Should you ever decide to help that along, I'd appreciate it. Otherwise, at least back up out of my personal space."

I caught his 'fair enough' expression before he stepped back and sat at his desk once more. That was about as much cooperation as I was getting out of Grey Walker. When he sat down, he didn't bother to turn away. He wasn't hiding the fact that he was staring at me. Studying and perusing, as if I were a statue in some museum. If it were anyone else, I wouldn't have minded the looking, so long as there was no touching. But with Grey, the looking was just as bad.

Though I'd attempted to go back to the book I was reading, I knew I wouldn't comprehend another page. Not with the way his eyes traced my lips, sending sparks crackling along them like the static gathering before a shock. The heat drifted away as Grey took note of the piercing in my nose. He then began to trace my entire profile and my breathing came faster and shallower as the study continued.

Irritated, I whipped around to glare at him. "What the hell do you want from me?"

"This." His eyes raised to mine.

Oxygen vanished. My lungs cried out in protest even as my heart shot into overdrive. Around us, sparks flashed through the air. It amazed me that no one else was attracted to the crackling and hissing that they gave off.

Triumph was prevalent along our bond, and I shoved my disgust back at him. For a moment, the lightning in the air grew wilder and more erratic, reacting to my temperament. At the same time, the heat grew stronger as it caressed our bond.

Beneath it all, I could feel the desire rising. The urge to get closer to him. To touch him. It grew within me, begging to have some sort of vindication. I wanted him. Even when I hated him, I wanted him.

Wrenching my eyes from his, I took in a ragged gasp of air. It felt like I'd been smothered. The heat had suffocated me and the lightning had stolen my breath. All the while, I still burned with a need I couldn't explain and had never felt the equal of.

It wasn't until I felt the desire saturating our bond that I realized that I couldn't tell whose it was. Whether mine or his, it raged with such a single-minded intensity that I was surprised we hadn't acted on it. I couldn't even figure out which of us would have been able to withstand it for much longer.

"Damn," he breathed a moment later, taking a deep breath and releasing it.

"Bastard."

Grey raised his eyebrows a bit in a smug expression. "Tell me it wasn't worth it."

"It wasn't," I practically snarled.

For a moment, Grey's piercing eyes studied me. His curiosity was getting the best of him, again. Especially now that I was able to beat back the desire and replace it with my anger. He really didn't understand why it all pissed me off so much. I couldn't understand how he couldn't feel the same. It was an irrational dilemma.

"Why aren't you angry?" I whispered. "How can you be okay with this *thing* binding you to a stranger?"

"What makes you think I'm okay with it?"

"Please. I can feel you, too. You're curious, not upset."

There was a slight smile on his lips when he answered, "I guess that would be because it is *you* I am bound to."

I had to roll my eyes. It was mandatory.

Grey released a low chuckle, sending a minor shiver down my spine. "If it had been anyone else, Alex, I don't believe I would react any differently from you. But it's not anyone else. Instead, it's this pretty new girl I've never seen before. Add in the fact that she's a powerful witch who, I am sure, could put me in my place, and I was hooked. It wouldn't have taken a connection like ours for me to be any more interested in you."

I wanted so badly to meet his gaze. Not to feel that flood of desire, but so he could see the truth in my eyes when I rejected him. So he would know just how little he meant to me.

"And without this connection, I would have shut you down hours ago. Your magick is an interesting characteristic, but not one that would make me give a damn. This is the last year that I have to coast through before I return to my life. The less drama I am a part of in the meantime would serve my purpose a great deal."

"Well, Alex, it seems to me that you'll have to adjust your expectations a bit. For one year, at least, you're stuck with me. And who knows how long this will last. I think you had better begin to believe that I am now a part of your current reality."

It was the first time I made the decision to cut that reality short. Thanks to the various curriculums of my other schools, I only needed one semester to see a diploma in my hand. Before, it hadn't seemed like a real option. My eighteenth birthday had been a close enough deadline. Now, I wasn't so sure.

The walk home was more comforting than I would have imagined it. For each step, I was taking in a long, deep breath of the precious oxygen. After the events of earlier, each felt more needed than the last.

When I got home, a weary smile pulled at my lips when I noticed the several trucks and van sitting in the driveway. My dad's crew had arrived and they were all bustling around the front of the house as they worked on the foundation. That was my cue to head around to the back door.

I made it past the industrial dumpster before I called it quits. Looking at the low-hanging branches of the hawthorn tree sitting in the backyard, it seemed like a good place to hide for a while. Lifting up one of the branches, I dragged my bag in after me as I crawled into the hidden space.

Placing my back against the trunk, I let myself connect to it and every other living thing I could touch. It was a therapeutic necessity. If I had to deal with any more in the next hour, I would go off on someone. And the one person I wanted to really rage at was about five miles away.

As my hour was nearing its end, my eyes snapped open as a rustling alerted me to an intruder. With as much concern as I had, my mother crawled under the branches and came to sit beside me. Her eyes traveled around her, taking note of my new haven. Then she nodded in approval.

"That kind of day? You need a sanctuary already?"

"You knew there were witches here." It wasn't an accusation. Just a statement of fact.

"I did."

"You could've warned me."

"That bad?"

I didn't answer that one. Mostly because I didn't know. The connection between Grey and I was certainly frightening and unwanted, but it had yet to prove itself sinister. Exhausting and irritating as it was, I didn't know that I could describe it as bad.

"Something weird happened today. I don't know how to explain it, or if I even want to. But now I have to deal with something that I didn't want to get involved in. Does that make sense?"

"A little bit," my mom said. "But you know, Baby, sometimes you have to be involved. I know you're anxious to get back to Cedar Creek, but you can't treat every day between now and then like it's another obstacle in your path. You might as well make memories in the meantime."

I raised my eyebrows at her. "Is that why we moved here?"

"There are people here who can understand you in a different way than us, if you let them. Not better, but different. I thought you might need that before you decided the rest of your life."

"Mom..." I didn't know what to say. I'd told her before that my life had been decided since

I was nine. She believed me, though it took a while. So there had to be something else here that I was missing. What decisions did she think I had left to make?

She shook her head. "If I made a mistake, we'll know soon enough. All the same, I hope I didn't. I want you to be happy, Lex. Always. Now, come on. Pizza should be here any minute."

"Pizza again?"

She shot me a smirk over her shoulder. "You haven't seen the kitchen."

Shaking my head, I followed my mother out from under the hawthorn tree.

Unable to help myself, I turned my head to the right and stared off into the distance. I could still feel him.

Chapter Six

EXPOSED

I felt exposed. Of course, that was the point. The shirt I wore had just enough sleeve to cover the top of my shoulders. Which meant my left arm and its garden of scars was on full display for the world to see.

My chest tightened as I stared at the calendar in my skin. Seven hundred and fifty-nine scars were burned into the flesh, starting from my left breast and trailing up and over my left shoulder. The bulk of the scars had crowded together all the way down to my wrist. Most of them were ivy leaves. Others, however, existed with more purpose. Oak leaves for the first day I went down Old Grove Road. Apple blossoms for the day I met Morgan. Oleander flowers for the day of my Ascension and the day Morgan committed suicide. There were so many others, but the two that held the most meaning rested on the inside of my wrist and in the crux of my elbow. An empty hourglass to mark two years since I said goodbye, and valerian to mark when I was asked to come home.

Releasing a breath, I turned from the mirror, grabbed my bag, and headed downstairs. Part of me was glad that the kitchen and dining room were in shambles. It meant there wasn't a location suitable for my parents and I to meet up before I left. Which was good, considering this was my day to show my scars. Even after a year, we still weren't in a place where we could ignore them or forget how they came to be. So, I did us all a favor and made sure the exposure was limited.

Except for today. The first day of school was all about getting my bearings and figuring out how things were going to occur. I chose the second day to reveal a little bit of the damage done to me. Not to incite curiosity or attention, but to push away those who saw them and didn't understand how I could do that to myself. It separated me from my classmates. Sooner rather than later.

I was almost to school when I felt him getting closer. My stomach twisted once more as I realized how potent our link had become. Even with time and distance, its strength hadn't diminished. Which had me worried about what would happen when we were within sight of each other. How much stronger would it be then?

Delaire and Catori both made their way to my locker once they spotted me. It took them all of two seconds to have different and opposing reactions to my garden.

"Blessed Goddess, Alex," Delaire murmured, staring at my arm in alarm. "What have you done?"

Cat tilted her head to the side a little as she examined the pattern. "It's gorgeous."

"How many?" Delaire demanded after shooting Cat a scathing look.

"Seven hundred and fifty-nine."

"A calendar?" Catori guessed. I nodded.

"Why?"

"To feel something at a time when I could feel nothing. When marking the days made more sense than living them."

"And now?" Cat asked.

My right hand reached over to cover the valerian. "Now I don't need a calendar."

"Good," Delaire sighed, her eyes flashing with pain each time they traced one of the scars. Cat's reaction still made the least sense to me, but she also didn't suffer the trials I had. She was able to keep her innocence intact, and I kind of wished it would remain forever.

As if to disprove my thoughts, the Native woman raised her eyes to mine and smiled. "Be proud of your scars, Alex. Each one you have is another that you have survived. You're a stronger person for that."

"Even when the wounds are self-inflicted?" I remarked.

"Would you allow anyone else to inflict them?"

Silence reigned and at last I shook my head. Catori nodded, proving that she understood more than I'd given her credit for. Whatever wounds she had, I now knew that she had inflicted them herself. Whether mental or physical, we were determined that the only people able to hurt us were ourselves. And we hurt worse than anyone because of it.

By the time I headed for my first period, I was anxious. Though I could tell that Grey remained on the other side of the school, I also knew that seeing him again was going to hit me far harder the second time around. Mostly because I'd spent all night under the delusion that our bond wasn't as horrific as my shock made it out to be. Lies. All lies.

Grey's power overwhelmed me. When I was just outside of our history class, I felt the same heated blast that had pushed itself into the room the day before. This time, it shoved out of the room as Grey went from being on one side of the building to right inside of the classroom.

The bastard could teleport.

Letting out the breath I was holding, I took a step through the door and found him sitting on my desk in the corner. There was something incredibly irritating about people that didn't bother to hide their smug condescension. Especially when they shared an emotional bond with an unwilling participant.

That same bond seemed to explode with intent the moment I walked into the room.

With his fiery magick still taking up space in the room, my own magick was eager to best it. A cloud of static entered with me, shooting sparks at his flames in the corners of my eyes. As I purposefully kept my gaze from Grey's, it was a far more subdued reaction than yesterday. It was still enough to steal my breath.

It was hard to avoid his gaze as I headed toward my desk. The way I was raised relied on a lot of eye contact, so being deprived of this one natural reaction was as frustrating as Grey himself was. A fact he wanted to cement while leaning against my desk and smiling at me.

Stopping well out of reach of him, I said, "Please get off my desk, Grey."

"Just saving your seat," he replied with an impish grin.

"They're assigned. You made sure of that." My tone was scathing and it took all I had not to back it with a glare.

Grey's mouth opened for another quip, but I knew the instant it died on his tongue. The heat of his gaze set off the lightning arcing along my skin as he traced the scars down my arm. His lips parted in astonishment and I somehow felt his speechlessness along our bond. He was stunned by what I'd done to myself. Which wouldn't have bothered me so much if he hadn't taken an unconscious step forward.

At once, I twisted my body so that my arm was out of his sight. His eyes shot to my face and I barely avoided meeting his gaze as I glared at him. A harsh warning snapped through our bond. If he touched me, I would break his hand. Simple as that.

It was the first time I felt that Grey's concern was genuine. His eyes shot to my shoulder and back to my face as I kept my arm out of view. He kept his voice low when he asked, "They're burns, aren't they?"

Without answering, I stepped around him and set my stuff on my desk. Grey turned to put himself between our desks, putting his hands on the surface of mine as he leaned toward me. In a moment of indulgence, I turned a bit so that he could see the devastation of my past decisions.

"Yes, they are burns," I answered. Already my arm was coated in a mixture of fire and lightning as he absorbed the garden.

"So many," he murmured to himself. "What

for?"

The bell rang at the same time that I said, "For reasons that don't concern you."

His eyes snapped up to my face, darting over my lowered eyelids. After my proclamation, I could feel a flash of irritation travel through our bond. Then he leaned even closer and lowered his voice.

"I only asked because they reminded me of my own."

It was my turn to be stunned and my eyes instantly sought his for confirmation.

The contact was just as heady, breathless, confusing, and intense as it was the day before. Worse, in its own way, because I knew what to expect. Our desire, especially, leapt to the surface and I felt myself drawn toward him. I thanked every deity I'd ever heard of that the desk was in the way. When my leg glanced off the chair, I was at last able to tear my gaze away.

For the rest of class, I did my best to ignore my curiosity. That was accomplished by burying it under the irritation I felt for him once he'd opened that can of worms. My Ryder Pride would not allow for me to ask. If my scars were none of his business, the reverse must also be true.

With that realization, it was surprisingly easy to put it out of my mind. It wasn't as easy to pay attention during class, since that same humming electricity existed between us, and Grey made a habit of checking on me to see if I'd pay attention to him. Almost as often, Summer would glance back and check on his reaction. I almost rolled my eyes the third time she did it and he was looking right at me. The last thing I needed was for her to start something.

As before, I leapt to my feet and bolted as soon as the bell rang. Though I knew I would be forced to see Grey in a mere five minutes, that was still five minutes I was able to catch my breath. Five whole minutes where a suffocating atmosphere didn't cling to us, waiting for one of us to set the world ablaze.

Chapter Seven

RULES

Once more, Grey appeared in the classroom a moment before I stepped through the door. I took one minute to brace myself before I crossed the threshold. My step faltered the second I realized that he wasn't looking at me. It was a blessing I was too suspicious of to be grateful for.

As I approached the corner, it was apparent that, in this class, my left side was exposed to him. Which meant he could sit and count every scar if he wanted to. It rankled a little that I couldn't stop him. I also had no one but myself to blame. That was the point of this exercise, after all. Let him see how damaged I was. If I was lucky, he would run from it.

Before I even had a chance to sit down, Grey

stood up and turned to face me. I was more than a little surprised when he began to roll up the left sleeve of his t-shirt. There, in a two-inch band around his upper arm, were several burns. I recognized them as runes, though I couldn't understand the words. Even if I could, half of them were hidden on the underside of his arms. What little I could make out, however, seemed to be a pledge.

"Initiation," he explained. Then he rolled up his right sleeve and revealed another paragraph. This time, a slight smile pulled at his lips. "Ascension. Sixteen."

All three oleander scars flared to life. The word fell from my lips before I could stop it. "Thirteen."

His impressed expression matched what I was feeling from him. "You must have had one hell of a teacher."

Without answering, I gave a curt nod and sat down. It took longer for Grey to follow my lead, but the bell ringing urged him to take his own seat. All the while, I clung to the numbness that the memories had reawakened. Though I'd never wanted to indulge in it again, this once I didn't fight it. It was better than Grey realizing how much hurt still existed. How much my wounds still needed to heal.

I wasn't allowed to indulge the thoughts for long. Mr. Watts had decided we'd had enough time to ease into being back at school, since he wrote an outline of the course schedule on the board in front of us. In a Creative Writing class, I expected poetry and various elements of fiction. In no way was I prepared for playwriting, which was the first subject to be covered.

After our lecture, we were given free rein to discuss it with our partners. Everyone around us turned and began going over their notes with one another. Grey and I remained silent. A fact which Mr. Watts noticed.

"Walker. Ryder. Is there something I can help you with?"

I shook my head. "No, sir."

Grey shrugged. "No."

"Then perhaps you'd like to tell me what you've been working on."

I would rather have bitten off my own tongue. Making my course grade depend on my ability to work with Grey Walker was a new form of cruelty. With such extenuating circumstances, Mr. Watts would never understand how difficult it would be for us to work together.

An instant later, a familiar magick wrapped itself around Mr. Watts. Once more, thoughts and ideas were being weaved into another's mind, forming so fully with his own personality and process that he would never know that the thoughts didn't originate from him. It was almost terrifying how good Grey was at twisting minds.

After a moment, Mr. Watts looked at us both and shook his head. "You know what, I can't make you talk to each other. But I can dock participation points for it. Being that it's only the second day of school, I'll let this slide. Tomorrow, though, I'd like to see you both a little more enthusiastic about the time I give you to work together."

The minute his back was turned to us, I unleashed a glare that would scorch the sun. Grey shrugged. "You wanted him gone. How else was I going to do it?"

"I want you gone, too. Can't seem to manage that one, now can I? Some things we just have to learn to live with."

The scathing remark didn't seem to bother him, but I felt his own flash of irritation. "Guess you'll just have to learn to work with me, then. We are partners for a reason."

My vexation transformed. There was no longer any heat to it. Now there was a coldness that I sent through our bond. A thorough sign that I was fed up, and my opinion of him was almost fully formed.

"Really? You wanted me to speak with you so badly that you coerced our teacher into making it a requirement? Then tell me, Grey, what is it about my obvious lack of interest in you that makes it so necessary for you to seek my attention?"

He threw a charmer's smile on his face, forgetting that I could feel the snap of anger that my words caused. "Well, Alex, did you ever consider that talking to me would be the one way for me to leave you alone?"

"I don't negotiate my values. I'm not going to do something I find unnecessary and tedious just to appease your ego."

"You really aren't here to make friends, are you?"

"I told you before that I had no desire to deal with any of this. I meant it. All I want is to graduate high school and move on with my life. Why should that plan involve you?"

"Do you think my plans involved you?"

"I think if any pretty girl with a decent drop of magick in her veins walked into this school, you would make it your mission to have their life involve you. This connection between us, that you *thought* would make it that much easier, is making it that much more difficult for you to succeed with me. And that frustrates you to no end."

"I told you that myself. I am interested in what and who you are. It's not something I intend to apologize for. But I am getting tired of you blaming me for something neither of us can control."

"I'm not blaming you for this thing existing, Grey. I'm blaming you for how you've reacted to its existence."

"So, I should bite your head off every time you so much as look at me? I should be angry and fearful for hours at a time, but refuse to question why this has happened? Well, Alex, I'm sorry but I don't have the energy to keep up that kind of pointless antagonism."

My stomach churned as each accusation bit into me. The worst of it was, I couldn't even call them unfair. Yet, if he thought that was the extent of my issues with him, he was sorely mistaken.

"I would understand you better if you did. Or at least I would have enough empathy to back off and let you work it out as you saw fit. But I never would have sent a Freshman to spy on you, nor would I manipulate our teacher into making it a requirement that we work with each other. You'd have had much better luck talking to me if you had tried to understand why I was pissed. Instead, you went from a non-starter to an asshole right quick in my book. So, no thanks, I'd rather not deal with you on any level."

"Why *are* you so pissed?" he groaned.

"One reason? I choose who I allow into my life, in what capacity, and for what reason. This thing has taken away at least one of those choices, so I damn well will not relinquish the others. You are in my life, Grey. That doesn't mean you get to fill any other role than the one I've assigned to you."

"That's it then?" he scoffed. "You've already set me in my place and I don't even have an option or opportunity to change anything?"

I shrugged. "It's my life, Grey. I get to make whatever rules I deem necessary. If it makes you feel any better, you have the same obligation to yourself. Make your own rules and don't let anyone else think they can change them."

Grey lowered his eyes, shaking his head from side to side. "Very well. Have it your way."

The bell rang, keeping me from questioning what just happened.

I was surprised to find Faye lingering by my locker, a penitent expression on her face. My suspicion spiked, thinking back to Grey's declaration that she liked me. If that were truly the case, there would be a few things she and I needed to sort out before we became anything close to acquaintances.

"Yes?" I asked as I moved past her to my locker.

Faye's teeth gripped her bottom lip. "I'm sorry." A pause followed that and I turned an expectant expression on her. She sighed. "I'm sorry for trying to spy on you. Grey and I were both curious and I wanted to get to know you, anyway. There aren't a lot of solitaries around and I thought it might be nice to have a companion, or something." The entire time she spoke, she refused to look at me. A sure sign that there was some humility in her family after all.

"Why bother spying on me? Why not just get to know me because you wanted to?"

Her eyes never left the floor when she said, "He's my cousin. He's ... pretty much the only person that doesn't want to see me stoned for my decision. We're bonded, Grey and I."

I barely held back the snort. Or the sarcastic remark that at least she had a choice in her bond. Instead, I shook my head and sighed. "Faye, I'm not one for making friends, but I do know what it's like to be lonely. If you don't mind hanging around me, I'm not going to avoid you. But you can't expect me to tell you things so long as I know you're just going to turn around and tell someone else. If I wanted anyone else to know about me, I'd tell them myself. It's not your job or your right to say anything about me."

She nodded slowly. "How am I supposed to prove it to you, then? That I'm not saying anything to Grey?"

I offered her as encouraging a smile as I could. "Stick around and pay attention. I'll know if something gets through."

"What if something does, but it wasn't from me?" she challenged.

"I'll know that, too."

Chapter Eight

SOMETIMES LESS

For the rest of the morning, I found myself thinking back to Grey's declaration. If it was as I hoped, it meant that he would cut off contact with me. It's what I wanted, after all.

It wasn't what I wanted at all.

When I entered the cafeteria, neither of us could help seeking out the other. My eyes shot to him as he threw a glance my way. Before our eyes could meet, I stepped into the lunch line. He went back to the quiet murmurings of his conversations. I wished it offered more evidence of his intentions, but we'd done the same thing only a day ago. No confirmation would be given to me until our study hall.

Delaire and Catori fell into the line behind

me a moment later, each one smiling at me as if they weren't studying my scars out of the corner of their eyes. So far, the only person to have not reacted to them was Faye. Which, if I thought of it too long, would seem suspicious. If I took it at face value, however, chances were that she had just decided not to comment on them.

Faye was already seated by the time the three of us made it to her table. Right as we sat down, Autumn and Summer approached. For one brief moment, I thought they were going to pass by quietly. Then Summer stopped and cast a condescending look on Faye.

"You know, Morgaine, when you are done rescuing strays and having this little rebellious phase, the Elders will welcome you back. All you need to do is cast aside the riff-raff."

For a moment, I was confused and a little stunned at hearing a name so close to my mentor's. Then Faye met her gaze with a cool expression. "You can't go back to where you've never been, Summer."

Summer's features flushed in embarrassment and I straightened my spine as I felt the magick gather in her. At the same time, a little of Faye's flared to life. While Summer was gathering all she could hold, Faye held but a fraction of her power in order to equal her. It seemed the reminder that the Season Sister needed in order to back down.

Baring her teeth at the younger witch, Summer hissed, "You are a fool, Morgaine. Turning your back on us will have its consequences."

Instead of answering, Faye shrugged. It unleashed something in Summer and the makings of a sharp spell not yet fully formed snapped out at Faye. Before I could react, she had a shield in place. Then a blast of heat rocketed through the room, throwing Summer back until her hip collided with the edge of the table behind us, the impact throwing her to the ground. As one, everyone looked at Summer. I looked at Grey.

Pure, undiluted rage burned through our link. It choked me as he rose to his feet and stepped around the table so that he could face her. Seeing how calm his features were somehow made his murderous intent that much more difficult to deal with.

When he drew abreast of our table, he stopped beside Faye while his eyes never left

Summer. His magick was holding her in place, making it apparent to all that she would be unable to escape his wrath. For a moment, Grey did nothing more than draw the net tighter.

At last, he said, "The judgment is yours, Faye."

His rage was so all encompassing, I forgot to factor in Faye's. Looking across the table at her, I could see the fury swelling. Her poker face was not as adept, but her intent was on par with his. Feeling like I somehow got trapped in a witchy soap opera, I held my breath and waited on her answer.

"Mercy." The single word echoed in the silent cafeteria. It seemed so deafening, most people didn't realize that Faye spat it with every ounce of vehemence she possessed.

Turning his face just slightly to Autumn, Grey announced, "Mercy is granted. Remove her."

It took a moment for Autumn to gather herself enough to murmur, "For how long?"

"To be determined."

Without an ounce of gentleness, Autumn marched over to her sister, pulling her roughly to her feet and shoving her toward the door. After watching them disappear, I turned my wide-eyed gaze on Grey. He didn't seem to notice since that's when Spring approached.

"Grey, she wasn't intending–"

"If you want to defend her, you can do it at her side," he promised in a low, lethal tone. "Otherwise, you can inform her that she is to keep her distance for a week."

Spring hissed, "School has just begun."

His eyes hardened even more. "There are consequences, and she will live with them."

For a moment, I witnessed a battle of wills filled with unspoken nuance, packed with years of history, and fueled by a kind of hatred I didn't know one being could feel for another. Then I saw the heartbreak in Spring's eyes the second before she turned away. When Grey's attention returned to us, I almost wish she had stayed.

Turning to Faye, he jerked her chin up until she met his angry gaze. The same level of intensity filled her, but it was less composed in its own way.

"You did well," he said in a low voice.

"Next time, I'll kill her," Faye swore in a voice as lethal as his. "The next time that bitch–"

"Not yet," Grey announced. "When you're strong enough, maybe. Until then, I will keep them in line."

"They won't stay in line and you know it," she hissed.

The anger cooled. In his voice, his eyes, even along our bond, it transformed into icy clarity. "Then maybe next time you won't say 'mercy.'"

The implication sat heavy in the air. It bespoke years of frustration and abuse, as well as a promise putting an end to all of that. A shiver rocked through my entire body.

I waited in my study hall with a sense of trepidation. Grey's rage had lessened a bit, but he was still roiling with anger. Enough to make me not want to sit beside him for another hour, trying to concentrate on things I wouldn't remember until after we were separated. At the same time, some inconceivable little part of me felt the need to comfort him. It was an instinct I was doing my best to murder by the time he walked in.

It was still disconcerting to match what I knew he was feeling against his facial expression. Grey didn't keep a plain mask over his face. Instead, he offered up an entirely unperturbed persona to anyone that otherwise might have thought him homicidal. Only I knew what was churning within him when he smiled and nodded to the classmates that wanted a moment of his time. I almost rolled my eyes when I realized he was placating them in the same way a prince would honor the peasants with his presence.

Then he sat down and we both made a decent show of ignoring the other, despite monitoring every movement. Then he murmured, "She'll need backup every once in a while, but she'll never admit it."

My head jerked up and I turned to look at him. For the first time, Grey didn't attempt to stare back at me. Instead, his magick produced a notebook and he kept his attention on his notes. Since he didn't seem inclined to say anything else, I turned my attention back to my own textbook.

"Are you prepared for that, or are you just going to let her handle things on her own?" His voice had grown a little harder and I could feel his frustration spike.

I didn't look up at him again as I answered, "You really think she can't take care of herself?"

"Faye is an asshole, Alex. One day, she will bite off more than she can chew, and she will need backup."

"And you're asking me to be her backup?" I scoffed.

"I'm telling you that it is a cost of her friendship. I'm asking what kind of friend you'll be to her." Once more, a wave of protectiveness washed through him, and I realized that he wasn't even trying to hide his emotions from me anymore. Either he was too pissed to rein them in, or he wanted me to feel it all.

Leaning back in my chair, I thought about what he said. I knew how he wanted me to answer, but we both knew that was a little ridiculous. Faye and I barely knew one another, and there was nothing about us to suggest we'd hang around each other enough to form a real friendship. If we did, however, then the answer was obvious.

"I will be the kind of friend to her that she is to me. Right now, we're not friends at all. But I will return loyalty and trust as far as it is given unto me. Sometimes less."

Another thread of curiosity darted through our link before he put a clamp on it. Without looking at me, Grey gave a curt nod and made a point of continuing his work. That was the end of the conversation.

For a moment, I considered antagonizing some answers out of him. While he put a clamp on his curiosity, mine had only grown in the past few moments. However, my Ryder Pride wasn't dead yet. After asking him to leave me alone, I was not about to begin any sort of conversation with that man if it could be avoided. So, taking a deep breath, I attempted to focus on my work, wishing the whole time that I could stop noticing every breath he took.

Chapter Nine

ALL FOR ONE

By the time I made it home, it looked like the guys were putting the finishing touches on the foundation. At least the front of the house no longer looked like it was going to fall flat on its face. Forcing a smile, I waved at them all before heading around to the back door. This time, I left my bag in the living room and snatched the phone off the cradle. Then I darted back outside and climbed beneath the hawthorn tree once more.

It rang three minutes later.

"Hey," I answered.

"Hey," Matt replied.

He would never understand the relief that flooded through me every time I heard his voice. Ever since the coma, Matt was a solid foundation for me. Had to be, considering he was the reason for it. When he'd threatened me with the truth, I'd lashed out. It came back to bite me times three. And when I woke up, the first phone call following it had started with two words, 'Don't apologize.' He never did let me say the words, and he'd never needed to hear them. We both knew. Which was why these phone calls were so precious to me. Because they didn't have to happen.

"How've you been?" he asked and I groaned loud enough for him to hear me. I was rewarded with a chuckle. "That good, then?"

"Mom set me up," I grumbled. The laughter stopped. Switching to a faux chipper voice, I said, "Guess what, Matt? I'm living in a town full of witches!"

"Oh shit."

"Yeah."

"So how bad is it, exactly?"

I opened my mouth to explain it all, and stopped. Even if it was Matt, I couldn't say it. Despite how well he knew me, there were some things he just didn't need to be aware of. Deciding what part of mine and Grey's interactions I could share was the difficult part of it. Because, deep down, I knew I wouldn't tell another living soul about our connection for a long time.

Instead, I said, "Well, it won't be easy. Pretty sure most of these witches are part of one giant coven, and they're not fond of outsiders. There's only one other solitary that I met, and today one of the coven members tried to pick a fight with her. The response was brutal."

"The other solitary kick ass?"

I smiled a little as I said, "No, the prince issued a decree."

"And 'the prince' is..."

"Their most powerful witch."

"And somebody who's caught your interest, judging by how carefully you answered that question. So, what gives?"

Leave it to Matt to pursue a topic I didn't even want to think about. "The other way around. I caught his. Not sure he's used to being outmatched, much less by someone outside of his bubble. I'm hoping he'll back off now that he realizes I'm not interested, but we'll see."

For a minute, Matt didn't reply. That worried me, considering my skill with half-truths had plummeted over the years. It would figure if Matt could see even what I didn't want him to look for.

At last, he asked, "Do you at least have an exit strategy?"

I grinned. "As a matter of fact, I do. Between all of the schools I've been to, I have enough credits to graduate at the end of this semester. If things here get too complicated..."

"You can come home." He said it how I would have: low and breathless. As if we were discovering the meaning of life or something. This was the treasure we'd been searching for; this opportunity that would set me free and lead me home again. And it was only a few short months away.

"Yes," I answered in the same tone.

A few seconds dragged on before he replied. I could hear the grin in his voice when he asked, "Yeah, but would you admit it if it was too much for you to handle?"

"Of course not," I scoffed.

His chuckle drifted through the phone and a feeling of contentment tugged at my heartstrings. I missed him so much. Out of some of the most trying days of my life, Matt had held his head high and hadn't been ashamed to be seen with me. Friends like that were hard to come by. Especially after what I'd done to him.

"So, how's Pennsylvania? Are you kicking ass at college?"

"If you mean getting my ass kicked, sure. Had my first classes last week and the reading list alone is enough to knock me unconscious."

"And what, you don't have the extra time?" I snorted.

"Hey! I'll have you know that I have a wide variety of pressing social engagements to attend to."

"Are you going out for Rush Week? Didn't you want to be part of some fraternity or something?"

"I said it was an interesting concept; not that I would commit myself to it. Besides, I've got you and Nathan. What brotherhood could top that?"

Though part of me was waiting for it, I was never quite able to control the mixture of emotions that flew through me when he said Nathan's name. First came the shame, considering everything I'd done to myself. Fear of never seeing him again followed it, and was chased out with the knowledge that existed in my bones that I would see him again. Nothing would stand in our way. Then I was overwhelmed with the longing. Nathan and Cedar Creek were as one to me. They were my home. Without them, it left a heartache that pulsed like an open wound.

"You all right there, Sparky?"

"Yeah. Just ... can't wait to go home. You know..."

"Yeah. I know."

"Thanks, Matt," I whispered into the phone. Sometimes the most important thing a good friend could do was know when to say nothing. He was a good friend.

I wasn't sure what I expected to come of the following morning, but I was pretty sure that Grey ignoring me for the entirety wasn't it. I'd also found it a bit unnerving when Summer didn't show for our first period. It made me really question how absolute Grey's power was as the prince of Crone's Crescent. If he could ban a witch from entering his presence, or even a building where he was located, what else was he capable of? And who sat high enough to stop him?

At lunch, I was witness to the one being who dared. Once more, Spring sat beside him, presiding over their own royal court. Again, he didn't look at her and she snuck glances at him. Even so, with his magick on display, everyone but her had theirs kept under tight control. Despite not having the power to be considered their princess, she had the enigmatic sway. That seemed to be enough.

"You're staring at them again," Delaire remarked, flipping the page in a catalogue she'd brought with her.

In an instant, I tore my eyes away. At least she was willing to tell me when I was making a fool of myself. I still didn't want to make a habit of it.

"You can ask me questions, you know. I've never been initiated, so whatever I know isn't top secret information," Faye said with a shrug.

I almost bit my tongue for real. As much as I wanted to know about Crone's Crescent, I didn't feel comfortable asking for that information. It would be unfair; like I was prying into someone's life without offering them a glimpse of mine.

Faye seemed to sense some of my resolve,

because she said, "Everything I know is public information. No reason you should be ignorant of what everyone else in this school already knows."

"She has a point," Cat remarked. "The coven may keep to themselves, but rumors have lives of their own. If you want the truth of something, Faye's the closest you're going to get to it. Might as well take advantage."

For a moment, I considered it. Then I looked at the young witch and asked, "How are you a solitary?"

"You mean because I'm coven-bred?" she asked with a smirk. "My parents are both coven witches, coming from many generations of other coven witches. To be a coven witch, you have to be initiated when you're thirteen, and only then do you learn the real truths of your community. When my birthday drew near, however, I refused. It's made life ... difficult, to say the least. But I don't regret it."

"Why?"

"'All for one, and one for all.' It's not a reality I'm comfortable living. I'm not going to stand behind someone and give them my support just because they're part of my coven. Nor will I bow to others just because they have a touch more power than myself. There are many reasons I chose to be solitary. Having control over my own life was number one on the list."

I nodded once, all the while fighting the urge to reciprocate. She'd given me a glimpse of her life, and my mind rationalized that it would be only fair to return the sentiment. It wasn't something I could do, however, and so I kept my mouth shut.

Before I could decide how to respond, Delaire's head jerked up and she shoved the magazine toward Faye. "Look at this coloring. It would work perfect for your outfit. Add a few white beads over the skirt and silver coins at the hips... If I order it now, it should arrive in a week. That'll be plenty of time for me to get it ready."

Faye's attention was redirected in an instant and the two began talking sizes, cuts, coloring, and style. All of which confused me to no end. Thankfully, Cat took pity on me.

"Del's mom is our dance teacher. We have a kind of performance scheduled in October and Del's been making our costumes. Every time she tries to find something for Faye, though, it somehow doesn't work out and it's been driving them nuts."

"What kind of dancing do you do?" I was still half-listening to Delaire and Faye discuss skin-exposure, getting more suspicious by the second.

At the same time, a sly grin pulled at Cat's lips as she announced, "Belly dancing."

Chapter Ten

PROXY

"Oh, this was a bad idea," I grumbled as I followed the girls into Delaire's basement. Considering the size of her house, I wasn't expecting a room so large, and the seamless mirrors covering the entirety of one wall creeped me out more than a little bit.

"Relax, it's all fun and games," Faye chuckled.

"Yeah, mhm," Del answered, shooting to a corner of the room where clear totes were loaded with colorful fabrics and a sewing center was set up. She returned with a measuring tape.

"Oh no!" I balked, taking a few steps back. "What are you doing with that?"

She released a dramatic sigh. "Relax, would you. It's not going to bite. Now stand still so I can get this done. Cat, pen and paper, please?"

"I am not performing anything, you know. This is a waste of time," I warned her.

"If you think I'm letting you leave this house without taking your measurements, you're delusional. Also, I can pretty much guess just by looking at you, so you might as well let me confirm. Now hold still."

I let her take the measurements. Really, there was no stopping her. Besides that, I had zero intentions of it being necessary for her to use them.

"Do you do any kind of dancing?" Cat asked, heading for the stereo against the opposite wall.

"Nope."

"This will be fun, then," Delaire said with a wide grin. "We'll be able to mold you how we want, instead of trying to contradict other teachers."

I tried to remember that I had wanted to do this, but that was hard when faced with the embarrassment that came with knowing I was about to make a fool of myself. They could say what they wanted about me just being a beginner and not catching onto things they'd spent years honing, but the failure would still be there. And I would still be humiliating myself.

All the same, I'd made a commitment and I had no intention of backing out. It wasn't in my nature. So, I stepped up to the mirror and paid close attention as Delaire explained the posture she wanted me to start off in. From there on out, it was a long afternoon.

To his credit, Grey tried to do as I asked. For about a week.

I'd been suspicious, at first. All weekend, I'd been unconsciously monitoring his every vicious, rabid mood. There wasn't a single time that I could have called him content all the while we were separated. He went from agitated to furious in moments, and it drove me crazy not knowing what was happening to cause his mood swings.

On Monday, I almost asked him what it was. It was on the tip of my tongue when he walked into our history class, and I was talking myself out of bringing it up. Then a sudden contentment washed over him the second his eyes landed on my face. The interrogation died then and there.

As I'd asked, he didn't speak to me. He was letting me have my way. In first hour, when he avoided looking at me. At lunch, when he thought I wouldn't notice every glimpse he shot my way. During our Creative Writing class, he even made it so that Mr. Watts didn't notice our lack of cooperation. All to avoid breaking with my wishes.

What got me the most, however, was when he sat down next to me during study hall and a rune appeared in the corner of my notebook. I had to take a breath when I recognized the X shape of the rune Gebo. It was the rune of fair exchange and sacrifice. In some circles, it could even be thought to mean: balance of opposites, dissolution of barriers, and gratitude. In itself, that single rune asked a question that I could not yet answer.

On Tuesday and Wednesday, the same pattern occurred. While Grey was refusing to talk to me, that didn't mean he was not making himself an accessible part of my life. The reason for which, I couldn't deny. He was offering me the chance to alter the role I had assigned to him.

It wasn't until Thursday that I realized that

he was doing that himself. Even if he didn't speak to me, I was learning things about Grey Walker that I hadn't asked to know. Without a single word, he was sharing parts of himself with me so that I could have all the facts before I made a decision. Bit by bit, he was reworking how I saw him. And making me want to see more of him.

That same day, Grey decided that he was done playing by my rules. I felt the determination set in a moment before he strode into the class. His eyes didn't leave my face for a second as he crossed the room.

Before I could move, one hand was on my desk and the other gripped the back of my chair as he leaned in. His lips were so close to my ear, I flinched away, afraid of what would happen if we touched. Then he spoke and I forgot how the sound of his voice was enough to set my body into overdrive.

"We tried it your way," Grey murmured, "and it's driving me crazy. Now it's my turn."

He sat down before I could respond, but my eyes followed. His features were set in a daring expression as he slowly raised his eyes to mine.

It was the first time in a week that I didn't look away.

A surprised hiss slid between my teeth as the intensity slammed into me. Fire blazed hot and furious between us. What I had thought of as sparks before now seemed like jagged arcs of lightning racing across the ceiling. The oxygen vanished as the storm surged throughout the room. Neither of us could break away. Neither of us wanted to try.

It wasn't until Summer walked between us that the connection shattered. Quickly, I closed my eyes and began breathing again. My lungs felt sore as the air dropped like ice into the bottom of them.

Beside me, Grey was doing his best to downplay how hard it was to breathe, or how drained the encounter left him. A weary smile pulled at my lips as I attempted to do the same. All the while, his promise replayed itself in my head and I tried not to be too pleased by it.

When I opened my eyes, it was to realize that everyone sharing the corner with Grey and I were subtly trying to decipher what had just happened between us. Summer, in particular, seemed anxious about discovering why we kept shooting glances at one another. The fact that I had to force away a smile and he wouldn't stop grinning didn't help matters. Which made me grateful when class started and we got a reprieve from the prying eyes.

For the most part, I understood his reasoning. He got what he wanted out of me and he was feeling triumphant. What I didn't understand was my reaction to it. When our eyes met, it was like riding a high. It felt so good that it was damn near addictive, and I wanted more of it. Which only added to Grey's triumph.

When class ended, I hurried to escape, as I always did. This time, I wasn't quite fast enough. I was surprised when Grey was standing in my way by the time I whipped around my chair. A sly smile pulled at his lips that had my eyebrows climbing up my forehead.

"May I walk with you?"

I tried to find an appropriate way to respond to that, but all that came to mind fast enough was, "We're going to the same place. I can't stop you."

His grin turned devilish. "I'm sure you could

if you wanted to."

I barely glimpsed the murderous look on Summer's face as we drifted out of the classroom. Part of me found it odd that she was serving as her sister's proxy when it came to being jealous of me, but I also found it kind of admirable. Summer was loyal to her sister, and she didn't have a patient temperament. When she saw what she believed to be a transgression, she attacked it. That was a sisterly bond I would never have a part in, but one I could admire from a distance.

"You really aren't interested in maintaining the goodwill of your subjects, Your Highness," I remarked.

A surprised chuckle escaped him. "You've heard the nickname."

"To be fair, I probably would have started calling you that myself after seeing you and Spring holding court at lunch every day."

His emotions spread taut, though his face betrayed no sign of reaction to her name. Some defensive little part of me didn't care that I was making him uncomfortable. I had my reasons for keeping my distance, and this kind of drama was at the top of it.

"You didn't answer the question. Why are you trying to antagonize Summer by talking to me?"

For a second, he tried to catch my eye, but I ignored the sensation. "I'm not trying to antagonize Summer by talking to you. I'm speaking to you because I want to. Antagonizing her is a bonus."

My stomach knotted again, remembering similar words I'd once expressed to my mother. When I was in the middle of punishing my parents for taking me from Cedar Creek, I'd told her that most of what I was doing was just to get through the day. Pissing them off was a pleasant side effect.

"Alex?" Grey questioned, his voice going low so no one could hear the honest concern.

For a moment, I'd forgotten that my emotions also traversed the link, so often was I focused on his. With him able to study my face, however, I was quick to throw a mask in place and shrug off my ordeal.

Grey didn't get the chance to ask again before we entered our classroom. Even when we took our seats and waited for the rest of the class to wander in, he didn't speak. Silence that I was grateful for. The less I had to dodge the subject of my past, the better.

Once we'd all taken our seats and the second bell rang, Mr. Watts stood in front of the room and showcased a broad smile. It should have made me suspicious. It didn't.

"All right, let's settle down for a bit. Today I have some good news for those of you who are already sick of this subject. For a final project to end your endeavors as playwrights, I am tasking each pair of one male and one female to create a scene. I will provide the overall theme, the general storyline, and assign each part to you. If your current work partner is not of the opposite sex, I will also shuffle you around. Your job is then to create a believable scene that follows my narrative while remaining true to the character arc your classmates provide.

"This will not be an easy project, nor is it something we will accomplish in a day. Therefore, we have one week. Next Friday, we will present our miniature play-with each of you acting out the parts of our characters-to Mrs. Lauren's second period drama class. While your acting may be critiqued, it is your skills as a playwright that will come under the most fire. Now let us begin."

Chapter Eleven

RECIPROCITY

I paid careful attention to the narrative of antagonistic detectives that Mr. Watts outlined for us. There were twenty-four kids in the class, which broke us into twelve groups. Since there were more males than females in the class, there were choices to have a pair of men either open or close the production. They chose the easiest route and decided to open it with a 'let me tell you a story' kind of setting. Which meant whoever had the last scene had to nail it.

That was me and Grey.

I literally let my head drop onto my desk the minute Mr. Watts assigned us the final sequence. Not only because I knew how difficult it would be to wrap up everything left for us by the other groups, but because Grey's sly grin told me that this was going to be far more complicated than I anticipated. And I was anticipating a lot.

For the rest of the hour, Mr. Watts worked with us as far as setting up the play. As with every form of expression, the story had to come first. Without that, it didn't matter what was written, because nothing would make sense.

Granted, there wasn't a lot that twelve scenes and a minimal cast could produce. Every scene relied heavily on the dialogue to explain what had come before and set the stage for what was left. In that regard, at least, being last would be easier. All Grey and I had to do was put an end to the story.

I might have felt better about that if Grey's magick wasn't running rampant throughout the room. My stomach roiled as he sat back and let the others do his bidding. The meager storyline laid out by Mr. Watts was already rife with his desires, but the way he was directing the scenes and other students into creating them was more than a little unnerving. By the end of the class, I was fuming.

When the bell rang, I was out of there before

Grey had a chance to even open his mouth. I was never more grateful for the fact that I had the next two classes without him. It might have ended with me strangling him, otherwise. Which was why I skipped lunch entirely when the bell rang, instead making my way to the courtyard.

I'd been sitting with my back to a tree and my eyes closed when the power surged around me, announcing his arrival. A groan was expelled as I covered my face with my hands. With my anger still faithfully broadcasted across our link, he had to be an idiot to come anywhere near me.

Without any care for my mood, Grey approached and sat beside me. He was too close for comfort, but I was too stubborn to move away from him. I was further surprised when a smooth surface brushed against the inside of my wrist. My eyes snapped open and looked down at the red and green skin of an apple.

Grey said but one word. "Please?"

Taking hold of the apple, I waited for him to release it and retract into his own personal space. I had no intention of eating it, but fighting with him about it was pointless. Something he seemed to sense, considering the trepidation that darted along our connection.

"You're a real prick, you know that?" I growled. "I mean, how can you be okay with this?"

"Was there another way?"

I didn't offer up an answer. Of course he couldn't see it in the same light that I did; the story was half his. Though it was wrapped in the fiction of two partners working to solve a mystery, our relationship was layered through every scene. Enough so we would have to address it in the finale. He was going to call me out, on a stage, in front of almost four dozen strangers.

"You won't talk to me, Alex. You're sitting here trying to pretend, even now, that this is something we can get over and move past. It's not, and you know it. So, we have to confront it. If you don't like how I'm doing it, you can always change it. Until then, this is what's happening."

"How could I change it, Grey? With magick? Should I just invade the minds of others and warp their thoughts without care for the conse-quences? No, thank you. They deserve their au-tonomy, and so do I. Maybe you're right and this isn't something we can just get over and move past. That doesn't mean it is something I need to mold my life around. It exists, for good or ill, but it doesn't get to call the shots here."

"And you do?"

"Is it always going to come back to that? Yes, Grey, I do. Because I take control over my life and how everything turns out. If you can't say the same, then I feel sorry for you."

"What's the difference between control and suffocation? How can you enjoy anything in life if you have to create rules for every aspect of it? Pity me as much as you want, Alex, but know that the feeling is mutual."

Without another word, Grey's magick wrapped around him and he vanished. For a moment, I sat there staring at the spot where he'd been sitting. Then I cocked back my arm and threw the apple across the courtyard.

Chapter Twelve

JOURNEY

I wanted to get back at him. It was all I could think about after class. As had happened the day before, he'd pushed them around. Invaded the minds of twenty-two teenagers and twisted everything they said or wrote. All so it could lead to a confrontation between us. At least I could give him credit for knowing that it would be a confrontation.

Still, getting back at him was going to be difficult. While Grey had been revealing pieces of himself–I still got a rune during study block–there was still a lot I didn't know about him. And when I asked Faye what the best way to piss off her cousin was, her response had been less than helpful. Even so, it gave me an idea. Now if only the execution matched the planning...

It took every single step of the walk home for me to get my nerves under control. Granted, Grey didn't know that my feelings were about him, but if I didn't keep them in check, he would. As little hope as there was for my plan, at least it was something.

When I arrived home, I was greeted by the sound of a sledgehammer biting into drywall and smashing against studs. My mother's plans called for an opening between the kitchen and dining room, with pillars to support the weight of the second floor. Making the whole house open concept would cost more than it was worth, considering there were too many load-bearing walls, but she was determined to at least do what she could to get a better flow.

I couldn't have picked a better day to take myself out of the house.

For the first time in a week, I entered through the front door, without once visiting my hawthorn cave out back. My dad spotted me between swings of the hammer. With ease, he let it drop to his side, offering me a tentative smile. I returned it.

I may not have physically hurt my dad like I had my mom, but those days had damaged our relationship in other ways. In my mind, he'd ruined my life, and I'd taken retribution by doing the same. While my mother was easy to forgive, my father wasn't. Even though he told himself that there was nothing to forgive me for, we both knew that wasn't true.

So, there we were, afraid to smile too widely at each other and shatter the fragile illusion that everything was going to be okay. As usual, we were saved by Mom. She spotted me a second after my dad did, and her grin was wide as she lowered the earmuffs.

"Hey, Baby. Thought you were going to be out again?"

"I am. Just not at Delaire's. I've got a project in Creative Writing and I'm heading over to my partner's house for a while. Not sure when I'll be back. Just wanted to let you know."

"And who is this partner?"

I almost groaned. Leave it to my mother to ask the one question I didn't want to answer. "His name is Grey Walker. I'll be back in a few hours."

My mom gave me a look that said we'd discuss it later. I got out of there before it became sooner.

Grey was located north of me by about five miles. Taking a deep breath, I calmed my nerves as much as I could before throwing in headphones and turning on my music. With the active bass in my ears, I smiled a little and set off on my journey.

I forced myself to lose track of time as I listened through the roughly three hundred songs I'd accumulated. All the while, I couldn't distract myself from monitoring our link. At first, it was in a state of turmoil. His emotions rocked between irritation and snide amusement before falling into a steady burn of anger. How he always felt when he was away from me. Then he surprised me when I was about twenty minutes away. Somehow, he let go of all of it and gave himself a clean emotional slate. I felt nothing.

My pace increased as I entered into the wealthier neighborhood of Grant. Larger houses were spread out by acreage of woodlands. Long driveways vanished between trees, cut off by ornate gates. And all the way, I could feel the magick boundaries that marked each witch's residence. Crone's Crescent Coven dominated Grant in every way.

Following our bond, I was soon directed down a private road. That was the official term for a ridiculously long driveway. At the end of the road, a magickally guarded gate barred my path.

My stomach clenched as I approached it, afraid of what enchantments lingered within the metal. All the while, the decision plagued me: either use my magick to pass through it without detection, or send a blast of emotion to Grey and reveal that I was there. In the end, I decided it depended on the barriers.

In an instant, I knew that this was a place where the coven met most often. Otherwise, there would be a negative-barring barrier that did not allow for anyone with ill intent to cross the boundary. If it was like the other estates I passed-or even like my own cottage-that would be the first spell laid down. No one hawanted to deal with pissed off people in their safe zone. Which also informed me that this was no one's safe zone.

Upon further examination, I realized that

the spells stitched together around the property were the kind that repelled magickal attack, discouraged unwanted guests, and warned off most individuals; most of it was a bluff. Upon the gate itself, there was a glorified, magickal intruder alarm. As soon as I passed through, no doubt every member of the household would know that someone had crossed the boundary. But none of it existed to cause me actual harm.

Taking a deep breath, I pushed the gate wide and crossed into the Walker estate. Behind me, the gate slammed shut.

It amazed me that Grey was still locked within the emptiness. Did he just ignore the gate's warning system? Did he assume it was someone else? How could he not notice how close I was? What kind of mental exercise allowed him to be that oblivious?

I blessed whatever it was as a new excitement entered my system. I was about to sneak up on Grey Walker. The man I had an irrevocable bond with from the second our eyes met. A man who frustrated and tormented me daily was now at my mercy. That kind of power made me feel giddy.

By the time I reached his house, I thought I was prepared for anything.

I wasn't.

Materializing straight out of a horror novel, the gothic building before me looked like an ancient cathedral, though it couldn't have been older than fifty years. The driveway looped around in front of the enormous building, a large, lichen-covered fountain towering in the center of it. Stone walls climbed upon one another until they reached the steep slopes of the roof. Above the door, however, they kept climbing until the tower was complete. A large, circular window existed in its center, looking very much like a watchful eye over the domain.

It was the only point of the roof where a person could safely stand without sliding to their death. I knew that because Grey's black cloak was framed against the roiling clouds being pulled in from the west. My breath caught, praying to myself that he wouldn't look down.

I was more cautious in my approach of the house. My eyes kept darting to him, even after he was blocked from my view. When that happened, I took a deep breath and reached out for the giant brass knocker attached to the door through a lion's jaws.

At the same time, I shoved everything I felt in that moment along our link and had the pleasure of feeling it shatter his emptiness. Pure shock replaced it as a woman opened the door for me. She looked me over in an appraising manner.

"May I help you?" she drawled, a slight Southern accent lingering on the words.

I almost had to clear my throat before I forced out, "I'm here to see Grey Walker."

"Mr. Walker is not available at this time." Her sentence ended with a sharp intake of breath as I felt Grey appear behind her.

"He will see me," I assured her. Then I looked pointedly through the door and asked, "Won't you, Grey?"

The woman leaned her head back a little, catching his reaction with her peripheral vision. He must have nodded, since she then pulled the door open wider. "Please come in."

When I stepped into the foyer that ran the length of the house, I had to do my best not to gawk. At the end of the corridor, I saw two doors that led out onto a back deck area. About at the halfway point, stairs framed the corridor, separating public space from private. It was strange that the two did not connect, instead leading into one wing of the house each.

When my eyes trailed upward, I was astonished to find out why. The corridor not only ran the length of the house, but it also had the entire vaulted ceiling available to it. Right about where the third and fourth stories would be, the light of the circular tower window shown down over the crystalline chandeliers that hung from arches that looked to be specifically for support and beauty. That is, until one spotted the doors at either end, and it became apparent that they were bridges that linked the two wings of the house at the upper levels.

"By the Gods," I murmured to myself, turning in place before my eyes fell back to Grey. He looked anything but pleased.

Chapter Thirteen

TRADITION

"Impressed?" he asked, drawing out the word. My awe had overpowered our link so diligently, that I hadn't noticed until that moment how furious he was. Though he leaned against the wall with blatant unconcern, I could feel the churning of his emotions. It was warning enough; if I lashed out, he would strike back.

If it was just his anger, I might have felt more tempted. There was more to the sea thrashing inside of him, however, and that gave me pause. In the span of seconds, I was hit with anger, distrust, paranoia, fear, a flash of jealousy, as well as a bitterness that I couldn't understand. One by one, they threw themselves along the bond, each volatile emotion chasing off the last.

"Yes," I said, finally remembering to answer his question. Even if it was asked in sarcasm.

"Have you ever seen so grand a building?" He gestured in a passing fashion to the room. His eyes never left my face, and I was growing more tempted to meet them as time went on.

"I didn't come here to discuss your living conditions," I announced in a far gentler voice than I had intended.

Grey shrugged off the wall, stepping close enough that I had to crane my neck back to see his face. "Why are you here?" It was a slowly spoken accusation.

Despite myself, I bristled at his tone. "You said you wanted to talk to me. Did you mean it?"

"Of course." Quick and curt.

"How about now?"

"It is not a good time."

"It wasn't a good time for me, either, when you walked into my life. When you manipulated our teachers or classmates. You can't have it both ways, Grey. Either you want to talk to me and we'll hash it all out right here and now, or you can keep trying and failing to get answers to questions you have no right to ask. Just because you're curious, it doesn't mean you've earned anything from me."

For a moment, we just stood there, staring at each other. Emotions roared across our link, and I was surprised that so few came from me. Though I'd wanted to get back at him, I didn't feel vindictive or spiteful in that moment. I felt exhausted. The sooner we could get this over with, the better.

"I'll tell you what, why don't you think about it? For one day, you and I will have an honest conversation. We will answer with the truth or we will pass on questions that we feel are too personal. After that, we work on this stupid project like it isn't about you and me."

An irritated snort left him. "What's the point of that, Alex? You consider everything too personal. What questions won't you pass on?"

"Then we'll set a limit. Five passes total."

"Two."

"Four."

"Three."

"I will concede to three."

"Very well. How about tomorrow?"

"It'll have to be later in the afternoon. I have

plans all morning."

"Lunch is out, then?"

I gave him a half-assed smirk. "Lunch with the girls. How's four?"

He raised his eyebrows. "Lunch lasts four hours?"

"Lunch isn't scheduled until two, since most people like to sleep in on Saturdays. And that could take two hours."

He nodded. "Where should I pick you up?"

"I can meet you somewhere."

"Here?"

That one surprised me, given his initial hostility. A hostility I was surprised to find had faded away as our conversation continued. Now, there was a playfulness in him. He was almost ... flirty.

"Sure," I answered, drawing out the word in a slow, uneasy way.

In an instant, I was treated to a devilish grin. I hadn't noticed before, but Grey had dimples. Especially when he smiled like that.

"I'll give you the full tour," he assured me.

In an automatic response, my eyes darted around the room again. I was actually kind of eager for that one. He'd been right on that count at least: I'd never seen a place so grand.

Shaking my head a little, I turned back to him. "I should get going. I'll see you tomorrow, Grey."

As I moved toward the door, he reached out and opened it for me. I was just about to pass through when he remarked, "It's a date."

It took everything in me not to respond to that.

When I paused in the doorway, I found the trees surrounding the house in the midst of a dance. Swaying one way and then another, a brisk wind forced them to bend to its own rhythm. All the while, the clouds pulled in darker and faster. Soon, they would release their burdens in a hard, savage downpour.

I grinned.

"Wait," Grey said, almost reaching out to touch my arm. When he realized what he was about to do, his hand snapped back to his side. Clearing his throat, he said, "Follow me. I'll give you a ride home."

For the first time, I really smiled at him. "No thanks. I'll see you tomorrow, Grey."

The moment I stepped outside, the rain started to fall.

I burst through the front door, soaked through to my skin. Leaning back against the door, my teeth chattered between gasps of hysterical laughter. What made the situation funnier was the pent-up frustration Grey was sending along our bond. Though I'd been poured on all the way home, I hadn't once used my magick. It was something he could not understand.

"Oh, I'd know that laugh anywhere," my mom announced. It sounded like she was in the kitch-en. Then she walked right through the space her and Dad had created between the dining room and kitchen. She was holding her laptop.

I didn't bother waiting to be given permis-sion. There was only one reason for this. Grin-ning, I strode across the room and lifted the computer out of her hands, turning it to face me at the same time.

Matt was grinning at the camera before he got a real look at me. Then he started laughing. "You look like a drowned troll."

"Shut up. I just walked five miles in the pouring rain."

"Five miles?" my mom questioned, crossing her arms and cocking a hip to the side.

"No pity for you. No one made you do it," he responded.

I rolled my eyes but turned toward the stairs. "How long ago did you call?"

"About fifteen minutes, I think."

"So, Mom gave you the full breakdown?"

"It's tradition," Matt announced, putting a grandiose note into his voice.

He had that part right, at least. Ever since we set up the video chat on my mom's laptop, any time that Matt called and I wasn't available, Mom would take him on a tour through the house, pointing out the layout. Then she would take him room by room and explain exactly what she intended for the space. It usually lasted them until I arrived or was able to snatch the computer from her.

"And your thoughts?"

"My dorm room is bigger than your bedroom. That's sad."

I rolled my eyes, knowing exactly what he

was referring to as I climbed the stairs to the attic. "I like my room."

"No, you think you deserve it."

Pretending not to hear the accusation layered in there, I said, "I do deserve it. It's cozy, quiet, and slightly out of reach of crazy guys who like to throw rocks against my window in the middle of the night."

"I did that one time and I was fourteen!"

"It still happened. And it was very adorable," I added in a patronizing tone.

"Shut up," he growled. "So, where were you this time?"

Just the way he said it tipped me off. Which meant my mother would have even more questions for me than I had anticipated. Ever since the coma, Mom and Matt had operated on an open-honesty basis. Anything I said to one was subject to being repeated to the other. That's how my support system worked: by making sure everyone involved in my life remained involved.

Since I told Matt about 'the prince' during our last conversation, it wouldn't have taken him long to guess who my partner was. Or why my Mom received a watered-down explanation of my whereabouts. Which meant he basically told her everything that he knew about Grey. At least it wasn't much.

Releasing a sigh, I said, "I hate being manipulated."

His expression became surprised. "Uh-oh. What's going on?"

"Nothing," I said, shaking my head. "Just some witchy high school drama."

"Don't they know you're too old for that shit?"

I snorted as I set the computer on my desk, facing the wall. "You would think," I replied, raising my voice to be heard as I rummaged through my dresser for clean clothes. The dry fabric sent a giddy feeling through me.

"Come on, Lex. Just come out with it. Get it out of your system."

For a moment, I paused in the act of dressing and let my head lean back. Staring at the ceiling, I felt a pulse of sadness before a flash of longing shot through me. Matt would never know it, and I almost didn't admit it to myself, but there were just some things I would rather didn't get out of my system. It frightened me how much the bond affected that thought process.

Turning the laptop back around to face me, I settled in to tell Matt almost everything. Without divulging the truth of our bond, I outlined what had been done to me, as well as what I'd done in return. As always, Matt took my side. Just what I needed.

Chapter Fourteen

CLASSIC OMISSION

"So, who's Matt again?" Catori asked, scooping up a mouthful of croutons.

"You know those are supposed to be mixed in with the salad, right?" Faye remarked, earning an unimpressed shrug.

"Yeah, and how come you haven't mentioned him before?" Delaire demanded.

"He's one of my best friends. He was also, very briefly, my boyfriend."

"How long ago was that?"

"I was thirteen the summer that we dated."

"Awe, you had a summer love," Delaire teased.

"Shut up. Anyway, back to what I was saying, we had a video chat last night and I told him all about you guys."

"Well of course. We're fabulous," Del remarked.

"*And* he would like a picture. So, if you guys are willing..."

"Did you bring a camera?" Faye asked.

I held it up as evidence. The freckled Freshman plucked it out of my hands with ease, immediately delving into its inner workings. Rolling my eyes, I left her to it.

"So why does he want a picture of us?" Cat demanded.

"I'm not sure. Probably so he can tell me that my friends are hot and I should get him your numbers."

"Okay, I think I have it figured out. Here, Alex, stand right here. The lighting's perfect from this direction. But you'll have to make it quick. It's almost four and I've still got a week's worth of homework to cram into the next two hours."

My eyes widened as they shot to the clock above the cafe doors. I had about ten minutes to finish up with the girls and head to Grey's. We were still two miles away from his house.

"Oh crap. Okay, come on," I urged Del and

Cat as they pressed together for the picture. I took two shots, just in case the first came out blurry, before I shoved the camera in my bag and started gathering my things.

"Where's the fire?"

"I'm supposed to be at Grey's at four. We've got a ... thing."

"You are a shitty liar," Cat said.

"It's a Creative Writing thing. We're assigned partners and I'm stuck with him. I told him I'd show up this afternoon so we could go over a few things."

Delaire's eyes narrowed. "Did that sound like the truth to you?"

"Yes ... and no."

Faye's smile was less amused while her eyes were more cautious. "It's a half-truth. Classic omission technique. And she's good enough at it to where that's all she feels she needs to say."

I didn't bother looking at any of them. Hell, I barely heard what they said. My stomach was too busy sinking to the floor as I felt him approach. I'd taken too long and now he was coming to pick me up. If it weren't for the girls, I would have groaned aloud.

Faye's head tilted to the side and her gaze turned toward the window. "He is impatient," she murmured. I'd forgotten that it would be easy for her to sense him the closer he got. All four of us were staring out the window when the silver Audi pulled up.

I felt like a little kid who'd been called to the Principal's office. There was a strange feeling along our link. Something akin to a superior amusement but with a hint of chastisement. Then the outright expectation.

Rolling my eyes, I said, "I'll see you guys later."

Faye's eyes shot to me and she grinned. "Have fun on your date."

"Shut up," I growled back at her, though I was already heading for the door.

I had no idea what I was getting into, really. Since I was late, I couldn't hold it against him that he came to retrieve me. At the same time, I wasn't keen on the idea that I was about to be sitting in a very confined space with him. Even if it was only for two miles.

When I stepped outside, a steady rain was falling, causing me to wrinkle my nose up at it.

Though I loved my downpours, I was never going to be a fan of light rain or even a boring, steady rain. Burrowing farther into my jacket, I trotted over and climbed into Grey's car.

I didn't mean to meet his gaze, but there was no help for it. He was staring straight at me when I turned to greet him. In a second, I was unable to breathe, much less speak.

Somehow, it felt more intense each time that it happened. Longing shot through me and my hands ached for want of touching him. My lips tingled and I sunk my teeth into the bottom one before I could betray my desire. In such an en-closed space, with his body so near to my own, all I wanted was to know how it felt if we touched. I wanted to feel his skin against my own, and I wondered if it would feel a fraction as thrilling as when our eyes met.

Jarred by my own thoughts, my eyes snapped away from his and we took a deep breath at the same time. Adrenaline coursed through me, making my entire body shake. Beside me, I could practically feel the vibrations as Grey worked through the same issue. For one endless minute, we sat in that car and tried to get over the desire that still roared through the link.

"Damn," Grey eventually said.

I nodded in agreement. Shaking his head, he reached over and started the car. As he pulled out onto the street, I leaned back in the leather seat and closed my eyes. For the rest of the ride to his house, I remained focused on my breathing. The last thing I needed was another jolt like that.

My eyes opened the minute I felt us cross the barrier along the gate. I scanned the forest as we proceeded up the driveway. When we got to the end, Grey began the circle before heading down a hill on the right side of the house. It surprised me when he pressed a button and a garage door opened beneath the house. A smirk pulled at his lips and he dared a glance at me-that I was quick to avoid.

"I don't use my magick for everything."

It was my turn to smirk. "Did I say anything?"

Grey chuckled a little, shaking his head in a dismissive gesture. Then he put the car in park and hit the button to close the garage door.

"Now, I remember promising you the grand tour. While I would like to start with the foyer and move on from there, I feel that it's a little impractical now. So, we'll start from the bottom and work our way to the top. Please, follow me."

My eyebrows rose as I followed him to a door in the corner of the room. "Oh, so you're not going to ask me what took so long or any of that?"

He shot me another devilish smile. Dimples and all. "I figured I'd wait until we started the official interrogation."

A slight shiver ran through me that I tried to hide. The idea of having only three passes did not seem comforting enough for me to go through with this. But a deal was a deal.

When Grey opened the door, I was surprised to find that it led into a hallway that was easily as long as the upstairs foyer. Several doors dotted the opposite wall, and Grey led me past most of them until we were closer to the back of the house. Then he grinned at me and pushed the last door wide.

As far as finished basements went, this was the most comfortably stylish one I had ever been in. While it wasn't huge, it was large enough to set itself apart as a gathering place. Along the right side was a large glass wall that I knew was one of those retractable doors. In the summer, this entire room would become part of the outdoors. A theme that was accentuated with the wood wainscoting and tile floors.

To my left, a pool table was set up, with the balls all arranged for a break. Beyond that was a wet bar tucked into the corner created by a bathroom. On the wall directly across from me was mounted a massive TV with an entire entertainment system set up beneath it. Between me and the couch, a long table was set up with eight chairs surrounding it.

Without a thought, my feet dragged me to the glass so that I could look out at the slope of the garden. From the doors of the basement, it ascended in a gradual incline, broken up by flower beds or herb patches surrounded by red mulch or with rock circles separating them from the lawn. A grin spread across my face as I noticed the fairy village centered around a rowan tree off to the right.

"That's where the kidlets spend most of the ceremonies. Mind, none of us has ever seen a fairy, but it's kind of tradition that they keep it up. In the spring, they'll repaint the houses, add fresh nesting materials, and make it all pretty again."

I wasn't sure what bothered me most. That even though I'd been distracted by the garden, I'd felt every step he took. That he was standing so close, our shoulders were almost touching. Or the fact that I was actually comfortable having him at my back.

Shaking it off, I turned to look at him and forced a smile. "Grand tour?"

For once, his smile was genuine. "Follow me."

Chapter Fifteen

COPE

An entire half an hour passed as Grey dragged me through his house. The official tour didn't touch on private rooms, and we skipped most of the guest rooms. However, I was treated to a few secret passages, the enormous dining hall, as well as the chef's kitchen that Anna, the woman with the Southern accent, was quite busy in. After he made a point to show me where his bedroom was, I'd had it.

"Alright, Grey, I think I've seen enough," I announced with an amused grin.

To be fair, I almost hated putting an end to the tour. For the past thirty minutes, I didn't have to deal with a cocky, arrogant, charming individual. Instead, I got an enthusiastic young man who was eager to show off his home to a stranger. Not because he wanted to make me envious, but because he wanted to share this with me. He did this because he knew how happy it made me to see it all.

Running a hand through his hair, Grey looked around him as if deciding what else I absolutely had to see. Then he sighed. "Very well. Everything else I could show you is outside, anyway. Maybe tomorrow you can see it."

I smiled, "Family day tomorrow. It might have to wait for Monday or Tuesday. Assuming I'm allowed back here after this discussion."

In an instant, his mood transformed. A new cunning slipped into his demeanor as he remembered my real reason for being there. And what it meant for him now that I was willing to part with some of my secrets.

"Very well. Where would you like to continue this conversation?"

I thought about each room we'd been in and found that there was only one where I felt comfortable enough. "The basement."

His lips twitched and he turned to lead me down yet another hidden staircase. Though I loved how many hidden passages his house had, I would never be able to understand where each one led. The place was a maze.

When we entered, Grey went immediately to the bar. I was surprised when he helped himself to the liquor cabinet, offering up a bottle to question my preference. Shaking my head, I moved to sit at the table. A bit later, Grey joined me, placing a glass of water in front of me.

Just when I was wondering where to begin, he asked, "So who were you having lunch with?"

"Faye, Delaire, and Catori."

"They're who you've been spending your afternoons with. What have you been doing?"

"Hanging out. Teaching each other a few things. Girl stuff."

"Am I supposed to be satisfied with such vague answers?"

"Aren't you going to give me the same kind of answers when I turn this back on you?"

He bowed his head in acknowledgment. "Very well. Turn it back on me."

I felt a jolt of pride when my first question hit him hard. "What is it with you and Spring?"

Grey did his best to hide the unease and

irritation that shot through him at the sound of her name. He looked perfectly content, however, when he answered, "We were friends once. Then we were lovers. Now she is nothing to me." He took a drink of amber liquid and I took the same opportunity to sip at my water. "What about you? Any lovers?"

I laughed a little, leaning back in my chair. "Not in the way you make it sound. I had a boyfriend once, then he became one of my best friends. He still is."

"How long ago?"

"When I was thirteen."

His eyebrows rose a little. "And you've been playing the field since?"

My mind flew back over the chaotic years following mine and Matt's breakup and I began to laugh so hard that tears formed in my eyes. Shaking my head, I managed to convey the ridiculousness of his question. At last, I was able to gasp, "No. Not even a little. There has only ever been one guy for me."

"So, you've never..."

"Had sex? Nope." Anticipation held steady in me as I waited for his surprise. Or snarky remark.

A moment later, he smirked at me. "Saving yourself?"

I shook my head. "Just disinterested."

"Why?"

Shrugging, I took another sip. "I've never been sufficiently enticed."

"Would you notice if anyone had tried?" He meant it as a barb, but I smiled.

"Grey, I know I'm pretty. And I've had the requisite amount of attention that comes of that fact. So yes, I've noticed the attempts."

"And you rebuff them as quickly as possible. Why is that?"

For a moment, a fist squeezed my heart as thoughts of home bombarded my brain. Running my tongue over my lips, I focused my eyes on the glass of water as I answered. "I avoid attachments wherever I go. We don't stay long anywhere, so it's best not to bother."

"You're forming attachments with Faye and the others."

A smile tugged at one corner of my mouth. "If Del wants to be friends, I don't know that anyone could stop her. As far as attachments go, ours is not of a lasting nature. We'll have fond memories, but ours isn't a relationship that will be missed."

"Would it be so bad if it was lasting?"

"It would mean regret. I'd like to avoid leaving as little of that behind as possible."

"You're carrying enough of it as it is," he added in a low voice.

I raised my eyes to his lips, feeling my jaw set and my chin lift. Grey chuckled at my sudden defensiveness, but not in an amused way. Instead, his laugh was built of irony and a little self-mocking.

"You are so determined to keep everyone away, and you wonder why we're even more curious about you. Why are you trying so hard to make me dismiss you?"

"Why are you trying so hard not to?" I demanded, not bothering to maintain a level of levity in my voice like he was doing. It was time to drop the charade. Before I could stop myself, my lip curled and I sneered, "Grey, if we had just been two people who spotted each other across a classroom and felt nothing, you would never have looked twice at me. So why are we letting this *thing* dictate our actions in response to each other?"

"We're not like everyone else!" The words came out in an exasperated rush as his composure finally broke. "Why are you trying so hard to pretend that there is nothing here?"

"Because there shouldn't be," I growled back. "Whatever exists between us *shouldn't*. There's no reason for it."

"Of course there's a reason for it," he snapped. "You know there is. Your problem is that you don't know what it is, and that pisses you off. So instead of trying to find out why, you're lashing out at me. As if I somehow want a complete stranger to know every single thing I'm feeling."

"Then say that! Tell me that you're upset or irritated or pissed off. Go ahead and take it out on me; that's fine. But don't sit here and act like it's the most natural thing on the damn planet and then wonder why I'm so pissed. This thing is an invasion in both of our lives, Grey. At least act like you know it is."

"So, because I cope better, that's not a proper enough reaction for you? I take things as the Goddess gives them to me, Alex. This is one more thing I have to live with and learn about. There's a lesson for both of us in all of this, and if you would quit your bitching for thirty damn seconds, maybe we'd be able to figure out what it is."

I almost bit my tongue as I let his words sink in. There was a restless itch forming inside of me and I could no longer sit still. Rising to my feet, I moved to the glass wall and began to pace in front of it.

"What if I don't care? What if I don't want to figure it out?"

He scoffed, "Does it look like you get a choice? This bond formed without your permission and it's staying in spite of your indignation. We have to learn to live with this, Alex, because it's going to take both of us to be rid of it. Which means you also have to learn to work with me. Are you capable of that?"

I shook my head. Not because I was incapable of it, but because I knew it was a bad idea. If I stopped to think about it for even a second, I knew exactly what rabbit hole I would be falling down. And I was desperate not to.

Swallowing hard, I almost met his gaze before asking, "Then what do you propose we do about it?"

The fight in him dimmed. "We get to know one another."

It was a simple request. The obvious choice. After all, how could we learn about a foreign connection when we didn't even know where it stopped and the other person began? His logic was sound, but it still left my stomach twisting. If I looked at my feet, would I see the edge of the rabbit hole right in front of me?

"And what if I'm not capable of that?"

Grey shrugged as he swallowed a mouthful of whiskey. "I'd say you have to decide which you are least capable of doing: getting to know me or having to endure this connection with a complete stranger. Your choice."

"Those are some awful choices."

He offered me a half-grin. "You can't really say that until you get to know me."

"I can say that because I don't *want* to get to know you."

"Why is that?"

My nose crinkled as I tried to find anything else to say, but we both knew the truth. "I don't want to know you, Grey, because I don't want to like you."

"And that is such an evil thing," he mocked, the smile spreading across his face.

"For you, it probably would be."

His eyebrows rose a little. "You have a high opinion of yourself."

I shrugged, not willing to share more with him. The truth of it was: I was right. I'd had enough experience with letting go, walking away, and moving on. If either of us were to survive the other, I stood a better chance.

"Some things I get over quickly."

"You think I'm one of those things?"

There was no doubt in my mind when I said, "I know you are."

Chapter Sixteen

DIFFICULT

That didn't stop him. Not that I thought it would, but there was some hope. Once I said it aloud, however, I knew that Grey would do everything in his power to make me like him. Part of me hated him more because I had an idea how easy it would be for him to succeed.

I was attracted to Grey. Not only because he was hot, but because he was cocky, arrogant, proud, and confident. I admired his self-knowledge and the authority and respect he commanded within his coven. There were qualities to him other than the snake charmer role he often played, and he was determined to make me see them. In the end, I knew how easy it would be for him because he reminded me so much of me.

"Well," he finally said, "then I guess that means I get a choice, too. I'm not scared of you, Alex. And whether you want to or not, we will get to know each other. You can't be this connected to someone and not learn about them. So, are you going to make this easy or hard?"

For a whole minute, I pondered my options. But logic had nothing to do with my decision. In the end, I didn't try to keep him from feeling the weariness seeping through me. With a grim smile, I glanced at his lips and said, "To be honest, I'm a little tired of difficult. What do you want to know?"

Draining the last of his whiskey, Grey got up and headed to the bar. His back was to me when he asked, "What's your full name?"

My teeth ground together for a second, but this wasn't a question worth passing on. "Alexandria Marie Ryder."

He stopped at the sink and smiled at me. "It's pretty."

I waited until he'd filled his glass with water and was headed back to the table before I asked, "What about yours?"

"Grey Walker. No middle name."

"Why?"

"Family tradition."

My eyebrows rose. "Family or coven?"

His lips quirked into a smirk. "A bit of both. My ancestors didn't hold with the new fashion of giving your child two names. They preferred not to have too many with the same first name. After a while, unique naming strategies were a staple of our coven. The few that do have them prefer them not to be used."

"Faye uses hers," I remarked, just to see how he'd react.

His irritation flared at the same time that he gave me an ironic smile. "Yeah, well, her first name put more expectation on her than she likes to allow other people to have."

"Smart girl. It's not worth it to care about other people's opinions. Especially when the only life you have control of is your own."

"Do you ever care what people think?"

"Define 'people.' There are some whose opinions I value very much," I said, a hand going to my arm. "There are also those who simply don't matter."

"And I'm not one of those whose opinion

matters," he remarked with a grin.

Raising my gaze to his lips, I gave him a small smile. "It's a short list."

For a second, I thought he'd dig into me about assigning value to people again. Instead, his next question caused my chest to tighten. "What happened to your arm?"

It took a bit before I could breathe again. When I answered, I wasn't looking at him. My eyes were trained on the valerian in the crux of my elbow when I said, "I kept a calendar."

"Of?"

"The days I missed."

"What were you missing?"

The word 'pass' was on my lips before I could blink. It almost flew out of me in a rush, trampling over any other answer I could imagine. I was grateful when I caught it just in time. It would save the pass for a harder question. This one, however, was easy.

"Everything. I am missing everything."

"Present tense," he remarked.

I nodded. "Present tense."

"Are the scars present tense too?" A subtle hardness crept into his voice.

"And if they were?" His jaw tightened and he glanced at the garden burned into my skin. "Relax, Grey. I stopped burning a year ago."

"Why'd you start?"

That required another deep breath and a question. How could I say it without revealing too much? At last, I answered, "We all have our dark times. These mark the darkest of mine."

"Are you better now?" The way his voice was pitched, I could tell that he was recovering from his own darkness.

Shaking my head a little, I said, "Right now? No. But I think I will be someday. I've put so much hope into being okay when this is all over, it'd probably rip my heart out if it somehow wasn't."

"What if you're not? What will you do then?"

"Am I supposed to know? The last time I thought everything could go back to normal, I entered a nightmare beyond imagining. Because of that, I have a garden of scars burned into my skin. If I fall down another hole as dark and deep as that, I will lose my bloody mind. No effort required."

For several seconds, he just studied me. At

last, he murmured, "What would you cling to if it all fell apart?"

I took a breath, monitoring how careful his voice sounded as he asked the question. In that brief moment, I realized that he and I had more in common than either of us had imagined. Because he was clinging to something, too.

"The same thing I am clinging to now," I answered.

"Which is?"

In one word, I could say it all. "Home."

Another silence fell between us and we took a few minutes to mull over what had been said. While I'd answered the most questions, Grey had revealed pieces of himself along the way. Pieces that left me even more curious and wary than before.

At last, he cleared his throat to gain my attention. Leaning back in his chair, a slight smile pulled at his lips as he turned his glass on the table. Without looking at me, he announced, "I will change your mind, you know."

"About?"

He smiled so that I could see his dimples. "Caring about me."

For a second, I would have rather bitten through my tongue than admit what came out of my mouth. "The sad thing is, I can see that happening. Which, I suppose, means the only recourse left is to make sure you stop caring about me."

Grey laughed. "You think you can?"

Lifting one shoulder, I let it drop. "Well, I haven't been successful yet, but there's a first time for everything."

My eyebrows rose a little as he lifted his glass up and toward me. Then I had to grin when he toasted, "Here's to a first time for everything."

I raised my glass to meet his. "First time for everything."

Chapter Seventeen

QUEEN

Lowering the glass to the table, I glanced at the clock hanging beside the interior door. "It's time to call it a night."

Grey's eyes appraised the clock as if it had committed a sin. I almost laughed as he double-checked his watch. Having a second opinion, he sighed.

"I'm afraid I have to agree. The coven will be arriving in about an hour and it's time to set up." That piqued my interest, but I held my tongue. "Come on, I'll give you a ride home."

"I can walk, Grey."

"No. I don't know what possessed you to do so yesterday, but it is not happening again. And we both know this is not the kind of rain you'd enjoy walking in."

I almost laughed at his stern expression, but nodded in any case. He was right on that count, at least. I really did not want to walk home in the boring crap.

We had just reached the door when Grey groaned. A rush of trepidation and irritation flared across the link and I raised my eyebrows at him. Then I felt what he did. What I would have felt far sooner had I been using.

As a vehicle pulled into the garage, two distinct sets of power were emanating from within. A breath escaped me as his mother's thick, fiery energy washed through the basement like acrid smoke. At once, it pushed in around me and it took all I had not to throw up a shield to push it back.

In comparison, his father was almost weak. Not in magick, but in attitude. He kept his magick reined in tightly, keeping a severe hold over it that was almost strangling. His way was not to scour out every change, but to evaluate every single detail in an instant.

No one could have explained Grey better to me than his parents in that moment. And I hadn't even met them yet.

I was about to.

"I apologize, Alex. I did not intend for this."

My voice was low when I asked, "Why do you think I would blame you?"

A forced smirk answered me. "You will see."

Nodding his head toward the glass wall, I followed him until we were standing before it, looking at the garden beyond. We remained in the same position until his father opened the door. We turned as one, each of us wearing a mask of polite intrigue.

"Hello, Mother. Father."

The use of the formal address weirded me out. By the set of Grey's jaw, however, I had a feeling it was the most civil thing he could manage to say. The tension vibrating along our link confirmed my suspicions.

I moved when he did, though I kept a foot of space between us as he introduced me. "Alex, these are my parents. This is Alex. She and I share a few classes together."

There was a sadistic pleasure he was taking in not saying my full name. Especially since his parents seemed to evoke a certain formality in their presence.

Taking a step forward, I extended my hand to his mother. Instead of opening with a lie, I said, "I'm sorry for the intrusion." Theirs. Not mine.

"Don't apologize. It is always interesting to meet new people." Her words were like melted honey, meant to draw me in. Too bad I could sense the poison in each lilting note.

Another stab of frustration flared through Grey and I almost sent a jolt of my own irritation back at him. As if I couldn't handle his mother. It almost seemed comical to compare her to even half of the things I'd been through.

"Will you be joining us for dinner, Alex?" His father did not make it into an invitation.

"Actually, I was just about to head home. My mom's expecting me."

"Have a good evening then," his mother said as Grey headed toward the door.

I waved goodbye to his parents and escaped out into the hallway. Grey set a brisk pace down the hall to the garage door. He didn't begin to breathe normally until we were in the car. Even then, the tension continued to roll off of him in waves until we were heading down the driveway.

When we were through the gate, he muttered, "I apologize."

"I'll accept if you stop using the stuffy formal talk."

That earned me a dimpled grin. "Sorry."

"Better. Now, again, why would I blame you?"

He shrugged. "You wouldn't have been there if it wasn't for me."

"Stop being so dramatic. So I met your parents. The floor did not open beneath my feet. There were no demonic creatures dragging me to the underworld. I think I survived quite well."

His eyebrows rose and he sent another sarcastic smirk my way. "You think it's over?"

"I think their opinion is irrelevant."

Grey released a heavy sigh. "Not to me."

The rest of the short drive was spent in silence. When we pulled up in front of my house, however, I lingered. I couldn't figure out why, but I suddenly had no desire to get out of that car. Or say goodbye to him.

Without looking at him, I said, "One last question before I go."

"Shoot."

Turning to him, I almost met his gaze as I asked, "Why is me meeting your parents such a bad thing?"

Grey sighed, closing his eyes and leaning back against the leather seat. "It has nothing to do with you, and it has everything to do with you. My mother is what you could call a 'social climber.' When it comes to the coven, she knows how to maneuver. To her, I'm a pawn on a chessboard. The minute she gets me across, I turn into something even more powerful. She wants me to be a king, and she wants to choose the queen."

"Spring."

"No, she'd prefer me to be with someone a little more biddable. For that reason alone, she has taken issue with anyone I've been with over the years. I prefer more independent women," he added with a knowing smirk.

"And your father?"

"Is a man of honor and principles. He believes that any commitment should be upheld, no matter the circumstances."

My eyebrows rose as I felt the unease and a little sorrow drift across our bond. "And the circumstances?"

Grey turned his head toward me enough so that I could see the weary smile. "Pass."

I wanted to bite my own tongue to keep from asking more. Instead, I nodded my head and unbuckled. A familiar heat traveled along my skin as he watched my movements. When my hand went to the latch, his voice stopped me.

"One more question before you go."

I turned back toward him, unable to halt the feeling of gratitude that I didn't have to leave just yet. Nor could I hide the hint of longing to stay. The closer we were to one another, the harder it was to ignore him. Now, there was no longer any chance of that.

My breath caught as he suddenly leaned close. I snapped my eyes shut when his face was within a few inches of my own, flinching back from the proximity. Then he asked his question and chills erupted all over my body.

"Can you feel it when I look at you, Alexandria? Does it move along your skin like fire and lightning making love?"

The words kept repeating in my mind long into

the night. Lying in bed, I could think of nothing else. More or less because there was no better way to describe it.

Fire and lightning making love.

He wasn't just talking about the feeling of his eyes tracing my lips or caressing my body. The phrase didn't apply to just how we looked at each other. It encompassed everything that happened to us the minute our eyes met.

Fire and lightning were making love.

Which was why the experience always took so much out of us. Why I was still weak from experiencing it again. Even why the desire had yet to dissipate, though the act of it was hours past.

The minute the words left his lips, I had been helpless to stop it. My eyes had snapped to his and the world stopped spinning. Everything inside of that car felt compressed, yet it seemed like there was a canyon of space between us. One that I had wanted to cross with every fiber of my being. Desire had damn near drowned me right then, and I couldn't remember how to break free.

I wanted him.

Wanted him enough to forsake even my own

defenses.

My terror saved me from that mistake.

The minute I realized the depths of my desire, my horror of the situation spiked high enough to force my eyes from his. More than that, it had me almost flying out the door. I couldn't even handle looking back before I ran into my house.

Being able to feel him that entire time did not help. Not even a little.

The desire in him was just as strong as it was in me. Strong enough to make me want to scream. I was burning alive with it, and I knew that Grey had somehow driven home while feeling the same.

It was a horrific nightmare with no end in sight. Even if I did manage to fall asleep, it was with the knowledge that it would be waiting for me when I woke. That was almost as terrifying as knowing that I would have to face him on Monday. And he might ask me to explain.

I wasn't sure I could pass on that one. I didn't even know the answer myself.

Chapter Eighteen

TEMPORARY

Passing notes was a thing of the past. Magickal note sharing had yet to be detected. As I found out almost as soon as I pulled out my notebook in first period on Monday.

Grey had entered later than usual, but a self-satisfied smirk was plastered all over his face when he made it to his seat. It set off a grin of my own, though I couldn't understand how. Then his eyes perused my body as was his custom. Only, this time I had his words flowing through my mind as he did so. A blush warmed my cheeks as I tried to force the embarrassment out of my system.

When I opened my eyes, a message was waiting for me in my notebook.

Are we on again for tonight?

For a moment, I stared at the words. Then I grinned and scrawled a hurried reply beneath them. *I'm not banished from the grounds?*

I'm not finished with you yet.

For one whole second, I felt a little indignant at that response. Then I felt vindictive. *Nor I with you.*

Beside me, Grey tried to turn a chuckle into a cough as Ms. Dixon called the class to order. For a few minutes, I tried to keep my attention on the task at hand. Then I made the mistake of glancing down. It was my turn to stifle a laugh.

You'd tell me if you were.

When. Not if.

Ouch.

I told you this was all temporary. You're not going to change that.

Grey shot me another grin. *You really don't give me enough credit.*

You really underestimate how stubborn I can be.

I think I'm starting to figure it out. You didn't answer the question.

A grin pulled at my lips as I thought about it. *If you remember, I only offered you one day.*

We still have five passes between us. It's not over

until we've used them.

And who made that rule?

I did.

I didn't agree to that.

You're agreeing now. Your smile says it all.

Damn him.

What was worse, I couldn't stop smiling. The banter was so light and quick and fun. It was easy to forget that we were in the middle of class and the world didn't stop so we could deal with each other. In that way, it was kind of nice. Whenever I had to go through something it was usually alone. This time, someone else was along for the ride.

We'll see. I made sure to shoot him a look letting him know that that was the end of it. Grey grinned and sent a mock-salute my way before the entire conversation vanished.

My irritation with him returned in our second hour. Of all the things I could handle, having to form a mini-play with characters based on us was not one of them. Thankfully, the plot didn't allow for him to direct it into more sensitive territory, because where he was nudging it was bad enough. Of course, half the battle was knowing that I could stop him, but by choosing to keep my penance intact, I was allowing this to happen. It was a hard pill to swallow.

At lunch, another unspoken rule was broken. He kept staring at me. While I waited for my friends at our usual table, his eyes never once left my face. It was easier to ignore until the girls showed up.

The first thing Cat said to me was, "Grey Walker has done nothing but stare at you since you sat down."

"Believe me, Catori, I know."

"So how did everything go on Saturday?" Faye's question sounded casual enough, but I could hear the genuine concern that lingered beneath her tone.

"It was okay. We're just trying to figure each other out for now."

"The purpose for that being?" Delaire asked, wiggling her brows suggestively.

I shrugged. "To be honest, I have no idea."

"Well, he's definitely showing interest."

"Yeah, I know. Just not sure I feel the same."

Faye snorted while Cat exclaimed, "Oh bull-shit! You've been sitting here smiling to yourself for the past five minutes while looking anywhere but right at him."

I couldn't help but laugh. "I didn't say that I wasn't attracted to him. Just that I don't think I'm interested in being with him."

"I can give you that one," Delaire said with a shrug. "Probably for the best, all things considered."

"You mean Spring?"

"I mean the coven."

"The more I hear about covens, the happier I am to be solitary."

"Then you haven't been seduced yet. Give it time. At least one of the Elders will see your worth and attempt to bind you. The worst one you'll have to watch out for is Mrs. Walker," Faye warned.

"We've met, and she didn't seem to take a fancy to me. Something about not being as pliable to her will making her dismiss me out of hand."

Faye shook her head. "She's dismissed nothing. Power determines rank in the coven. The Walkers hold a high hand because of their children. Broke everyone's hearts when Azure left."

That piqued my interest. Grey hadn't mentioned a sister.

"Anyway, you'd be a sort of consolation prize if it was because of Grey or the Walkers that you joined the coven. After you were totally initiated, you'd rank even higher than them. Which is why Mrs. Walker is undoubtedly weighing the pros and cons of having Grey seduce you."

"Well then," I said, a little laugh in my voice.

Faye shrugged. "I'm coven-bred. I know how it goes."

"Either way, it'll never happen. And Grey knows better than to try it. He knows how temporary my being here is."

Faye's eyes latched onto mine and I could see her storing that information for later. Without acknowledging what she was thinking, she simply remarked, "Don't bet on it."

Chapter Nineteen

OBSTACLE

I'd intended on walking home, talking with my mom a bit, and then heading toward Grey's. None of which seemed likely to happen when I found him leaning against the wall just outside of the doors. When he saw me, his lips pulled into a wolfish grin.

"Seriously?" I asked, rolling my eyes.

"I'm ready when you are."

"I've got to check in with my parents," I told him.

He shrugged, reaching into a pocket. Pulling out a cell phone, he held it out to me. "You call your mom; I'll go get the car."

For a moment, a silent dare hung between us. He wanted me to get close to him. Something we both knew I avoided like the plague. Even now, there existed a foot of space between us. And I would almost have to touch him if I wanted to grab that phone.

Unless I used my magick.

There was no choice. In one move, I stepped forward, plucked the phone from his hand, and whirled away again. I'd already begun to dial when I heard him chuckle right before he vanished.

"Ryder Housing, Melanie speaking."

"Hey Mom, it's me."

"Oh, hey Baby. What's going on?"

"Just wanted to check in and let you know that I won't be home until later. Grey's giving me a ride to his house. I'll have him drop me off when we're done."

"You'll have him drop you off?" she asked, a hint of sarcastic humor in her voice.

I grinned. "He's the one having a fit about me not walking in the rain. If that's the case, then he can be responsible for avoiding that outcome."

"Okay. So, what are you two going to be doing at his house?"

"Learning to live with each other, mostly," I

said with a snort.

The Audi pulled up just as she said, "Keep talking like that and I'm going to worry about the two of you eloping."

I couldn't help but laugh. "Gotta go, Mom. The brat is waiting. See you when I get home."

"See you, Baby. Be careful."

Rolling my eyes, I snapped the phone shut before heading toward the car. Once I was inside, I casually set the phone on the console before I turned to buckle up. I could feel Grey's amusement practically fill the car. It was almost equal to his anticipation.

"I'm not looking at you, so you might as well drive," I announced, unable to help the wide grin.

Beside me, Grey chuckled before we pulled out of the parking lot. As we started toward his house, another question popped into my head. Turning my head, I noticed the relaxed smile. It was something that I saw only when we were alone. When it wasn't part of an act.

"Why do you drive to school?"

"You mean because I can teleport? When you were using, did you never use other means of transportation?"

It felt like ice had slid down my spine. "What do you mean? I never said I wasn't using."

His eyes slid over to me in an expression that clearly indicated he wasn't stupid. "Alex, it wasn't something you had to say. You're living in a town full of witches. Magick isn't something we gawk at here. *Not* using magick makes us take note."

My arms crossed over my chest and I tried to sink into the seat, away from his knowing expression and placating voice. It was something I knew I should have expected, but I somehow thought that it wouldn't be remarkable. I was wrong. Which meant most of his curiosity about me could have something to do with that one fact about myself.

"I won't ask you now," he said, "but I hope that when I do, you'll trust me enough tell me the truth. Either way, that's not what I want to know about you right now."

In spite of my own defenses, that caused me to sit up straighter. "What do you want to know now?"

Grey didn't answer until we had pulled into his garage and he shut off the engine. Then he looked over at me and I was surprised at the amount of trepidation filling him. "Do you see every day as an obstacle?"

I didn't know what thought process led him to that conclusion, but I could not deny its validity. For some reason, I looked away when I said, "Yes."

"And so is everyone in it," he added with an almost sad smile as he got out of the car.

I was quick to follow. "Don't take it personally, Grey. My whole life has been an obstacle since the day of my Ascension. Until I can go back to the beginning and reset the balance, everything is something else I just have to get through."

He shook his head. "I don't know how you can look at it like that. I don't know how you can't see that every day is an opportunity."

I paused in the act of closing the door, staring at him over the top of his car. My head tilted to the side as I studied his earnest expression. At the same time, I felt his genuine confusion and emphatic belief through our bond. Suddenly, I was happy for him.

"That's what your dark times taught you. To be grateful for every single second, and to make it count. It makes sense, now."

I could see the wall forming in his eyes as he attempted to shut me out. Not that he was successful. We both felt the sharp pain that came with my words, and I was almost shocked at how familiar his heartache was, and how much it had once resembled my own.

Feeling a little more in tune with him, I closed the door and moved to the front of the vehicle. He met me there, and this time there were only six inches of space between us. I raised my eyes as far as his lips.

"My dark times didn't teach me that. They taught me that there is no such thing as coincidence. That you meet people in this life that are only meant to be there for a short time. And it taught me that those people will be important. Whether or not I want them to be.

"I know you're important, Grey, and that's what terrifies me. Because I don't want you to be. I am so close to the moment I've been waiting three years for, and I don't know how to handle anything that steps in the path that I can envision so clearly.

"I may be making a mountain out of a molehill, but even molehills have a tendency to trip you when you least expect it."

Leaning back on his car, Grey crossed his arms over his chest and released a deep breath. "And there I am, being an obstacle again."

My throat grew dry as I asked, "What do you want to be?"

"Important." He said it with a mocking little smile, but it was overshadowed by the sudden loneliness that traversed the link. Sensing that I was reading his emotions, he let his arrogance go and shrugged. "I want to matter to you."

"Why?"

His gaze slid to the floor and a self-mock-ing grin tugged at his lips. Then he seemed to gather his confidence and his eyes raised to mine; I looked away. "I don't fight my feelings like you do, Alex. When I fall, I'm going to try my damnedest to take you down with me."

A fist squeezed my heart and I couldn't figure out what to say, or if I should say anything. There was a challenge there that my Ryder Pride almost lunged for, but there was a huge portion of me urging a step back. The worst part of it was knowing that it wouldn't take much for him to trip me, either.

Grey leaned closer and my breath caught. "Why do you always feel ... distraught when the idea of you and me comes up? You know I wouldn't hurt you, right?"

For a moment, his own emotions wavered between indignation and shame. As if he might have given me the impression that he was a horrible human being. Beyond that, they moved into his confusion, probably as he wondered what he could have done to make me think like that.

Taking a deep breath, I lifted my shoulders and let them fall. "Honestly, Grey, I don't know. It's how I've always felt about it. As if it shouldn't happen; and with how much I want it sometimes, that scares me."

"Why shouldn't it happen?"

I shook my head. "I don't know, but something is telling me to quit while I'm behind. I've come too far to ignore my instincts now."

"And they're always right?"

I almost looked him in the eye before I announced, "Always."

He nodded in a thoughtful manner. "Then what can we do to set them at ease, do you think?"

"I don't know. I'm not sure we can. Or that we should."

"Okay, but how much of this do you think is because of the link, and has nothing to do with me?"

A rueful chuckle escaped me. "I have no idea." Then I released a sigh and said, "You know, we only started talking to each other the other day. Isn't it too soon for this conversation?"

He grinned at me. "You know it's not. The only reason it takes some people longer to get to this point is because they waste time trying to figure out how the other person feels before taking the plunge. In that way, you and I got lucky. And we're both direct enough not to bull-shit the other."

That much, I could not deny. "So, what now?"

It wasn't hard to imagine that he could sense my fatigue. With the topic, the locale, and thinking about him and me as more than separate identities. Therefore, I wasn't surprised when he nodded his head toward the door and took a step away from me. "Now we continue the interrogation. We still have five passes to go."

Chapter Twenty

ALONE

Suppressing a sigh, I nodded once and followed him to the basement hangout room. I decided then that I was going to start the interrogation this time.

"Where is your sister?"

He whipped around in an instant. In that split second, his features matched his emotions for a change, and the heartbreak left the hole in his chest exposed for the world to see. The second I felt it, I almost thought it was my pain, because it was the same pain I felt when I thought of Nathan and Cedar Creek.

In a blink, his features smoothed and he shoved back at the heartache until it no longer marred our bond. Taking its place was a cold determination as he said, "She's traveling."

For a while there, I thought sharing emotions meant he wouldn't be able to lie to me. That thought was suddenly turned on its head. If he could focus hard enough on forcing it out, he could say anything he wanted to. I was tempted to let him.

"Oh? Where to?"

Grey shrugged, making it a really convincing scene as he moved over to the bar. "Not sure. I only see her around holidays."

"That must suck. You guys were pretty close." I didn't bother making it into a question; we both knew the answer to that.

Another flash of longing before the frustration forced it back. Then he forced a smile and remarked, "You're an only child."

Even though I knew he was just trying to turn it back on me, I couldn't keep from saying, "Doesn't mean I don't have someone like that."

As a point, I thought of Nathan. I thought of the times my mind used to go to him when things were at their worst. When he was fixing the roof on the cottage, playing lacrosse, when he'd spend hours in the lake, swimming laps even when the water got cold. Every time he felt me watching, he stopped. Whatever he was doing, I became his focus. As if he knew that I needed that from him, even if it only lasted a few seconds. As I stood there in front of Grey, I let him feel that same heartache and I didn't bother to hide the tears filling my eyes.

After a minute, I shoved the memories back behind the black wall. It didn't take me much longer than Grey to regain composure. I had the numbness to thank for that. When it was over, I let our eyes meet for a second before I lowered them to the table.

"It's not a treasure you get to keep for yourself just because you and she share blood. Pain is universal, and it likes it that way."

Grey swallowed hard and the layer of determination seemed to crack a bit. "Who is it?"

"My best friend." I think we both knew that was all I was going to say. Either way, I wasn't going to let him turn this back on me. Not yet. "Your sister's name is Azure?"

He nodded. "Yep. She doesn't have a middle name, either." It was a sad attempt at humor, but I smiled anyway.

There was more I wanted to ask about her, but I had learned long ago that people had the right to their own stories. It wasn't Grey's place to tell me, and it wasn't my right to ask it of him. I decided that it was a good time to stick to me and Grey.

"What was it like growing up with a sibling?"

A rueful smile was forced onto his face. "Well, I grew up in the coven, so it felt like I had several siblings."

"You can tell me about that too, if you want," I suggested as I made my way to the couch.

Grey followed and took a seat at the other end. "We don't have the time for that, and it's not as interesting as it sounds. As for me and Azure, I somehow don't think I need to explain anything. She's the most important person in my life, and I know I'm the most important person in hers. That's how it's always been."

Silence fell between us and I didn't feel like breaking it. There wasn't much I could say, other than I knew what that felt like. There were few things as certain in my life as Nathan and Cedar Creek. They were what I was enduring each day to return to. Judging by how Grey felt about Azure,

I imagined he was waiting for the day she would return to him. I wondered if their deadline was similar to my own. When Grey turned eighteen, would Azure come to claim her brother?

At last, Grey asked in a low voice, "What's it like being alone?"

My stomach twisted as the words registered. While I knew he'd turn it back on me, I didn't realize how I would feel when faced with the word 'alone' versus 'only child.' When I realized how appropriate it was, that made it worse.

Shaking my head a little, I said, "Normal. I've never had other kids around, really. I never wanted them or needed them in my life. I never needed other people, Grey."

A wry chuckle was his response. "If that were true, Alex, you wouldn't feel like I do."

"You know what I meant. Don't be an ass."

"So, you didn't have any friends and you were the poor little witchling freak?"

It was sad watching him force the levity, but I was starting to understand that it was his default setting. He didn't like things to be too serious, even when he wanted serious answers.

"No. I was the witchling freak that they were

afraid to talk to. For a long time, the kids knew their place in my book, and I knew my place in theirs. We didn't need to interact because most of us couldn't find the others worthy of our attention." I smiled a little as I realized, "Damn. As children we had a far better sense of what our time was worth, didn't we?"

"Probably."

After a minute, I asked, "Were you always the prince?"

A pleasing chuckle answered me and I smiled in response. "No, not at all. Compared to Azure, I wasn't much of anything. It wasn't until after she left that my parents tried to make me worth something to them. Which, of course, meant I was happy to disappoint them. If Azure was the only one who cared about me before, then I had a pretty good idea what false idolization looked like when she was gone."

"Why didn't they care about you before? What made her so special?"

"She was the oldest," he said, as if that explained everything. When I didn't wipe the expectant look from my face, a thread of confusion wove through our link. "Come on, you have to know. In most magickal families, the eldest is the most powerful. Any child that follows after is a disappointment in that regard. It's why the coven can't arrange marriages for the eldest children; they're the most powerful and thus deemed the future leaders. Which means they get to make their own decisions."

It took me a bit to get over my initial shock. When I did, I waved him to a stop. "Wait a second, just wait. Are you telling me that Crone's Crescent believes in arranged marriages?"

He snorted. "You act like we're the only ones. All of the major covens do it."

My head was going to burst. "What major covens?"

Once more, he looked at me as if I were being sarcastic. He was waiting for a punch line to a joke that didn't exist. The second he realized I was serious, his shock shoved across the link.

"What rock have you been living under?" he asked with his mouth hanging wide open.

"Does it matter? Tell me what you know."

Shaking his head, Grey did his best to compose himself. Then he said, "Crone's Crescent is one of five major covens in the continental U.S.

In the northwest is Sacred Summit, below them is Blessed Endeavors, and just beneath us is Maiden Falls, with Coral Creator in the southeast. You've never heard of any of these?"

It felt like a boulder had settled in my stomach. Knowing about Crone's Crescent was one thing. In a way, it made sense that witches like me, who could harness real magick, would flock together and form a coven. Even a large one. I had no idea that it was massive or that it was one of five. My head was spinning.

"Who's in the northeast?" I asked, still trying to remember the names and locations of each of them.

"No one." There was a slight wistfulness in his voice as he said it. "As many small covens that exist in New England, no real coven has a chance of staking a claim there. While most of the witches in Salem are little more than basic diviners, there's enough of them to put up a fight if someone else tried to tell them how to run things. Can't imagine the witches farther north would deal with outsiders any differently."

A slight smile pulled at my lips. "No. No, we wouldn't."

His eyebrows shot up and our eyes almost met for a second. "You're from the northeast?"

Sensing dangerous territory, I shrugged my shoulders. "I'm from all over."

"Including New England."

It wasn't worth it to pass on, but I wanted to. "Including New England," I confirmed.

Grey had just opened his mouth to say something else when his arm jerked up so he could read his watch. In the same instant, I looked over the back of the couch to see the clock on the wall.

Turning back to him, I raised my eyebrows. "You set a magickal alarm just to notify yourself when you'd have to take me home?"

"Did you want to wait around until my parents got home?" I leapt up off the couch. "Yeah, I thought so," he chuckled.

"Don't act so superior. You wouldn't hang around with my parents either."

I'd made it around the couch by the time he asked, "Is that a bet?"

"What? No," I scoffed, turning to face him.

A wide grin spread across his face, stretching out his dimples. My stomach dropped a second before he said, "Well you did meet my parents. Fair's fair, don't you think?"

Chapter Twenty One

LOST

"You're either brave or stupid," I reminded him for probably the fifth time since we left his house.

"Is there a difference?" He was still grinning wide enough to showcase his dimples, making it hard not to stare.

"Not much of one," I said as we came to a stop in front of my house.

Grey cut the engine and turned to face me. The feeling of fire and lightning traced over my lips, which made me direct my own gaze anywhere else. What was worse than feeling where his eyes roved my body was knowing that he could tell when I was doing the same to him. It made it much more difficult than it needed to be to check him out. Of course, he probably thought the same about me.

"Is this your way of telling me you don't want me to meet your parents?"

That was a no-brainer. In zero possible realities was I ready for this. "Yes."

His grin widened. "Fair's fair."

Grey opened the car door and I jumped out of the vehicle. Scowling at him, I tried one last deterrent. "You know my dad will want to shoot you, right? Is that really what you want to walk into right now?"

Stopping in the middle of the sidewalk, Grey turned to face me, a devilish smile spreading across his face. Then his voice came out in low, husky tones. "Why would he want to do that? I haven't even touched you. Yet."

Blood suffused my face and it was all I could do not to duck my head and run for it. As it was, I felt every centimeter of skin that his gaze traveled over. It took only a second before Grey's longing flared to life, rushing along the link to bash itself against my brain. It was met with my own intolerable need.

Then I raised my eyes and knew what lost truly was.

It was a climax. The second my eyes met his, my body exploded in pure satisfaction. My lightning wrapped around his fire, forcing it to respond to every jagged stab of bliss. It spread through our link and assaulted every one of our senses. Between the sensitivity and the ecstasy, I was also surprised to find how powerful I felt in that moment. That in itself could have kept me looking into his eyes for days.

I didn't hear the front door open or see my mother lean against the doorjamb. Somehow, though, I heard her voice clearly as she asked, "You coming inside or staying out on the curb all night?"

My eyes snapped shut and I took a much-needed breath. Long enough for me to register how humiliating it was to be standing in my front yard having an apparent staring contest with Grey. If my mom didn't think something was up before, she would have no doubts now.

Opening my eyes, I glanced at her and gave over an embarrassed grin. Then I decided to play along. Taking a look back at the curb, I then turned to give the house a once-over. My eyes shot back and forth as if debating my options.

It might have worked better if she wasn't impatient to meet Grey. "Get in here," she called as she turned around. "And bring the boy."

For a second, I almost made the mistake of meeting his gaze again. "Well, it's too late now. Time to face the music," I warned.

"I did sign up for this, you know."

I pretended to ponder that. "Yes, you did. Suddenly the lines between bravery and sheer stupidity seem a whole lot clearer."

"You really hate this, don't you?" he asked as we walked across the porch.

"As much as you hated me meeting your parents, but for different reasons."

"Really?"

My eyes traced his lips before I murmured, "I'm afraid they'll like you, not hate you."

Grey pulled open the screen door right as he whispered, "So was I."

He left me standing there for a heartbeat as he walked into my house. As if it was something he was used to. The worst part was that it seemed natural to me too.

"Hello. You must be Grey. I'm Melanie Ryder," my mom said as soon as we walked in.

"Hello, Mrs. Ryder. It's a pleasure to meet you," he said with one of his signature smiles, holding out a hand to her. For one second, I thought he was going to be stupid enough to kiss the back of her hand, but he just shook it and let go.

"So, Lex tells me that you guys have a project due on Friday?" my mom prompted.

His embarrassed but endearing laugh *had* to be rehearsed. There was no way I'd believe that sly smirk and the defensive shoulder shrug weren't meant to make her think of a wounded animal. Or a toddler afraid of getting in trouble.

"Well, to be honest, Alex and I haven't been working on it."

"Oh?"

Again, he tried to act coy. "I think we just really wanted to get to know each other."

I'd had it. "Grey, this is my mom. Dig yourself deeper if you want, but don't expect her not to call you on your bullshit."

"Ruin my fun, why don't ya?" she pretended to scoff as I wrapped my arms around her waist and she pulled me into the hug. "How was your day?"

As a point, I let my eyes trail up and down Grey. "Interesting," I said at last.

My mother performed the same survey and declared, "She gave you hell. Did you at least give it back?"

For one second, I could feel his gaze teasing the edges of my eyes. There was no doubt in his voice when he said, "Yes, I did."

"Good," she said with a satisfied smirk. Then she turned to me and said, "Your father is upstairs."

"I know."

They both raised their eyebrows at me in apparent expectation. Grey even sent me a knowing smile that I could almost read the words 'fair's fair' on. As if he wasn't already a glutton for punishment.

Rolling my eyes, I said, "I'll be right back."

I didn't want this to be a big thing. There should never have been a formal introduction, and I shouldn't have felt like an idiot going to my dad for something as stupid as this. Grey wasn't a permanent fixture in my life; having my parents meet him made him far more stable than I liked. At the same time, I couldn't deny them this. It was part of our silent promise to get through anything together. No matter what I wanted, Grey was a something. Ryders dealt with the somethings, good or bad. Plus, I could at least count on my dad not to like him. He didn't like anyone that annoyed me.

Even with my magick dimmed, I could still tell that he was in the third bedroom that had been turned into the home gym. It would have been my room had I not taken a liking to the attic, so they'd made appropriate use of the space. When I stepped up to the open door, I found him running a towel over his face and obviously preparing to come downstairs. As soon as he saw me, he beckoned me into the room.

Shit.

"Give it to me straight, kid, what's with the boy?"

For a second, it almost felt like a reversal of what I'd done to him when I was thirteen. The most awkward conversation we'd ever had was when I confronted him about the puppy love I was feeling for Matt. Now he was throwing the same level of awkward back at me, and this was so much worse.

"The whole, undiluted truth?"

"Just tell me."

"Okay, I'm really attracted to him and he's really attracted to me, and that freaks me out a bit. I don't want him to meet you because I don't want to get that attached to him. I don't … want anything to do with any of this. I just–"

"Want to go back to Cedar Creek. I know." As long as he lived, that sentence would never lose the bitter edge, no matter how well he buried it.

A lump lodged in my throat and I could only nod.

Rubbing the towel through his sweat-dampened hair, my dad met my gaze with one of those delving looks I knew so well. Unlike my mother, my father and I couldn't make decisions in a split second with minimal information. To him, he didn't have enough to go on. He'd have to meet Grey himself to understand the situation better. Then he'd decide how to react. I stifled a sigh as he threw the towel over the bench and promised that he'd be down in a few minutes.

Making my way back downstairs, I realized that my mother and Grey had moved into the living room where he'd made it his mission to make her laugh. If he hadn't been aware of me, I would have taken a minute on the stairs and listened to the conversation that drifted over to me. As it was, there was no hope for it, so I passed into the living room and flopped down onto the couch at the other end from Grey.

"Dad'll be down in a minute."

Mom nodded at me to acknowledge she heard. Grey shot me a grin before turning back to her in order to finish the story he was telling. It was so hard not to laugh a little when he described how Faye decided to sit him down and teach him how to do makeup one night. Without magick. Just imagining how that could have turned out was making me press my lips together. I'd have to ask Faye for proof.

There had to be something to being married, because my mom was the first to notice my dad's approach. From where she was sitting in the armchair, she'd have first view as he walked into the living room, and her eyes were trained on the doorway well before I realized he was just outside the room. Even Grey was late to pick up on his presence compared to her.

Then he entered the room and Grey bound-ed to his feet. The manipulative bastard. There wasn't an ounce of nervous energy anywhere in him, yet he leapt up like he was in a panic to meet my dad. It was enough to send a surge of anger through me and to him. He could try his tricks on a dozen other people, but if he so much as attempted it with my parents, I would flay him alive.

All at once, motion in the room ceased as Grey's head whipped around to stare at me. For several seconds, it was just me and my fury. Then I registered him. His shock and contrition. When that happened, it registered that our eyes were locked. I tore my gaze away before more could occur.

The spell broke.

My mom was still looking at me, but Grey cleared his throat and turned back to my dad. This time, his nervousness was real as he held out his hand. "Hello, Mr. Ryder. I'm Grey Walker."

For a second, my dad gave him the same once-over my mother and I had performed. At last, he shook Grey's hand. When he let go, he looked at me. "What was that?"

Chapter Twenty Two

INEVITABLE

Grey's shock raced through our link, along with a hint of panic. He wasn't used to being out of his element, and my family was about to give him apoplexy. More than that, I knew his fear resulted from our secret, because it was ours and we didn't want to share that with anyone else.

"That," I said, "was one of the reasons I'd rather not get attached."

"He's like you." Though I knew my mother must have told him some of our previous discussion, I could still see the effort it took for him to say it out loud.

I nodded. "A lot like me."

"And you're not," Grey remarked, looking over both of my parents. His expression was pure puzzlement.

They both shook their heads. "No. We don't know where she gets it from, but it's not something we were ever involved with," my mom explained. Then she shrugged a little. "It's why we came here. I heard a few rumors about Grant that I thought we might prove or disprove."

"You set her up." I swear, he was becoming more in awe of her every second. Then he glanced over his shoulder at me before looking back at her. "Do you regret it?"

Her smile was the placating kind that basically said she didn't have to respond to that, and implied idiocy on the person asking. What left her mouth, however, was, "I'm not sure yet."

Unable to stop himself, Grey turned toward me, appearing completely dumbfounded. "This would never happen in my house."

My gaze traveled over my parents before I said, "It didn't always happen in ours. Especially when it should have." A hand went to my arm before I could stop it.

Turning back to my dad, he shook his head and said, "I'm sorry. This is just strange to me. For you not to be like us but to know everything that's going on." Somehow, he knew the word 'witch' would put him on treacherous ground.

"Oh, we don't know everything," my dad interjected. "Far from it. But the lines of communication are more open now than they were, so we'll take it."

"It amazes me," Grey admitted, taking a moment to look at all three of us.

He wasn't lying. His shock was being replaced by his awe. Not just for my mother, but all of us. Everything said in this room was so foreign to him, I was surprised his head wasn't bursting. It wouldn't take much more to accomplish the task.

"Your head is going to explode," I murmured.

"Probably," he agreed.

Smiling a little, I rose from the couch and said, "Say goodbye, Grey."

He forced a smile to his face and shook my father's hand again before waving to my mother. I moved around him to the door and had just opened it when my mother's voice called out, "No eloping."

Grey didn't miss a beat. "So I should cancel Elvis?"

While I wanted nothing more than to growl at him, I couldn't halt the laugh. When I stepped out on the porch, I took a deep breath and waited for him to close the door behind him. He joined me at the railing as we stared out over the quiet suburb.

After a few seconds he asked, "How much do they know?"

"They don't know about the bond, if that's what you're asking. They do know that a coven is here and that I've had interactions with them. Including you."

"How much will you tell them?"

"Whatever I feel they need to know, or what I don't think needs to be kept secret." His anxiety spiked a little and I said, "Relax. I don't tell them other people's stories. It's not my place. If they don't hear it from you, they won't hear it from me."

"Really?"

"Everyone deserves to share their own stories. They're the ones that lived them."

"What happened? I mean, why are you all so...?"

"Open? Forthright? Prideful? Intimidating?"

"Sad?"

"Oh." A fist squeezed my heart and it took me a second to remember how to breathe. There was only one answer for that. "Pass."

"Pass?"

"That's a part of my story only one person has earned the right to hear."

For a second, I expected him to protest. But he knew that there was someone else as important to me as Azure was to him. Grey knew how far from that position he stood, and he didn't bother to contest it.

"Fair enough," he said. Then he turned to look at me and I had to close my eyes as the feeling of fire and lightning making love traveled over my skin.

Then he took a step toward me and I took a step back. "You should go home now."

"Why do you do that?" he asked, ignoring my suggestion.

"Do what?"

"Why do you flinch or back away every time I get close to you?"

"I thought the answer to that would be obvious. I'm afraid of you touching me."

"Why?"

"Fire and lightning making love, remember? I know what it feels like when you look at me. I know what it feels like when our eyes meet. I'm not sure I'm ready to know what it feels like when our skin touches."

A small grin pulled at his lips. "What if we experimented with it, then? In a controlled environment?"

"Controlled environment?" I scoffed.

"I'm serious. My house, tomorrow after school."

I sighed, rolling my eyes for added measure. "Tempting as that *doesn't* sound, I'm hanging with the girls tomorrow."

"Wednesday then?"

"Maybe. And if I do agree to it, you have to promise me we'll work on this stupid scene."

He placed a hand over his heart and declared, "On my honor, I dare not agree to that request."

I couldn't help but crack up over that. "Go home, Grey."

"Goodnight, Alex."

Wednesday couldn't come fast enough. As much as I hated to admit it, my anticipation was to the point of strangling me. Every time he looked at me, every time our eyes met, even thinking the word 'Wednesday' was enough to make the desire spike. It also set off a string of thoughts I didn't dare travel down. That was a snake pit lined with too many 'what ifs' that was best left untouched. And I was about to slam into it with zero hesitation, because Wednesday had arrived.

"And I thought you were jumpy yesterday. Why the hell are you so wired?" Faye sighed as she sat beside me.

I'd made a point of sitting with my back to Grey just so I could relax a bit more. Considering every time I stood up his gaze landed on my ass, it was far less comfortable than I had imagined. All the same, I couldn't understand how she picked up on it.

With a sigh, I explained, "I'm about to do something that I know is stupid, but I'm also not about to stop myself."

"Oh Goddess, do not tell me you're going to sleep with my cousin. I literally just got my lunch."

"No!" I gasped, my eyes darting around the room to make sure no one else heard her. "Thanks for that, by the way. Of all the things I was trying not to think about."

"To be honest, I didn't think the two of you stopped thinking about it. You always look like you're going to jump each other in the nearest darkened alley or something."

"Yes, because I so needed that mental image," I remarked in a dry tone.

"Hey, what you do with him is your own business. Just do not mistake me for the type of friend that needs all of the details."

"You're right: you don't need details, and I don't need innuendos invading my brain. Especially about something that isn't going to happen."

"In the near future," she added, grinning at me. My unimpressive scowl was met with laughter. "Oh, come on down from your high horse, okay? For a minute. It won't kill you. Now, after you do that, can you honestly say that you will never have sex with him? Ever?"

Until that moment, I hadn't considered it.

Not really. In my head, it was bad enough I was going through with this 'controlled environment' experiment. Sleeping with him was in that pit of snakes I didn't want to fall down. At the same time, every time I felt his eyes on me, it was like he was writing the word 'inevitable' into my skin and it was glowing with neon lights. It wasn't something I had to think about, because it was a place we'd get to at one point or another. That scared the hell out of me.

Scowling at Faye, I muttered, "You know, that high horse was precious to me."

She snickered a little as Cat and Del approached. Thankfully, the conversation was dropped as Delaire launched into her own tirade. I was grateful that no one else seemed to notice how anxious I was. No one but Grey.

Chapter Twenty Three

GREED

A minute after the last bell rang, Grey appeared in front of my locker. His excitement was at the same level as my dread, and we were both doing our best to ignore our anticipation. He waited just long enough to drop his cell into my hand and inform me that he was getting the car. I rolled my eyes when I found that he'd programmed my mother's number into the phone.

"Ryder Housing. Melanie speaking."

"Hey, Mom. You should probably save this number as Grey's. I don't think this is the last time I'll be using it," I said as I put away my things.

"Not coming straight home then?"

"Nah. I'm going to try and get some real work out of him today, but I doubt my efforts."

"I'm doubting your efforts, too." There was another innuendo there, and I wasn't about to take that bait twice in one day.

"I'll be home by dinner."

"See you then. Love you, Lex."

"Love you too, Mom."

I snapped the phone shut just as I was stepping outside. Grey had pulled up right to the steps. The passenger side window was down and he was giving me a pointed stare. Unable to help myself, I grinned a little and made my way to his car.

As before, once I entered the vehicle, I set the phone on the console before buckling up and staring straight ahead. "Just drive, Grey."

He didn't even let out an aggrieved sigh before he stepped on the gas. We made it to his house in record time, and he grinned the whole way. Our link was drowning in our anticipation, and even my dread was giving way to his excitement.

"I was so bored yesterday," he admitted as we pulled up to the house. "Is it weird that I'm already used to having you around?"

"Yes."

He shot me a grin. "Admit it, you're getting used to this, too."

Turning my face away, I said, "I admit nothing."

That much, at least, I could say was true. I was not getting used to it. While it was becoming easier to deal with the connection between us, it was still something that made my skin crawl if I thought about it for too long. What Grey thought of as acceptance was really avoidance.

"Okay, so what's first?" he asked as we got out of the car.

"We're going to work on our scene, remember?"

"So, basement then?"

For a moment, I shot a studying look at him. With a sigh, I pushed open the door to the basement room. "We're not going to work on our scene, are we?"

"Not at all."

Glancing over my shoulder at him, I said, "We're going to fail this project."

"I don't really care."

"You staged it," I pointed out.

"What are you talking about? Mr. Watts has

been doing this project for the past decade, at least."

"Really? Then what was with the magick overload the first day of school?"

He smirked at me. "I had a few schedule changes to make. Maybe a few seating assignments to arrange."

My face blanked. "How many classes did you have with me originally?"

"Just the one."

"And you changed it so we'd have more time together?"

"Yes."

"You're a prick." I wished I could have said that with more vehemence. Instead, it came out like a statement of fact rather than an insult.

Grey grinned at me. "I think you'll find that fact matters very little if the end result is that I get what I want."

"Is that how you justify everything? It's all okay as long as you get what you want in the end?" I asked as I flopped down on the couch.

"No, not everything. Of course, there aren't a lot of scenarios where I'm denied what I want, either. I have no problem admitting to being a spoiled prat. It's just something I've learned not to feel guilty for."

Well, I couldn't argue with that one. For one, I knew I was a proud and resentful bitch, and I wouldn't bat an eyelash at anyone else calling me on it. If Grey heard all his life that he was spoiled and pretentious, eventually he'd identify what made him that way. When that happened, there were only two things to do: change, or accept the inevitable. Grey accepted what he was in the same way that I did. Now, no one could use our truths against us.

"So, if we're counting on the Seven Deadly Sins, yours would be gluttony?"

"Greed," he answered, not missing a beat. "Why stop at one thing when you can have them all?"

I nodded my head to him, satisfied with that answer. "Mine is pride. Ryder Pride."

"It has a name?"

"It does. My mom coined it after meeting my dad. I have it worse than he does, but not by much. If the stories are true, there isn't a being in our family to escape it."

"What are you most proud of?"

"You honestly think I can answer that?" I scoffed.

A tiny smile teased his lips, but I felt it when his determination solidified. "Okay, so what are you most ashamed of?"

Every scar grew a little warmer. Running a hand over my arm, I let a bitter smile pull at my lips. "I don't think I need to answer that."

His features stilled before he shook his head. "No, you don't."

I was about to ask him about his greed when my stomach rumbled. Loudly. For a second, we ignored it. Then it rumbled again and we both started laughing.

"Come on," Grey said, "let's go feed you."

"I'm fine," I snickered. "I don't even feel hungry."

Again, my stomach rumbled. "You've been outvoted. How do you feel about popcorn shrimp?"

"If I don't have to cook, it's good enough for me."

"Fair enough," he said with a shrug as we climbed the stairs that were hidden in the wall behind the bar.

When we entered the kitchen, I sat on one of the barstools at the island and watched as he set the preheat on the oven. For a few moments, I watched with a feeling of amusement as he went about the tasks of a domestic witch. A cookie sheet flew out of a cupboard near the ovens, the bag of shrimp jumped out of the freezer and opened itself, while a pair of plates glided out of their cupboard to come to rest in front of me. All in the same time frame that it took Grey to open the drawer in front of him and remove a spatula.

When he turned around, he was grinning at me. Behind him, the shrimp was arranging itself on the cookie sheet and the heat on the oven was rising much faster than should have been possible. Chuckling to myself, I shook my head.

"What's so funny?"

"Nothing. It just reminds me of when I began learning."

"Oh?" he asked, leaning on the counter. "How so?"

"The day after my Wiccaning, my mentor had placed all of these baking supplies on the table. I was told to bake. Magick only. No recipe. Everything had to be done by intuition and I couldn't touch a single thing with my hands."

Grey raised his eyebrows. "How long did it take you to get it right?"

I shrugged. "I didn't really get anything wrong. If I made a mistake, I fixed it. Then and there."

He leaned back, his face growing impassive as he threw his mask in place. All the while, his emotions flickered through surprise to distrust to suspicion. He thought I was either lying or joking. I almost let him believe it.

"Yes, Grey. Either I'm more powerful than you can tell, or I was trained in ways you can't comprehend. Both are true."

Shaking his head, Grey turned to focus on putting the shrimp in the oven and setting the timer. When he turned back, he was relaxed enough to lean on his elbows, with his hand landing close beside mine. So close, in fact, that our fingers could touch.

Our adrenaline spiked at the same time. My breath caught as anticipation flooded my system. Though this was the professed reason for my visit, I still couldn't help the little flash of panic that shot through me. Which was why I needed it to be over with.

Releasing the breath, I whispered, "Do it."

My voice was so low, it was hard to believe I'd said the words aloud. I knew I did, however, because the anticipation between us burst outward. It was similar to when our eyes met as the air deadened in preparation. In a single motion, we were about to change our dynamic. I was far from ready for it, but it couldn't be stopped.

With the most casual of motions, Grey slid his pinky finger toward mine. My teeth sank into my bottom lip and I forced myself not to jerk away. I couldn't tear my eyes away as the distance between us was crossed. Until there was no distance at all.

Lightning sparked, hot and furious, as it shot up my entire arm. Every nerve in my body raged to life, feeling raw and exposed. The minor stimulation was enough to make me want to scream. It felt so good that it was borderline painful. And like grabbing onto an electric wire, I couldn't let go. I couldn't stop it.

Grey jerked his hand away, curling his hands into fists as he leaned against the counter. His breathing came in the same hard, desperate gasps that mine did. And I could see his entire body shaking from the contact.

After a minute, he said in a hoarse voice, "I ... didn't think it would be like that."

If I could have laughed, I would have. "I did. It's why I didn't want to."

Grey's eyes raised to mine, and I let them meet for a second. Then mine lowered back to his fists. Swallowing hard, I held out my hand, palm up. My entire body was still shaking.

"Again," I ordered, not bothering to look at him.

For a minute, he didn't move. We both stared at my shaking limb and I could feel each hard beat of my heart in my wrist, just beneath the hourglass scar. As always, it reminded me that I had my limits. I was willing to push them.

At last, Grey raised his left hand off of the marble and let it hover over my own. It could have been my imagination, but I thought I saw a jagged bolt of electricity jump between our palms. I didn't have time to contemplate it more before he lowered his hand onto mine.

My mouth fell open in a silent scream as the sensations assaulted me. Lightning ravaged my skin, causing each precious nerve to burst with energy. Blistering heat washed through me in a wave of pleasure that was almost pure agony. With it came the *need*. A desire so forceful and desperate pounded through me with a relentless ferocity. Then it coiled deep within me and I suddenly felt so hollow, I thought I might die if the desire was not sated.

I couldn't take it anymore, but I couldn't let go. I wanted more of him. Any part of him that I could have, I would take from him. And Grey would give me all, if I asked for it.

Before I could ask, I felt the magick gathering. Powerful, willful, prideful magick. It wrapped around me in a loving embrace. Then it dove into me and my hand was torn from Grey's as I was ripped through space.

My head hit the wall in my bedroom as I stumbled backward. I was shaking so much, it was hard not to fall straight down from there. With my teeth chattering and my vision blurred, I eased myself to the floor and tucked my knees up under my chin. Tears rolled in steady succession down my cheeks as I continued to battle that fervent, potent, insatiable lust that roared through me.

All around me, the magick continued to pulse in silent promise.

Chapter Twenty Four

BASIC CHEMISTRY

I was in the middle of showering when I felt him drawing closer. At first, there was no cause for alarm. Until he passed his turn off to the school. Then I began to rush.

He arrived before I had a chance to finish up. I wasn't dressed yet when the doorbell rang and I groaned when I heard my mother answer it. If I was using my magick, I wouldn't have a second thought as to eavesdropping on them. As it was-except for the instinctual teleportation performed out of desperation-I was still maintaining my mundane existence.

After throwing on my clothes and tearing a brush through my wet hair, I almost charged down the stairs. As soon as I rounded the corner into the living room, our eyes almost met before I was quick to turn to my mother. Her amused expression hid her curiosity well, but I knew that she was waiting for just the right moment to dig for details.

"Hey," I said, including them both.

Grey stood up, giving me no choice but to focus on him. When he took a step toward me, my breath caught. Then he surprised me by holding out my bag.

"You forgot this at my house yesterday." He said it so casually, I would never have known how riotous his own nerves were. My mother couldn't possibly be aware.

"Thanks. But you could've just given it to me at school." I was careful about retrieving it from him in front of my mother. Last thing I needed was for her to witness a similar scene.

A wide, charming smile spread across his face as he announced, "I was hoping I could give you a ride."

I wanted to punch him. After what happened to us yesterday, being in a confined space with him was the absolute last thing I needed or wanted. For him to say so in front of my mother meant he was trying to manipulate the situation. One could almost pity him.

"Thanks, but I'm going to walk today. It's nice enough out and I prefer the fresh air. See you later, Mom," I said around him and headed for the door.

An exasperated sigh escaped him before he turned and bid my mother a good day. I waited for him on the front porch, my eyebrows raised and my arms crossed over my chest. The minute he closed the door behind him, I laughed.

"Did you honestly think that was going to work? Like I can't be rude to you in front of my mother," I scoffed.

He shrugged as we moved down the steps. "It was worth a try. Are you getting in or not?"

I shook my head. "No, I meant it when I said I needed the fresh air. Especially when you're around."

Grey nodded and I was surprised when he turned with me. "Then I'll walk with you."

My eyebrows rose. "What about your car?"

"I'll return for it in a bit. I'm not actually going to school today."

"What? Why?"

"Mabon," he said with a little grin that was meant to chastise me for not remembering.

"Ah, yes. I forgot that was today. Do you take all of the sabbats and esbats off from school?"

He nodded. "Don't you?"

"Sometimes. Mabon I usually don't do much ritual for, so it doesn't bother me to maintain a regular schedule. However, you won't find me anywhere in town come Samhain. Yule my parents celebrate with me. Everything else I've not had much cause to celebrate, though I do pay my respects."

"And Beltane? It is opposite Samhain in the calendar. Tell me you don't ignore it."

I chuckled a bit at that. "And how do you propose I celebrate a day of fertility by myself?"

Grey shrugged while giving me a suggestive look. I busted out laughing while I smothered the urge to shove my shoulder against his.

"Regardless of what it is possible for me to do, the most I do is pay my respects. I have really no desire to set up a whole ritual just to pleasure myself, thanks."

"Isn't that the best reason for a ritual?"

Heat was building in my face and I did everything I could to banish the blush. It wasn't that I was uncomfortable with the banter, but it was putting visuals in both of our heads that didn't need to be there. Especially considering the already heightened chemistry that existed between us. We were not in need of any form of encouragement.

Suddenly, Grey turned serious. "Listen, Alex, about yesterday–"

"Please, let's not talk about it."

"Are you okay? I wasn't... I didn't mean for that to happen. If I had known..."

"You mean: if you had known that I wanted you to stop, you would have stopped. That wasn't the problem, Grey. There were no mixed signals, because there were no mixed feelings. I wanted it. You wanted it. And we were enjoying it."

"Then what happened?"

"It was too much. I'm sure you felt it, everything that was going through me. When it got to that point, I couldn't take it anymore. But I also couldn't let go. My magick acted of its own accord when it ripped me away from you."

His voice lowered. "I can't tell how you feel about that. It's all jumbled."

I shot him a weary smile. "It is all jumbled. And I have no idea how to feel about it. I suppose it scares me, more than anything. The last time my magick acted on instinct, people got hurt." Including me.

"So wait, you're confused how to feel about your magick usage? More confused than how to feel about you and me and what happened?"

Amusement drifted through the link and I rolled my eyes. "Do you want me to say it, Grey? Is it really that important to you?"

"A little bit, yeah."

"Fine. I'm not confused about you and me or what happened, because it's basic chemistry. I want you and you want me. What happened was a whole lot of wanting and not an ounce of doing anything about it. Believe me, I've felt quite enough not to be confused about it."

"But you're not going to act on it," he said with a wry smile.

I shook my head. "Not if I can help it."

"I understand. It's still too early for that. But are you thinking about it?"

"After what we felt last night? Are you really asking me that question?"

His smile became even more smug. "You know I won't push you into anything, right?"

"One: it wouldn't matter if you tried. I refuse to be forced into doing things I don't want to do. Two: I know you won't. If only because you need to maintain your ego."

"Ego? You think *I* have an ego?"

"Your ego could rival a Greek god's."

"This from the girl whose idea of a family tradition is her own brand of pride?"

"Oh, I know I have an ego. Doesn't mean I'm incapable of identifying it in other people."

Having reached our destination, I turned to face him. He was still grinning at me with his signature cockiness, his ego on full display. As was mine, I knew.

"What if I pushed you?" I asked, my head tilting to the side a little.

"What do you mean?"

I shrugged. "Well, you said you wouldn't try to push me into anything, but I never agreed to the opposite circumstance. So, what would you say to that?"

At once, the sexy smirk was in place. Then he held out his hand to me. "Push me."

It was stupid. I was going to regret it. There was no way I wasn't going to do it. Taking a deep breath, I placed my hand in his.

My breath left me in an explosive rush before I gritted my teeth together. Though the burning lashed through me, I was determined to work through it. I had to. The other thing I had to learn was how to let go.

For several long minutes, I tried to pull away. I wanted to stop, but I couldn't. Touching him was addictive, yet unsatisfactory. Even with something this mild, it awoke in me a need for more. So much more.

Grey dropped his hand and I stumbled back a step. For a minute, all we could do was catch our breath. Then a fist squeezed my heart when my eyes raised to his, threatening to consume us in equal measure. As was usual, it was up to me to break contact.

"We're opposite there," Grey murmured. "Our eyes meet, and I can't look away. Even if I want to. But when we touch..."

"I am the wanton," I remarked with a wry smile. "It makes sense."

"Does it?"

"I've been intimate in a mental way with others before you. It does not consume me in the same way it does you. But I've also never been that physical with another being, and actively avoided physical touch for a time. Therefore, it makes sense that it would ensnare me more easily than you."

Grey released a mock sigh. "Must you explain everything?"

He'd moved closer as I was speaking. Our bodies were mere inches apart and I was staring at his lips in an effort to avoid locking gazes with him. When he leaned in farther, I had to close my eyes and take a step back. One more second with the man and we would kiss.

I couldn't have that.

"I'll see you tomorrow, Grey," I breathed before I turned on my heel and darted up the stairs. I forced myself through the front doors before I risked a glance behind me. He was already gone.

Chapter Twenty Five

FORGET

I was anxious all morning come Friday. Part of me was eager to have it all over and done with. Most of me dreaded that it had arrived. For the most part, it was because I knew that Grey and I would be winging the entirety of our scene onstage in front of everyone. Of course, the worst part could have been that we were going onstage in the first place.

Our first period flew past, and I felt a knot of despair twist in my stomach. Normally, I'd have looked to Grey for some of his cocky assurance that it was no big deal. But I could feel that he was just as anxious as I was, with a hint of anger that kept flashing through the link before he could shove it aside. It made no sense, but I had the uncomfortable feeling that I was about to find out the reason for it.

As soon as we entered the class, Mr. Watts handed out four coats: two black overcoats for the guys, and long, tan trench coats for the women. They were all the costume we were getting and we would trade off in rapid succession as each scene progressed. My dread increased.

"All right, everyone listen up. We're all going to head to the auditorium now. As I've mentioned before, we're doing this in front of the second period drama class, and they'll have full license to critique you. We'll be going over all of those in class on Monday. As we only have this class period, we're going to have to get moving now and get through this as quickly as possible. Let's move."

In a surge, we all followed him from the classroom. Grey and I lingered behind, as neither of us was quite ready for this to occur. Though I knew why his trepidation spiked the minute we got close to the auditorium.

My eyes narrowed as I shot him a disbelieving look. "Spring? She's in the drama class?"

He nodded but didn't say anything else.

While I knew how he felt about her, I still took it as a bad sign that he refused to speak. Even when we took our seats in the auditorium to watch the first scenes, all he did was stare straight ahead. What was worse was feeling his emotions rocket between anger, resentment, anxiousness, determination, guilt, and sadness. There was a knot of them forming in his chest and I could almost feel it burning him up inside.

At last, we were three scenes from our finale. Grey and I rose from our seats and eased into the wings of the stage as we waited for our turn. A minute later, we were handed our coats and prepared to fail our first real Creative Writing assignment of the semester. Years ago, the idea of failing anything was anathema to me; now, it was simply a matter of having my priorities in order.

When the time came, I strode out onto the stage with Grey a few steps behind me. I had just reached the center when a blast of fury erupted along our link. In an instant, I whipped around to face him. His eyes snapped back to me from where they'd been scouring the audience. Then I was overwhelmed with his guilt.

"It's almost over," he announced. Neither

emotion marred his mask, making my nerves jolt a little.

I nodded once. "It is," I agreed, trying to figure out what my character would say next.

"What will you do when it is?"

Screw the character; this was about me and Grey. The second the words left his lips, I knew that he wasn't acting. Which made my walls and their spindly defense system shoot up a thousand feet between us. But there was never any protection that could keep him out. That was the problem.

Swallowing around the lump in my throat, I said, "Go home."

"And if I asked you to stay?"

"You wouldn't," I said in a voice just loud enough for the others to hear.

"Why not?"

"Because you're not that stupid."

A mocking smile spread across his face. "I beg to differ." Then he took a breath and said, "Ask me why."

I was going to regret this. "Why?"

"I can feel you inside of me, all the time. I know everything that you're experiencing, and I know you feel the same."

All at once, the blood drained from my face. At first, it didn't want to register. While this whole thing was about our relationship, he'd never hinted at the link. Grey felt the same way that I did about our connection. There was no way he'd announce it to forty strangers. Except, he just did.

In a flash, my face suffused with color and I rounded on him. "What are you doing?" I snarled.

Ignoring me, Grey trudged on, "You can't be this close to someone, and want so much from them, and just be able to walk away. Life doesn't work that way."

A sharp, harsh laugh burst from my chest. "Life doesn't work that way? Do you have any idea how life *does* work? You said it yourself: you're a spoiled prat who is rarely rejected. Outside of this little fiefdom, you've no idea what reality is. What life is.

"You think that you hold some all-powerful sway over me because we're stuck together for now? I have walked away from *everything* I hold dear in this world. You are nothing compared to that. Don't you dare flatter yourself."

While his face didn't change, I could almost see each blow land, fracturing his fragile ego. All the same, he hit back with, "And you think this is something you can walk away from? As if it won't haunt you every step of the way?"

For a minute, I couldn't find words to respond. I was so pissed off that the betrayal felt but a pinprick. Then, when that last sentence left his lips, I shot him a cruel smile.

"You say you know what I feel? Then you know what haunted truly is. Do you honestly believe any of this will matter to me in a few months or a year? Do you think I can't forget you, or are you too arrogant to realize that I can't wait to?"

"I'm going to make sure that you don't want to."

I spread my arms wide, releasing an exasperated sigh. "And how are you going to do that?"

Nothing could have prepared me for him taking three long strides across the stage. I had no idea what he was doing when he reached out and grabbed my wrist. The contact was enough for me to cry out as every scar beneath his hand screamed at the sensation. Lightning flashed through me, ready to strike. Ready to burn and blister his body. Instead, I took the ultimate revenge. I forced him to meet my gaze.

I don't know how long we stood like that. Around us, the entire auditorium was filled with flames and lightning, while our bodies felt afire for each second that we stood there. Neither of us was willing to let go of our respective holds.

A moment later, Grey yanked on my arm until my entire body was pressed against his. Even through our clothes, I could feel the electricity flashing between us. A gasp escaped me and that was all the opportunity he needed.

One of Grey's hands held tight to my lower back as he pressed me against him. Then he let go of my arm and his fingers dove into my hair. Dragging my face toward his, he paused just long enough for our eyes to clash one last time.

I closed my eyes as Grey's lips pressed against mine.

Chapter Twenty Six

RABBIT HOLE

From the moment he grabbed my arm, it was a never-ending battle with the lust. It was quick and forceful as it burst along the skin. The scars acted as a channel, letting it flow deeper into the muscle and bone. There was so much of it, I almost became weak in the knees.

Then he pulled me to him and I couldn't breathe. Shivers ran up my spine in rapid succession as one hand pressed against my lower back, keeping my chest against his. My entire body tingled when his hand dove into my hair, grabbing a large, controlling fistful and drawing my face nearer.

It all meant nothing the moment his mouth closed over mine. The kiss was a mix of passionate desire and wanton desperation. We were so consumed with what was happening that we couldn't think outside of the moment.

There was nothing gentle about the kiss. Aggressive as we were with each other, I wouldn't be surprised to later find bruises or learn that I'd left scratches. All of our passion and fury was being channeled into that one moment, and it was coupled with the chemistry and lust that we couldn't escape.

For us, it was the perfect first kiss. All fire and lightning, mixed with desire and fury.

At last, it became a suffocating experience. Our kisses slowed as we were desperate to drag out the experience. After another minute, we couldn't put it off any longer.

Stopping for breath wasn't the worst thing Grey did. Letting go of me was.

Somehow, he'd convinced himself that I was okay with everything that had just happened. He found out how wrong he was when I took a step back and caught my breath. Before he could finish catching his, I took a step forward and threw all of my weight into the punch that landed on the side of his jaw.

Grey stumbled back and I stormed past him. Four kids dodged out of my way as I stalked backstage. When I shoved open the stage door into the main auditorium, Mr. Watts was standing beside it with a palm held up in expectation.

"Script?"

"He has it," I spat without even looking at him.

With the pace I had set, I thought that I was going to make a clean getaway. Then the shadows next to the light booth formed a shape. I sensed Spring right before she let the camouflaging spell fade.

Part of me wanted to snap at her, demanding what she wanted. The smarter portion gritted my teeth together and watched her in the same way a mongoose watches a cobra. While Summer was impulsive and forthright, I knew how insignificant she was. Spring wasn't insignificant. She was the princess of Crone's Crescent, and she had earned that title through sheer willpower and manipulation. I wasn't about to underestimate how much of a pain in the ass she could be to me.

"Are you okay?"

Out of everything I was expecting her to say,

that wasn't it. Which led me to another revelation: Spring could lie to my face and seem one hundred percent genuine.

Forcing my face into a blank mask, I shrugged. "Why wouldn't I be?"

Her eyes flashed to the stage before returning to me. "That seemed pretty personal up there, and it didn't match the overall narrative."

Subtle.

"Isn't the point of acting to make it personal?"

"I'm sorry."

I was done. Turning to her, I asked, "Why? He did what you wanted."

At once, her cool, superior expression was in place. "Excuse me?"

"Cut the crap, Spring. Grey and I know each other better than we wish we did. Did you think he could hide that from me? You wanted to know what was going on between us; now you have your answer. If that's all, I'd like to be on my way."

I had just passed her when something made me stop. Looking over my shoulder, I added, "By the way, if you attempt to pit us against one another again, you will answer to me. My remorse for hurting people isn't what it once was."

Satisfied, I kept walking. Until her voice lashed out at me, "He was right, you know. Grey won't let you forget him, and you won't want to."

That night, I slept fitfully as I drifted in and out of consciousness. Each time I started to pull out of the blackness, I felt the urge to dive back in. Within the dark, at least, I felt nothing. Burning accosted me the minute its hold was loosened and I panted from the heat as I tossed the covers aside. Though it was a recent phenomenon, I knew that the desire was an all-consuming ordeal. Even in my sleep, I would find no refuge from it.

After drifting through the dark until almost an hour past dawn, it was suddenly unbearable. I was dragged awake not by the familiar desire, but rather the proximity of its cause. For a moment, I could do nothing but lay in bed and marvel at the nerve he had.

Then I did something that I hadn't let myself do in a year; I let the numbness take me. In an instant, it all switched off. My rage at being betrayed drifted back behind the black curtain in my mind. The desire I thought of as unmanageable was locked behind a heavy door. Even my disbelief at his presence vanished within the shadows. For as long as I could, I would cling to the numbness that afforded me some measure of sanity.

As I went about my morning routine, I could feel Grey's emotions becoming a tightly coiled ball of wire. Each thread wrapped around the other until some things were suffocated. What I could feel, however, held a lot of sadness. More potent than that was a layer of concern. I couldn't pinpoint which one pertained to me, but his chagrin was all of my doing.

I didn't rush. It didn't bother me that he was sitting with my mom in the living room. Soon enough, I finished making myself presentable and made my way downstairs.

My mother took one look at my face and the blood drained from hers. She knew what the numbness looked like, and neither of us had ever hoped to have this side of me present ever again. Her eyes flickered to Grey and I gave a slight nod. At once, her demeanor shifted before she excused herself from the room. Grey and I were left alone.

Without looking at him, I announced, "You are not welcome here. Please leave."

Grey leapt to his feet and twisted toward me, almost hitting the arm of the couch. "Alex, please. I just want to talk."

A smidge of pleasure shot through me as I took note of the dark purple bruise marring the left side of his face. If he wanted to pursue a conversation with me, I was pretty sure I could add a sibling or two to the other side.

"I don't want to hear it."

"Alex, I'm sorry. I just–"

I held up a hand to stop him. "You don't understand. I don't want to hear it. I've been listening to a lot of what you've had to say recently. I've had more than enough."

Determination set in along the bond and I almost sighed. "Well, then, this will be the last time. Hear me out now and I won't bother you again, as long as that's what you want."

A sarcastic laugh flew past my lips. "As long as it's what I want? I told you in the beginning that I didn't want any of this. What did you do? Went and manipulated everything so that I couldn't get away from you. You have no respect, Grey. I can't trust your word when you've already proven it's worthless."

"That isn't fair," he growled. "You know why I can't–"

"Oh, don't even! I have the same damn problem as you and I didn't jump you the moment you arrived. Clearly self-control has more than a little to do with our reaction to this. Not that you seem to have much of that to begin with."

"Is that all you're going to do? Hurl insults at me in the hopes that I'll get pissed off and leave?"

I shrugged. "Tell me it's not true. Is anything I've accused you of really something you can call a lie?"

He shook his head and his lip curled as his own disgust flashed through the link. "We've been speaking to each other for less than a week. Don't pretend to know me."

My expression was nothing short of imperious as I announced, "You are a fool if you think I don't know you. Every single day I've been forced to sift through your emotions, I've come to know you. With every word, and rune, and random note, you've let me know you. And you've displayed quite clearly the kind of man you are."

He took a step closer and dropped his voice. "And what kind of man is that?"

"The kind of man that lets another manipulate him. The kind of man that is capable of justifying a decision he knows is wrong. A special kind of fool who chose not to respect my wishes and found himself falling down a rabbit hole."

It was the first time I'd ever truly seen him in his natural form. Without the arrogance and natural charm he clung to. Now I saw that his face paled, his eyes widened, and an icy fear slithered through the bond.

"You spoke to Spring." His voice was as inflectionless as my own.

"I did."

"And?" he demanded, heat flickering through the single word.

"And what? Did she tell me how she was blackmailing you? No."

Grey turned away from me, a hand running through his hair. It was in that moment that I realized there was something that he was desperate to keep from me. Something he knew would drive me away if I knew about it. With Spring involved, I wasn't sure that he was wrong.

Clenching my jaw, I felt the numbness crack. "She won't attempt it again."

In an instant, he whirled back to me. "What?"

"Well, if she's as smart as she looks, she won't attempt it again. If she does, she'll be answering to me. And that is a match she knows she is unfit for."

"Why?" he demanded, stepping closer.

I held my head high as I declared, "Because it doesn't matter."

He scoffed. "You say that now."

"I will always say it. She means nothing to me, and I can't believe a word that leaves her lips. You know that better than anyone, I'm sure. Even if she does come running to me with a story about you, I'll be sure to ask for your version of events."

For a moment, he looked as if he would continue, but then he shook his head and turned away again. With his back to me, he leaned against the fireplace and said, "You're never going to accept my apology, are you?"

"No."

"Will you even let me say it?"

"I don't see the point, considering it'll change nothing."

"I can't pretend nothing happened yesterday."

"I don't want you to. I need you to remember everything you did yesterday. You need a constant reminder to know that what you did was despicable. Somehow, though, I have yet to believe you feel any remorse for that."

Once more, he was in my face. "How can you say that?" he hissed. "You feel everything that I do. You know how I feel about this."

"No. I know that you are worried about getting into trouble. What you're feeling can be attributed to you being afraid of pissing me off more than it can be connected to your actions. Tell me, Grey, do you even understand why I'm pissed? Or did you just realize that I was angry and decided to try to make amends?"

"Stop. You don't believe any of it, so just stop. I know what I did, okay. It wasn't just you who was exposed on that damn stage. This was about me as much as it was about you. The only difference is that I had to live with the fact that this was something I was going to do. She didn't give me a choice."

"That is bullshit, and you know it. You had a choice, Grey. Betray my trust to appease her, or tell Spring to shove her threats up her ass. What could be so horrible that you chose the first option?"

For a moment, Grey kept his eyes trained on the floor without saying a word. Then his eyes raised to my lips and he said one word. "Pass."

That single word felt like a punch to the gut. Not only because it reinforced the idea that he had done something unforgivable, but because it reminded me of the past week. It was a part of a game that we wouldn't play anymore. Knowing that this stupid, budding relationship was going to collapse on that word pissed me off.

I took a step back, shaking my head as my arms crossed over my chest. Without looking at him, I announced, "I'm done. You can see your-self out."

I had just turned toward the doorway when I felt him reach for me.

Twisting in the opposite direction, I did something I was aching to do from the moment I felt him in my house. I hit him again. This time, it was just a quick, stinging slap to remind him where we stood.

"What–?"

"If you are going to attempt to touch me without my permission, I am going to make you pay for it. That was your only warning. Keep your hands to yourself."

"I was trying to–"

"I know that you were trying to do. You were trying to immobilize me so I'd have to stand here and listen to your bullshit. But you can't, and I won't. Get out of my house, Grey."

With that, I left the room and headed for the backyard. I needed fresh air and the comfort of hiding beneath the hawthorn for an hour or two.

Chapter Twenty Seven

UNFORGIVABLE

My numb shell busted apart the minute Grey appeared behind me. "By the Gods!" I snarled, turning to face him. "Are you really incapable of telling when someone wants nothing to do with you?"

"I can't leave it like this."

"It's not up to you."

"It's not up to you, either," he snapped. "I understand that you're pissed and I know that it's my fault. Just let me apologize for it. Tell me how I can fix this."

"Damn it, Grey. Why do you think this can be fixed? You and I went round and round about this stupid thing between us. We fought and snapped and snarled at each other over it. But we were moving past it. I was getting over it. In spite of it, we were... And then you went ahead and let forty strangers know what it is that has us so connected. You took the one secret that we shared and threw it away as if it meant nothing. How can you apologize for that? What makes you think you can fix it?"

Seconds passed as he absorbed what I said. At last, he held his arms out to the sides while his eyes filled with silent pleading. "I don't know, but I have to try."

Again, I shook my head. "No, Grey, you don't. You don't *have* to do a damn thing, and that's something you really need to learn. There are options here, just like with everything else. Don't make the wrong one again."

"This is the right one," he announced.

"And how can you be sure of that?"

He shrugged. "Because you and I never got a choice."

The truth of that stung.

"We were never a pair of lucky idiots who stumbled upon each other and were able to walk away. You and I never got that option. This feels the same way."

"Did you ever stop to think that it shouldn't? It shouldn't feel like something you can't avoid. It's either something you want to do, or something you can ignore."

"I want to fix things," he said without an ounce of hesitation.

I wanted to say that I didn't. That I could just ignore it all and get on with my life. With every logical thought in my brain, I desperately wanted Grey to know how little I cared.

He would know it was a lie.

While we had been only talking for a week, I felt like I knew Grey. I also felt like I wanted to know more about him. A week was long enough for the attraction to sink in its claws, and I didn't know how to get them to retract. Maybe I never would. But I also knew that I didn't want them digging any deeper.

"I don't want to do this, Grey. We tried it and you ruined it. It's not a mistake I plan on repeating."

Some part of him sensed what was coming next. I watched his features stiffen as his emotions seemed to still. Waiting. Preparing.

"What are you saying, Alex?"

To save us both, I would have to be cruel. I would have to tell him a truth he didn't think could still exist. I couldn't think of a time where it would ever be a lie.

"I don't want you in my life, Grey. I never did."

My eyes closed as the hurt crashed through the link. Magick gathered in a heated sphere a second before I felt Grey vanish. Five miles away, he reappeared and my eyes opened to an empty backyard. And for the first time all morning, I had to fight the urge to cry as I crawled beneath the hawthorn.

"You'd think I would know better than to ask you a direct question when I know you don't want to answer, but I guess I don't. What happened, Lex?" my mother murmured an hour later when she eased beneath the overhanging boughs.

Without thinking about it, I leaned my head on her shoulder and closed my eyes. There was only one way to describe everything that had just occurred, and she deserved to know it.

"I was disappointed in someone I hoped

would be more than a passerby."

"You liked him a lot, didn't you?" she murmured.

A self-mocking smile pulled at my lips. "Yeah, I did."

"Is it unforgivable, what he did?" she murmured, brushing hair out of my face.

"To most people, it wouldn't be."

"You are not most people."

Taking a deep breath, I let it out in a rush. "No. It's not unforgivable. But it should be."

"You mean that if you didn't like him so much, it would be."

"Yeah."

"So, what are you going to do?"

"Nothing," I sighed. "There's nothing I can do. If he really wants to be part of my life, even for a short while, then he'll earn it."

"And if he doesn't?"

"Then I'll get over it sooner rather than later."

"How much sooner?" Her tone of voice caused me to sit up so I could meet her eyes.

"I don't know yet," I answered honestly. "But I was thinking of just finishing out the semester."

"I thought as much."

"How did you know?"

Her sardonic smile was as self-mocking as my own had been. "I'm your mom, Lex. There's plenty I know, and a whole lot more that it wouldn't take me long to figure out. Plus, I've never seen you as spooked as the day you came home from your first day of school. At first, I thought it might have been the other witches. Now I know it was him."

My eyes dropped to the grass I was picking and my voice came out in a whisper. "Would you be too upset?"

"Not enough to ask you to stay. If you can't stay away a single second longer, then I want you to go and be happy, Baby Girl. But if you leave here because you are running from whatever this is, you will never forgive yourself. Before you make any decision, you better figure out which it is."

She was right. Of course she was. It was the same thing I had accused my parents of doing when we left Cedar Creek three years ago. If I ran from this, I would be the same kind of coward that I believed them to be. And I would have to live with that every day.

"Thank you, Mom."

"You're welcome, Baby. Now, it's Saturday and we're both sitting out underneath a tree. Not very productive of us, is it?"

I rolled my eyes. "Which room is it today?"

"Well, your dad is going to pick up the siding. I thought we could go with him and start picking out the tile for the kitchen and bathrooms. Floors only," she added with a grin.

"I vote we pick out windows and the patio door first," I said as I followed her out from under the tree.

"Patio door?"

"Yeah, for the living room. We'll put the deck in later, but if we want to get the living room done before winter, we should start there. And let's face it, all of these windows need to be replaced before snow flies. Oh, did you guys pick out a new furnace yet?"

Just like that, we'd shifted gears and become absorbed with something far more productive. Which meant I felt like I'd accomplished something with my Saturday. Something I desperately needed.

Grey wasn't at school on Monday. It was the first thing I realized when I got there, and it was something I had to be reminded of most of the morning. Without him sitting next to me, I was suddenly very aware of how dull my day was, and I seemed to focus less without him there than when he was with me.

While I was still pissed at him, I hadn't thought he'd be too much of a coward to face me. At the most, I expected things to revert back to that week he left me alone. I was hoping for it, anyway.

Then I got to lunch and suffered the uncomfortable realization that Spring wasn't there, either. Instead, the mass of coven members seemed less taut and contained with the absence of their royalty. Considering the amount of involvement Spring had in the events surrounding Grey and I, there was no stopping the jealousy that hit me a second later.

"Sign this."

My eyes snapped to Delaire as she pushed a sheet of paper and a pen across the table to me. "What is it?" I asked, moving to pick up the paper.

Her hand slammed down on it, covering most of the print. "What is the point of bullying you into something if I let you become aware of it?"

It was the first smile I cracked all day. "Now I'm curious. What is it?"

"Sign it and I'll tell you."

"Tell me or I won't sign it."

"Alex, I know you might not understand how this whole bullying thing is supposed to go, but generally someone like you would comply with the instructions of someone like me."

"Ah, but that's supposing someone like you has a substantial threat to encourage the compliance of someone like me. So, what's your threat?"

Del gave a dramatic sigh. "I was hoping it wouldn't come to this. Catori, the video."

My eyebrows shot upwards even as I directed my attention to the camera Cat was holding out to me. In digital pixels, I was forced to endure the spectacle that was me trying to learn what they knew. It was time for my poker face.

"And your intentions for this travesty?"

"Sharing it to a social media site and spread

it amongst our classmates. Threatening enough?"

I nodded once. "The threat is adequate."

"So, you will comply?"

"Now, I didn't say that. First, while it is an adequate threat, I can't prove that signing this document isn't going to lead to an even more compromising position. Second, you have to take into account the nature of the person you are threatening. For the threat to be effective, I would have to care about the backlash of said video. Since I value no opinions above my own, it would seem that your efforts will be ineffective at best."

"Damn. You should be a lawyer," Faye chuckled.

A shiver shot down my spine. "No, thank you."

"You're a pain in my ass. Just sign the damn paper," Del growled.

"Tell me what it's for, and I will think about it," I insisted.

"No."

Cat groaned. "Oh my god. We want you to dance with us at the ren fest in October. You're not a pro, by any means, but you pick up choreography pretty quick and it would be a confidence builder for you. Plus, it'll be fun. Now will you sign?"

My head was spinning. "You want me to what?"

"I want you to dance with us. Back-up only. No solo dives. Just so you get a feel for it and everything. Plus, we'll be at the festival all weekend and they're super fun and we want you to be there."

"And this paper you want me to sign is...?"

"Your registration sheet. I already filled it out; it just needs your signature."

I almost rolled my eyes. "Really? Then why bother asking me instead of forging my signature and tricking me into coming along?"

"We thought about it," Faye said with a shrug.

"Then we realized we suck at forgery. Now sign the damn document."

With a sigh, I picked up the pen. "We are all out of our bloody minds," I muttered as signed my name.

Chapter Twenty Eight

SUCCESS

"My dad would kill me if he saw me in this."

"Hold still," Del admonished as she adjusted the skirt over my right hip.

"Seriously," Cat growled, a makeup brush held between her teeth. My left arm stiffened as she traced over yet another scar with silver body paint.

In the corner of the tent we were sharing with Delaire's mom's troupe, Faye was practicing our simple steps to the beat of the drums outside. Watching as she hit every step, I felt a surge of mild envy. While I was jealous of Delaire's proficiency and Catori's grace, Faye I was envious of because she was a natural. Her ability to keep time and rhythm and anticipate the music was astounding.

What teased my pride most, however, was the fact that she had only been studying for six months. Delaire, at least, had grown up dancing, and Cat had almost five years under her belt. Faye, however, was a fast learner and dedicated to the dance in the same way I had been tenacious about learning to play the piano. Though Del and Cat still outstripped her by miles, it was also clear that there was a vast distance between her and me.

My eyes drifted over to Catori, admiring the green outfit she wore. It appeared that Delaire did her best to match us with our closest elements. Cat's outfit was made of a dark green material with brown accents, with her hair done up with woodland accessories. In the opposite spectrum, Delaire was dressed in a pale yellow costume. White and gold were used to draw even more attention to her.

Faye was a water being, if it could be believed. At first, I couldn't understand how difficult it was to match her. Then I saw the steely blue silk of her costume with the gray accents and knew that Del had chosen well. There was more of a storm inside of Faye than a calm, summer's day on a lake.

I had been the hardest for Delaire. For a week she muttered about fire and lightning and 'showing the thunder.' None of which had made sense to me, until now.

The outfit I wore was meant for a fire element. A sheer, orange fabric was layered over a brilliant red skirt; both of which attached above my right hip, leaving the entire leg bare when I moved. Playing on the theme, the top was technically a scarlet color as well, but there were enough gold accents on it that it was hard to see any of the red underneath. Her reference to the thunder wasn't understood until she had told Catori to paint my scars.

By the time I was able to look in the mirror, I almost didn't recognize myself. Unlike the makeup I usually did for myself, what they had done to me was a lot more colorful. I had a sunburst blend on my eyelids, my face had a slight sheen to it from the highlighter they used, and my lips were a classic red that I had never tried before. One glance at my ravaged arm was enough for me to decide that I couldn't stare at it for too long before my eyes darted away. Altogether, I looked far more prepared for the performance than I actually was.

"If you're going to stare at yourself, you might as well practice with the mirror. This is the last chance you'll have, and I want to see how you move in it," Delaire announced as she and Catori began cleaning up their materials.

I did as I was told, going through the routine in front of the glass while Del watched and critiqued what she could. Then we all gathered together and went through it one last time. By the time we were announced, there wasn't a calm one among us.

Just as we neared the dance area, I felt him coming. My eyes closed the minute he arrived. Then the music started and I tried to shove Grey Walker from my mind.

I could not have blessed Delaire more for making Faye and I backup dancers. Our routines were simple compared to hers and Cat's highlights. It also kept me as far from Grey as the stage would allow. Though his eyes barely left me, there were enough times I was granted a reprieve by one of the other girls moving in front of me.

When the dance was over, we were all forced to line up and give a bow before Delaire led us offstage and back to the tent. It was empty, since her mom's troupe was performing another dance after us. Which was good, considering it would make our sub-par performance something people could forget. I hoped. Delaire and Catori were each going to perform solos of their own later on, so that would be a much more enjoyable experience for us.

As soon as we made it back to the tent, I turned to find that Faye was grinning from ear to ear. "I'll be right back," she announced. Whirling in place, she darted out of the tent without a backward glance. As if I'd needed to guess to know why he was there.

"Anyone see my backpack?" I asked, forcing my voice into a casual tone. Out of everything, I wanted to be in real clothes before Grey showed up. Del had other plans.

"No. Don't even think of it. I did not slave away over that outfit for weeks so you could wear it all of fifteen minutes. This is a ren fest. It's about the only place on the planet you can wear that in public and not be judged for it."

My arguments couldn't compete with that one. It wasn't even that cold out, so I couldn't cover my bare stomach with a jacket even. Considering my options were to traipse about in front of strangers wearing minimal clothing or wait around until Faye returned with Grey, I was willing to take on the strangers. Faye was faster.

Chapter Twenty Nine

CONSUMED

The second I felt them coming, I knew it was over. Best to accept my fate and try to act like it didn't bother me as much as it did. Though with Grey being able to feel all of my emotions, hiding it was a fruitless venture.

"Look who I found," Faye announced, throwing out that innocent act like any one of us was going to buy it.

When Grey followed her into the tent, his eyes stayed carefully away from where I stood beside the table. Instead, he greeted Cat and Del as they greeted him. He even complimented them on their dancing, though we both knew he hardly noticed what they were doing. The sly smiles they were casting around seemed to indicate that they were also well aware. At last, it got to the point where we had to acknowledge one another.

"Hey," he said, his voice coming out soft and low.

I cleared my throat as Faye made a point of ushering Cat and Del out of the tent. Then my eyes raised to his.

Weeks had passed since our eyes last met, and it felt like an explosion rocked through the tent. A raging inferno sprang up around us, driving any sort of chill from the atmosphere. Lightning leapt through the air, snapping between us with sharp consequence. Even more, I felt a magnetic pull toward him. The bond spread taught as it encouraged us to close the distance. All the while, desire whipped through it in a savage attack.

I fought the pull. Grey didn't.

He was a few feet from me by the time I was able to break contact. My head snapped to the side as I leaned back against the table. Shuddering breaths escaped me as a new chill traveled over my skin, raising goosebumps as it went.

Then his eyes lowered and the feeling of fire and lightning making love began to assault my skin. Tracing across my jaw, it was a long, slow caress he performed as his gaze trailed down my neck. He paused at my collarbone, taking one second to glance at where I was biting my lip, before his eyes returned to their previous place.

After spending a few long seconds in appreciation of my top, his eyes began to travel down my bare stomach. The nerves there exploded at this new sensation and the lower his eyes went, the fiercer my desire grew. By the time his eyes returned to my face, our bond was radiating with nothing but pure lust.

"You have no idea how hard it is for me to keep my hands off of you right now." His voice was low and husky, making him that much more desirable.

My hands gripped the table behind me so hard that it hurt. Releasing a breathless laugh, I gasped, "I beg to differ."

"It was almost worth it. The weeks of ignoring me. To see you like this." Each fragment of a sentence bore its own meaning that I wasn't capable of understanding. Not now.

Then he stepped closer and I couldn't find the breath to tell him to stop. Nor the desire to. Reaching out a hand slowly, Grey kept a careful eye on my expression as he swept my hair over my shoulder. Lightning traveled through each follicle, causing my entire body to tingle. Before his skin could touch mine, I held up a hand to stop him. I had so little self-control left, all I could do was trust him.

"Don't, Grey. Please don't touch me."

"Why?" he asked in that same husky voice. The need rolling off of him was absolutely equal with my own. No more; no less. That would make it harder for him to understand.

Another breathless chuckle escaped me as I admitted, "Lack of self-control."

"I promise you, Alex, I will go as far as you want me to and no further."

The closer he was, the more erratic my breathing became, until I couldn't speak more than I gasped. At last, I was able to force out, "It isn't you I'm all that worried about."

A hiss erupted from my throat as Grey took my chin in his hand. He pulled my face toward his and I was quick to squeeze my eyes shut. Tilting my head up, he surprised me by placing a gentle kiss on my forehead. My eyes snapped open even as he placed another kiss on my cheek.

Then his lips were brushing against my ear.

"This is as far as we'll go, then. Just a kiss. No further."

Grey pulled back just far enough for him to guide my mouth to his. I couldn't stop myself if I wanted to. The minute his lips met mine, I was consumed.

The kiss was gentle, at first. It was not enough. Not for me. Not for us.

I was the wanton. I was the aggressor. I was the one to pull him closer after sliding up onto the table. I was the one to deepen the kiss, so desperate was I for his touch.

My skirt fell away from my right leg and Grey placed his hand as high as it could go, sending bolts of desire straight to my core. His other hand rested on my hip, his thumb creating little circles over the sensitive skin. If it wasn't for how firm his hold was, I might have attempted more than a kiss. Though how he kept it at just that, I had no idea.

Of course, his kiss didn't have a specified location attached to it. Which I found out when he tore his lips from mine and left a burning trail down my neck. I released a moan as my head tilted to the side, encouraging him to torment me further. After leaving a playful bite on my shoulder, his mouth found mine again and we were back at war.

"Incoming!" a voice called outside of the tent.

I wasn't of a mind to listen. Grey was more reasonable than that. Stepping back, he removed the hand on my thigh, making the skin feel as if it were frostbitten. The hand on my side remained, however, as he turned to face the girls. I averted my face, trying my hardest to breathe normally while his skin was still touching mine.

"Well, it looks like you two have kissed and made up," Cat remarked and I could hear the grin in her voice. My face grew red as I refused to answer.

"Don't get your hopes up," Grey warned. "A kiss between us means nothing."

My entire body stiffened as my head snapped around to face him. For a moment, I wanted to demand how he thought that was possible. Then I remembered what occurred the last time and my face turned away once more. He was right; a kiss between us didn't mean a thing. But it was almost worth it to forget that fact when his lips were on mine.

"Looks like you two could stand to have a private conversation, but my mom and her friends will be back soon…" Delaire hedged.

Swallowing, I nodded as I eased off of the table. As I was heading for the entrance, Grey's hand slid from my side before he caught my fingers. Another hiss escaped me as the exposed skin readjusted to a normal temperature. Then I glanced back at Grey, reading the emotions he sent me along the bond. He was asking me a question, and his magick made it clear what he was asking. A question I didn't need to answer aloud.

I took one step closer to him before his magick enveloped me. In a blink, we were gone.

When I teleported myself, it was like taking a step from one place to another. Simple. Quick. Zero side effects. Not so when traveling with Grey. It felt like we had spent a whole minute being dragged through quicksand, though I knew less than a second had passed. When we arrived, it surprised me even further considering the short distance we had traveled.

Grey released my hand as he looked back toward the fairgrounds where the festival was being held. "I'd have taken you farther, but I think that outfit would stand out anywhere not close to this." He shot me a devilish smirk.

Once more, I looked down at my belly dancer costume and muttered, "My dad would kill me if he saw me in this."

Grey chuckled. "He'd kill me just for seeing you in it. Not to mention my reaction..."

I snorted. "You reacted better than I did."

It seemed like he was trying to make a point as the desire between us surged, stealing my breath. There was still a smirk on his face when he remarked, "Not by much."

Looking away, I took a deep breath before I asked, "A kiss really doesn't mean anything between us, does it?"

His expression became aloof as he answered, "It doesn't seem to."

I forced a smile. "To be fair, we've only done this twice."

"You've only hit me twice, too, but I'd prefer one of those things to outnumber the other."

Nodding, I let my eyes travel through the trees as I gathered together what little courage I had left. My mother's words drifted through my mind and I knew that this was something I couldn't run from. It was something I had to face.

Taking another step back, I put my fingers on my temples and closed my eyes. "That was a mistake, wasn't it?"

I could hear the amusement leave his voice. "Are you asking me?"

"I think I'm asking me," I admitted.

A thread of hope snaked along our bond before he quashed it. "Why wouldn't it be?"

For a second, I was impressed with his choice of wording. It showed that he knew why I would think it was. That fact that I wasn't convinced was the questionable part.

"I don't know. If I want to keep you at a distance, kissing you counts as the stupidest way to go about it."

Grey waited the length of a heartbeat before asking, "If?"

The urge to bite my tongue was strong. Shrugging my shoulders, I said, "Clearly I have mixed emotions."

"Very well. Let's clear them up."

I snorted. "This will not end well." When he held to his silence, I took a breath and let it go. "Okay, fine. I'm still pissed at you. This was our secret-it's something I haven't even told my parents about-but you went and told forty strangers. You also ambushed me at the behest of your ex, which is so pathetic, I don't have the words to describe it. Also, it really hurts considering how much I like you and how hopelessly attracted to you I am.

"If you had done it to be cruel or malicious, it would have been easy to deal with. I could have hated you for that, but I would have gotten over it and on with my life. Instead, every time I look at you, I think about your hands on me or that kiss, and it becomes so difficult to stay pissed off, even when I have the right to be. So yeah, I would say my feelings about you are a little conflicted."

He took it pretty well, considering most of that was full of body shots. All the same, he remained stoic for a few minutes before he said, "I still want to fix things, you know. But I understand why you wouldn't be able to trust me again. I betrayed you, deceived you, and manipulated you. Those are things I should not be forgiven for. I know that."

"Then what are we doing here, if you know all that?"

"Because I've been in the same place before, and I know how I would have wanted it to turn out."

At once, my own curiosity filled the link, and I did my best to stamp it out. It didn't matter what he'd gone through. What mattered was what *we* were going through.

"What did you want to be different?" I asked instead.

His eyes lowered to the ground and I could feel every flicker of emotion as he dredged through his history. "First, I wouldn't want there to be any justifications. There are no excuses for betraying someone's trust that can erase the act. Second, I would want a real apology. Not one meant to ease someone's anger, but one that results from knowing what was done was wrong. After that, I don't know. I have no clue what could be done or should be done to bring things back into a better version of reality."

There was no point in pretending. "What would Spring have to do to earn your forgiveness?"

Grey shook his head. "Honestly, I don't know. There's so much that has happened between us—including this—that I don't know how I would even try."

"But you're asking me to forgive you based on a similar level of betrayal."

His smile was grim. "It's not that similar. Not that it matters. You're the one that has to decide what it would take for you to forgive me, and I can't answer that for you."

Taking a deep breath, I went to cross my arms until I glimpsed all of the paint covering my left. Afraid of smearing it, I placed my hands on my hips instead and tried to figure out how best to say what was going through my mind. Because it was anything but simple.

"I don't want to forgive you, Grey. I don't think I should. If it was anyone else, it wouldn't be a question or a decision I had to make. But everything with you is complicated, and I wish it wasn't."

"*I* wish it wasn't. I wish it didn't have to be. But everything about this is nothing short of complicated. The only thing that will make it simple is if we make it simple. So, give me a yes or no answer right now: can we move past this?"

I was tired of thinking. I was tired of justifying my reasons. I was tired of all of it. So I didn't think about it.

"Yes."

Chapter Thirty

RIFT

For about one whole minute, Grey seemed stunned. He looked at me as if that wasn't the answer he was expecting at all. Then it clicked and a wide smile spread across his face.

One would have thought I'd accepted a marriage proposal by the way he reacted. In an instant, he reached for me, grabbing hold of my waist and pulling me against him. A startled laugh escaped me before his hand found the back of my head and dragged my face to his. Once more, I was consumed by my desire. As before, I was completely reliant on Grey not to go further than a kiss. He didn't.

I lost track of time. Minutes passed that we clung to each other. Even when we paused for breath, it was impossible to determine when we had started or when we would end. At last, Grey released his hold on me and took several steps back, grinning at me like a boy caught doing something naughty. I was grinning the same way.

"We should get back," he suggested when our breathing settled into a more normal rhythm. I nodded and he stepped close enough to take my hand.

Once more, I felt as if I was being dragged through quicksand before we reappeared outside of the tent. I could feel Grey cast out his magick in search of anyone around. Then his head turned toward the stage. He didn't bother to release my hand as he dragged me toward the sound of the drums.

We arrived just in time to catch the last half of Delaire's performance. My breath caught as my jealousy and admiration each hit a peak. At the same time, I was kind of glad I couldn't do half of what she could. It looked like an awful lot of work to maintain that level of skill.

Once the performance was finished, we were joined by Faye and Catori. Casting a quick glance at our linked hands, Cat raised her eyebrows and grinned like a feline as she sauntered past us to the tent. Faye was even more smug as she noticed.

"So, it's official then?" she inquired.

Grey reached out a hand and ruffled her hair. "It is official. Which means I am finally able to do this," he remarked before turning toward me. "Alex, will you go to homecoming with me?"

It was the first time I had ever been asked to a school dance, and it felt ridiculous how excited about it I was. Which made the answer a no-brainer. "Yes."

Faye rolled her eyes. "Yup, this'll end well," she pretended to grumble as she strode past us.

Smiling to myself, I nodded my head toward her retreating figure. "She dropped that cute and innocent act soon enough, don't you think?"

"Changelings can't keep up the act all the time," he remarked with a grin. Then he came to a stop outside the tent and released a sigh. "I've got to get home soon. See you tomorrow?"

I snorted. "No."

A growl rumbled through his throat and I laughed. "Why not?" he asked as he placed both hands on my hips and pulled me closer.

I hissed. "Touching while conversing ... it

doesn't work." I bit back a groan as the lust began to travel through my bloodstream, spreading to every part of my body.

Grey didn't bother to relinquish his hold. Instead, he leaned close to me and put his lips to my ear. "You'll have to get used to it eventually. I'm going to do this every chance I get."

It had never been so hard to glare at someone before, but I gave it my best shot. Then I said through gritted teeth, "Sunday is family day."

He grinned. "Valid reason not to see me tomorrow, then."

"How are you handling this?" I growled.

"How can you look away? Same principle, swapped scenarios."

Shaking my head, I forced myself to take a deep breath. I tried not to focus on the sensations shooting through me. "I'll see you Monday."

Grey nodded before placing his lips against my forehead. "See you Monday." I received one more gentle kiss on the lips before he vanished.

For a minute, I let myself feel the regret that he was gone. Then I let myself feel the grief for what would come next. But there was no running from this, either, so I turned and walked into the tent where I was immediately accosted for details. Of which I gave few.

By the time class ended on Monday, I couldn't remember a single second of what I just lived through. Between my anticipation and Grey's impatience, the whole day had rushed by on a continuous hamster wheel. Everything we did was by rote, but our minds were on vastly different tracks. The final results of which ended with a cell phone waiting in my locker and my boyfriend pulling the car up to the front steps.

I barely had time to close the car door before Grey reached over and turned my face toward him. His mouth was on mine a second later. After a few minutes, he let me go and sat back in his seat.

"I've been waiting all day to do that," he said.

My thumb ran over my bottom lip as I tried to limit my grin. All the same, I was grateful not to be the only one with self-control issues. Of course, had I started it, I still wouldn't have released him.

We made it to Grey's house in record time,

and as soon as we were out of the car, he grabbed my wrist and dragged me to the basement room where we spent most of our time. The minute the door closed, Grey twisted around and backed me against the wall. I had just enough time to grin before his mouth was on mine in the same frantic, desperate kiss as before.

Quite a few minutes later, I managed to push back on his chest in one of the moments where we stopped to breathe. An instant later, Grey backed up, hands in the air, and a grin spreading across his entire face. I wiped at my mouth a little, glad that I wasn't wearing makeup.

"Is that all I came over here for?"

Grey was not at all ashamed when he answered, "Yes. Pretty much." I laughed as he lowered his hands and leaned against the table. "Tell me you had another motive for coming over."

"Fair enough," I answered.

Then my head tilted to the side and I shot him a grin before sauntering past him to the couch. As we had done before, I took up one side of the couch and Grey took a seat at the other. It seemed so natural.

"So, what's the big deal about homecoming?

Faye didn't seem too enthusiastic about us going together."

He shot me a dimpled smirk. "It's tradition that all coven members attend public functions in whatever capacity is allowed. For all of us in high school, this means we will attend homecoming and Prom, as well as any other event the school chooses to impose.

"It is also tradition to attend with other members of the coven. It is a display of our strength, unity, and adherence to tradition. If you do not wish to go with a date, you are expected to be a part of a group of your peers."

"You bringing me is a statement."

"It is."

A weight settled on my chest, though his eyes sparked with mischievous delight. "And what statement will that make?"

His demeanor sobered a little as he registered my hesitation. "There are a number of ways it can and will be taken. In the first instance, you are a solitary outsider. It will convey a break with the unity that makes up the coven, as well as showcase my disregard for tradition. Secondly, you are the most powerful witch in Grant. By attending with you, it will put them on edge. Two of the most powerful people united can either mean that I am drawing you into the coven's embrace, or you are pulling me from it. The fear of losing me will test their resolve more than anything has done, since they have already lost my sister. Last of all, it will convey my independence and ability to choose who I am going to be with. Without their interference."

Out of all of his reasons, I could feel that his determination spiked with that one. "And that is the true intention, isn't it? To showcase that you have made a decision."

I was surprised when his hand reached out and laced his fingers with mine. "No. The true intention is to be able to show off my sexy new girlfriend. But I am perfectly content with the other outcomes of that desire."

"Why? What do you gain by pissing them off?"

Grey lifted a shoulder and let it fall. "A rift."

It clicked in an instant and I felt the breath whoosh out of my lungs. "You're going to take the coven."

Chapter Thirty One

JUSTICE

"To be fair, I'm already going to inherit it from my aunt. I'm not called 'the prince' for no reason. The position of High Priest has been mine since Azure cut her ties, and it's one I've embraced. That doesn't mean I'm not impatient. I love my aunt, but she's a product of the politics, traditions, and demands that define her generation. They are the very same things I have been able to dodge and duck at any given opportunity. However, if I succeed in creating a rift between the traditionalists and the visionaries, it will make it easier for me when I come into the position. Picking sides won't work, but mending a wound you opened is easier than most people realize. And after years of going at each other with bared fangs, a compromise will seem like the Goddess has blessed each and every one of them."

"You're going to let this go on for years?"

"Of course. I'm not a total asshole; I'm not trying to oust my aunt. But if she sees that maybe I should take her place sooner rather than later, I will humbly accept."

"I feel like I should apologize to the world right now for dating a politician."

Grey chuckled and I could feel that strange sensation flutter through me. "Well, you knew most of this about me before we even started dating."

"'Fool me once, shame on you. Fool me twice, shame on me,'" I said with an exaggerated sigh.

"Now why do I think fooling you is a damn near impossibility?"

I shrugged. "A hazard of the trade, I suppose. I learned a long time ago that going into a situation naïve was the surest way to have my ideals disappointed."

"And what about our situation would disappoint you?"

He wanted a serious answer, but the first thing that jumped into my head was, "Well, I did come over here for one reason..."

Grey needed no more invitation.

For the rest of the week, Grey and I did our best to make it seem normal. Though I'd spent Monday afternoon with him, that didn't excuse me from time with the girls. Therefore, a kind of schedule was being worked out between Delaire, Catori, and I on Thursday. We were about halfway through when I felt the magick spike nearby.

Faye was nearing our table with Winter close behind. Both of them were trying to act unaffected, but Faye's stormy nature was about to produce lightning. At once, my attention was arrested.

All of a sudden, Faye stopped in her tracks and twisted on her heel, causing Winter to take a hurried step back. "Is there something I can help you with?"

Winter's expression suffered a flicker of her disapproval before her face became blank once more. "It is my duty to inform you that we will be leaving the Solas house at seven."

Faye's chin lifted as she stared down the Season Sister. "And?"

Winter's eyelids lowered into a patronizing expression. "We will expect you at no later than six thirty."

The smirk that pulled at Faye's lips was every bit one of Grey's. Superiority poured out of her, though Winter would always remain on her level of power. In that moment, however, it was impossible not to know which of them held rank over the other.

"You may have as many expectations as you wish, but I will never step foot in your house."

With each word, Winter's anger and frustration was becoming more apparent. It was strange enough, however, to watch the visual decision taking place. Which sister would she emulate? Spring or Summer? In the end, the eldest was her role model and she reined her temper in with a cold aloofness.

"It is deemed the gathering place for all coven members of our age."

"So why are you telling me?"

Winter opened her mouth, but it was apparent she had no response for the question. A fact which made Faye give her a grim smile before she took a step back and turned to scan the entire section where the Crone's Crescent members sat watching the display. Then her eyes locked on Summer and her features went cold.

Turning back to Winter, she warned, "They're using you to get a rise out of me. It's sad and pathetic, and I'd be pissed about it if I were you." Then her attention returned to the coven and she raised her voice so the whole cafeteria could hear her, "I am a solitary witch. I have no coven. I need no coven. And I will never follow the traditions of a coven that are not my own. While you may not like it, you have no choice but to accept it, because there is nothing you can do about it."

For a second, I wanted to applaud. Then I felt Grey's emotions harden and realized what this meant. While Faye had never hidden her status as a solitary, announcing it to a cafeteria of people probably wasn't her wisest move. Considering how the magick began to gather in several different witches, it wasn't hard to guess why.

None of it seemed to affect Faye. In fact, she seemed quite superior to them all as she tossed her hair over one shoulder and turned her back on Winter. One look at the wounded pride spread across Winter's face and I knew it was a mistake.

Winter gathered her magick and hurled it in a single clean motion. Faye's shield materialized without a thought as she twisted back around. Then her magick lashed out, catching Winter across the middle and hurling her back several feet. My stomach twisted as I realized how mild a throw it was. If she had wanted, Faye could have sent Winter flying into a wall with enough force to snap her spine.

Summer intended much worse when her magick lunged toward Faye.

Faye's magick lashed out in a spell that created a bubble surrounding Summer. Her spell crashed against the inside of the shield before it bounced back and slammed into her. A scream reverberated throughout the room as she dropped to her knees and began to claw at her face. While the attention of the magick users shifted, I made my way to Faye.

At once, Spring was before us, her body serving as a barrier between me and her youngest sister, just as I was standing between her and

Faye. "What have you done?" she spat.

Faye opened her mouth to justify her decision, and I waved my hand to shut her up. Despite the fact that Faye's shield only gave back to Summer what she had sent out, Spring was in no state of mind to hear it. Two of her sisters had been attacked, and she wasn't willing to see either situation as self-defense.

"It is over now, Spring. Perhaps you should see to your sister," I suggested in as placating a tone as I could muster.

"It is not over," she snarled. "You dare attack my sister?"

"An attack was prevented, Spring."

Her lips curled back like a wild animal as she snapped, "You have prevented nothing. Justice will be done–"

"It already has been," Grey announced, moving to stand between us.

Spring turned her wrath on him. "How can you say that? My sisters–"

"Brought it on themselves. Winter picked a fight she could not win, and should be grateful Faye did not cause her more harm. And Summer knew the consequences of her actions before she made them."

"That is not justice! By the laws of the coven–"

Grey whirled on her, fury blasting throughout the room in a heat wave that smothered almost everyone else's magick. Striding up to her, his face was within inches of hers when he hissed in a low, soft voice, "Justice is what I say it is. By the laws of the coven."

Out of everyone I would have expected to cower beneath his rage, I was shocked when Spring didn't. Instead, she grew as cold. As forbidding. As lethal as Grey.

"By the laws of the coven, outsiders are not to get involved in coven matters."

Despite his rage, Grey forced the barest smirk into place. "It's not a coven matter. Winter and Summer performed a coordinated attack on a solitary witch. She defended herself and they were taught their place. Now get out of my sight, or your sisters will learn the consequences of attacking one of mine."

Naked fear flashed across her face so quickly, I almost didn't catch it. Even when her face had stilled into a familiar mask, I could still see the haunting in her eyes. A moment later, she turned and strode toward Summer, who was already cradled in Autumn's arms. Winter hovered nearby, looking almost as if she would burst into tears. As one, the Season Sisters rose to their feet and exited the cafeteria.

We all watched them go with the same forbidding silence that had drifted through the room since Faye's announcement. When we were sure they were gone, Faye and I released a breath while Grey melted back into the mixture of magick users. His voice was low as he issued orders. I turned around to look at Faye and got a shrug for my trouble.

"She always has to make things so damn difficult," he grumbled, running a hand through his hair.

"Spring?"

"Faye," he growled. "Everyone in the whole damn coven knows she's a solitary, but she likes to just keep rubbing it in."

"Should she keep it to herself?"

"She could not antagonize everyone with the fact."

"Well, if the coven is antagonizing her for it, she has a right to fight back."

"Which is why I defend her. That doesn't make her any less a pain in the ass."

"Well, I can't really deny that one."

Grey sighed as he ran a hand through his hair. "It'd be different if she was old enough to make a clean break, but she's not. Which means the Sisters are always on her case about falling back into place, and I'm stuck playing the buffer. Some days I think Faye keeps pushing just to see how far I will go. Other days, I see the look in her eyes and I know that if they push her too far, half the coven will be burned to ash before I can blink."

I'd seen that look too, and it caused a shiver to run down my spine. Grey was right on that count. If Faye got pushed past her breaking point, she would take them all down with her. It seemed amazing to me that the others couldn't see that, or learn to tread carefully around her.

Yet, I'd watched her grant mercy even when she wanted to kill Summer. I was witness to the control she executed when she tossed Winter on her ass. If Faye was pushed enough, she would snap and someone would die. There was no doubt in my mind. But it would take a whole lot to shove her past that point. And whoever the casualty was, they would probably deserve it.

"Faye knows how to take care of herself, Grey. One day, you're going to have to let her."

He gave me a grim smile. "No, I won't. Faye is one of mine. I protect what's mine."

Chapter Thirty Two

LIE

The same day that Grey had asked me to homecoming, I'd mentioned to Delaire that I needed a dress. I was ordered to leave it to her, and if she found out I went dress shopping, she'd have Cat scalp me. That Friday, while most of the school was at the football game, I was having my final fitting. She did not disappoint, and the first word to come to mind when I saw myself in the black lace gown was 'regal.'

I no longer felt regal.

When we pulled up to the school, Grey turned off the car but made no move to leave it. I knew why. The emotions roiling through him were of the conflicting variety. While I knew he was excited to share this night with me, I also knew that defying coven tradition in this way meant that he would have consequences to face for it.

As if he were getting it all out of his system, Grey allowed a wave of anger, defiance, determination, and almost a malicious violence rush through him for several seconds. Then, all at once, he shut it down.

Then he sighed. "I'm sorry, Alex. I shouldn't be making you deal with all of this."

"What do you mean?"

He reached over and took my hand in his. It made it harder to concentrate when he said, "I don't want you to be a pawn in coven politics, and I'm afraid that you're going to think that's all you are after tonight. If I wasn't 'the prince' then this wouldn't mean so much. But I am, and it does. So, if you don't want to deal with this, tell me and we'll leave."

I took him seriously. That was what he wanted most from me, so I had to consider it. There was likely to be a volatile reaction to the two of us dating, and neither of us was in a position to have a normal relationship. So, if I wanted a relationship with him, it would mean taking on every aspect of what that entailed.

"I'm not a pawn, Grey. I'm a queen. I am not walking into this blind. You told me the outcomes, and I'm still here. Though I'd like to know what you're hoping for."

Grey shook his head. "I would *love* to go inside and be able to enjoy showing you off. But I would happily settle for going in there and having everyone just step back and shut up."

I grinned. "Now be realistic and tell me what you really want to happen. What's the goal out of all of this? What message do you want to send to the coven?"

"Honestly? I want them to be afraid of losing me in the same way they were devastated to lose Azure. I want them to worry."

"To what end?"

"Their fear feeds me. It's why I can let the Season Sisters get attacked and no one will challenge my word. If the Elders fear they might be losing me, they'll get hostile and divided. It'll make them easier to conquer."

Taking a deep breath, I waited a minute before I nodded. "Okay. So, let's go form your rift."

"You're sure?"

Instead of answering, I got out of the car.

They were waiting for us. Though most of our classmates wouldn't understand the significance, each one of the coven members standing still and staring at the door would have alerted even the most obtuse individuals. One by one, I watched the blood drain from most of their faces.

As a reminder or a warning, Grey's magick preceded us into the room. It traveled over the crowd in a thick blanket, ready and willing to smother anyone who seemed to get out of line. A smile pulled at my lips as I thought, *The prince has arrived.*

The princess was already there. Spring watched our entrance with the single-mindedness of a cornered predator. It was the first time I actually considered her dangerous. Not in a volatile way like Summer, but in a far more calculating manner that reminded me that she and Grey had a history.

I was still in the middle of my royal survey when Grey pulled me out onto the dance floor. The minute he put his hand on my side, my attention was diverted. He offered me one more sexy smile before he leaned in and kissed me.

Spring caught the curse a split-second after Summer released it. My appreciation for her talents rose when I felt her cage collapse in on itself, smothering the spell. At the same time, Grey's shield sprung up around us and his fury flowed through the air until it fell in choking waves around the sisters. As usual, it was Spring alone who was able to hold her ground.

Then her eyes met mine. A different kind of understanding passed between us. Her eyes asked a question, and mine answered. As one, we stepped away from those closest to us.

Grey caught my arm before I could take another step. "Where are you going?"

For one moment, I turned to him and allowed our eyes to meet. Desire and passion sparked through the atmosphere. Then I broke the contact and sought out Spring.

"I'm going to talk to Spring."

"It can wait." At once, I was surprised by how pained his voice sounded, as well as the panic that raced through our bond.

Stepping closer to him, I held my palm

against his face as his eyes closed. "What is it, Grey? Tell me."

Instead of answering, he murmured, "Please, let it wait. Let's enjoy ourselves tonight."

It meant too much to him for me to say no. Nodding, I turned to find Spring still staring at us. When I caught her eye, I gave her an expression that clearly read 'later.' In response, her nostrils flared and she nodded once. She would hold me to that.

Grey and I enjoyed the dance as much as we could, for as long as we could. It didn't last, however, as the time drew near to announcing Homecoming King and Queen. While everyone was waiting in anxious anticipation, Spring chose that moment to pass close to us and whisper, "Now."

I waited a few seconds before I turned to follow her from the gym. Grey grabbed my hand before I could make it a couple of steps. Instead of begging me to say, he leaned close and whispered, "You said you would come to me for confirmation of anything she said. Please don't let that be a lie."

A shiver ran down my spine as he let me go.

Without looking back, I followed Spring from the room.

"Do you know what you've done? Did he tell you?" she asked in a soft, weary voice once the bathroom door had shut. A silencing spell shielded the room while the door was convinced not to allow anyone else entrance.

"Yes, Spring, he told me."

Her shoulders tensed. "And still you came. Knowing what it would do to us."

"Yes."

The magick surrounding her pulsed and faded every five seconds. It was the equivalent of someone making a fist before releasing it. Then she sighed. "I suppose I shouldn't be surprised. Solitaries don't have much respect for covens and their traditions."

My eyebrows rose a little. "I respect what you are and how you operate. That doesn't mean I will allow those same terms to dictate my life. But we're not really here to discuss my insult to your coven, are we?"

She didn't try to pretend otherwise. Instead,

she offered me a gracious smile and shook her head. "No, we are not." Then she took a deep breath and said, "He is our next High Priest."

"I know."

"Do you know, then, what role you will play in his life? Have you decided?"

The words were soft. Innocent questions. As if she were asking if I knew what I would have for dinner, or wear to school. Yet, there was a meaning within them that pushed the air from my lungs in a startled gust, because she just asked me if I wanted to be his wife.

"The role I play in his life is the same role he plays in mine. For a year, I will take from him what he offers and what I can endure. Nothing more."

"A year?"

"One year," I confirmed.

Spring's head tilted a little as she studied me. Even her magick pushed in a little closer, as if it could somehow leech my motives from my skin and expose them to her. In a low voice she asked, "You are going to leave him?"

"Yes."

"Why?"

A sarcastic smile tugged at a corner of my mouth. "My life is elsewhere; his is not."

"So, you will love him and leave him." The expression on her face tried to come off as mildly interested, but I caught the flash of pain in her eyes.

My eyebrows rose. "Aren't you relieved?"

A mirthless smile pulled at her lips. "More than you know. Sad, too. It has been a long time since he has been this pleasant to be around. I'm grateful for that."

"Are you? The way he reacts to your name, I can't imagine you've done a lot to help the situation."

At once, her demeanor shifted. "Of course I haven't. I did blackmail him, didn't I? And do you know why I did that, Alex? Do you know why I had to know what bound you to him?"

"No clue."

"Because I had to know if his interest in you was genuine. Grey has taken more than one opportunity to punish me, and I wanted to be sure you weren't part of the same old tired game. Neither of us deserved it if you were."

"You should have known better when you

had to blackmail him into revealing it."

Spring released a rueful chuckle. "Spoken like someone who has not dealt with his lies. He is exceptional at what he does, Alex. Never doubt it. To know the truth of the matter, I had to see your reaction. Hear it from your lips that this wasn't all some elaborate manipulation. If it was real, it had to be you to tell me."

Raising my arms a little, I asked, "And why did it matter so much? What if I was just a game to him?"

"Then I would have put a stop to it," she vowed.

"Why?"

"Pick a reason, Alex," she said. "I'm a decent person that cuts loose girls about to get hurt. I'm a bitch that likes breaking innocent young hearts. Or maybe I'm just tired of him trying to punish me for something that I have already suffered for."

"And what was that?" As soon as the question was out of my mouth, I knew I would regret it. Before I could take it back, however, she validated my fears.

At once, she shook her head. "No. *That* I

won't tell you. For that, you will need to ask him. Please, Alex. Ask Grey what became of our son."

Chapter Thirty Three

WEDDING DAY

I had no words. No reaction. Her suggestion hit me like a battering ram. Everything I could have felt was thrown back by the shock.

It was somewhere in the numbness that I felt the heartbreak, and I knew it wasn't mine. Out in the corridor, I knew Grey waited to face me. To finally lay bare the one secret he'd kept from me above all others.

Turning toward the door, I strode out of the bathroom as a fiery determination began to alight inside of me. If I was going to have this nightmare presented to me, it would be from the man I knew wouldn't lie to me about it. For the first time since my penance began, I was making a conscious decision to use my magick. I needed to know.

"Come with me," I murmured, taking his hand in mine. Before I could get too caught up in the sensation, I closed my eyes and released the magick.

I'd almost forgotten the high. The sweet, blissful rush that spread through my body as the magick gathered in my chest. My intent sank into the pool of power and I was a silent witness as it heeded the spell. In a cool, calm act, it embraced us both and moved us from one location to another. So smooth was the transition, a normal person might not have realized, but I felt the faint jolt of sensation in my stomach a second before it receded. Opening my eyes, I relished in the silence of my backyard.

For a moment, Grey seemed as if he wanted to be impressed. Instead, his eyes scoured my face and he waited for what I would say next. He knew what was coming.

"I told you that I would ask you first. I am doing so. But I don't want to hear a word. Will you give me the memories, Grey? Show me what happened?"

His back straightened as he drew up to his full height. He looked like a man about to go into battle, though the black shirt and crimson tie weren't quite the armor he was probably hoping for.

Grey nodded before taking my hand in his. There was zero hesitation in him, which made me feel a bit better. Then a white mist gathered over my eyes.

"I'm pregnant, Grey." The words came out in a soft whisper from a young girl who couldn't raise her eyes from their joined hands.

Though I'd known going into this what I would find, the revelation still caused my stomach to twist. Looking at the children in front of me, it was all I could do not to cut the vision short. Neither of them was older than fifteen.

As soon as the words left her lips, a younger Grey raised his eyes to the ceiling and I could see the emotions going to war on his face. The anger was most prevalent. Anger, guilt, defeat. They flashed over his features like pages of a book. When he finally lowered his face to look at a solemn Spring, however, he'd set his features into resignation.

"What do you want to do, Spring?"

Her pale green eyes widened. "Every life is sacred. The laws of the coven–"

"Don't matter. What do you want to do?"

There was the slightest shift in her expression that made me suspicious. Though she was nervous, she had not seemed afraid. Until now. When he was giving her a real option, Spring didn't know how to respond, because she'd held the coven's laws as unbreakable.

"I ... I'm not sure. What do you mean?"

"I'm asking you what you want, Spring. That's all. If ... if you don't want to ... have it ... there are options. If you do, there are options for that, too," he finished in a rush.

At once, Spring's hands clasped over her womb. "I am not killing my baby, Grey."

There wasn't even a flicker of disappointment in his eyes as he nodded. "Okay. So what else are we going to do?"

Hope flared to life in her eyes as soon as 'we' left his mouth. I was surprised to realize she'd doubted him. That made me wonder if she had reason to.

Shaking her head a little, Spring's voice dropped into a pleading tone, "I can't give it away, Grey. I'm sorry, but I can't do that."

He was almost convincing when he said, "Okay,

so we won't."

It was the first time she dared to meet his gaze. "So, we're in this together?"

Not once did he hesitate. "We're in this together."

I still felt ill. Knowing that this could only go from bad to worse didn't help matters. My chest constricted as I let go of his hand, stepping back to breathe as much as possible.

"You saw when she told me?"

"Yes."

Grey's jaw set as he stared off into the distance. "I would have taken care of my child." For a moment, I didn't know if he was trying to convince me or himself.

Taking a deep breath, I stepped forward and offered my hand. "Why didn't you?"

His hand took hold of mine and I was lost in the mist once more.

Despite all of the times I'd gone to Grey's, we'd never ventured into the backyard. That didn't mean I was incapable of recognizing it, even before I turned to see the house towering over the manicured flower beds, organized herb patch, or stretch of lawn that looked as if it were frequently trampled by dozens of feet. Right now, however, there were only four setting up the ritual.

It felt like someone had punched me in the stomach. There was no denying what I saw being formed in front of me, and I found myself drawing closer in the need to confirm it.

Grey finished laying the cedar boughs in a circle, leaving one set aside so as to leave the circle open. Within the circle, a woman who resembled Spring stood before a tall, narrow table with an altar cloth spread over the dark wood. Three cords were arranged on the purple silk between two silver chalices. Moving around the circle Grey had created, Mr. Walker formed the pentagram, invoking the elements into this travesty. Along the path that I walked, I recognized Mrs. Walker scattering flower blossoms. The meaning of each was to ensure a blessing on the couple that walked over them.

For the first time, I understood what Grey meant when he claimed his father believed any commitment should be upheld, no matter the circumstances. He had prepared his son's handfasting when Grey was only fifteen. To him, Grey and Spring must have been set *in stone.*

The memory was far from over, but I already knew that I could not forgive him for this. If he went through with the handfasting–if he took that child as his wife–I could not forgive him. For both his sake and hers, I couldn't imagine how he could make a mistake with so many horrific consequences.

At last, everyone ceased their preparation and took their positions. While the entrance to a handfasting was different for every practitioner, the Walkers and Spring's mother seemed to like the idea of a traditional wedding march. Or maybe it was Spring's romanticism which fueled it. In either case, Spring's mother kept her place at the altar, acting as High Priestess in the absence of Grey's aunt. Flanking the entrance to the sacred circle, Grey's parents waited expectantly for their new daughter to emerge from the house.

Once everyone was in place, music began to play from speakers hidden in the garden beds. It wasn't the standard wedding march, but a light, lilting melody created with pipes and wind chimes, if I had to guess. As one, we all seemed to take a deep breath.

Minutes passed. Instead of fidgeting or looking around like normal people, the four of them seemed to grow stiffer. I couldn't wait. Something was off.

I was halfway along the path when the screams began.

I froze. Their spell broke. At once, four people were sprinting toward the house as the screaming continued. Then something snapped and I sprinted to the stairs leading to the balcony. The second I made it through the doors, I skidded to a stop as my hands flew up to cover my mouth.

Grey charged into the house a few seconds later. Like me, he froze for one moment to take in the scene before him. Spring leaning against the wall, a hand holding tight to the leg of the table in front of her. Her other hand cradling the small bulge where her child had lived. And the blood creating a streak across the carpet, smeared over her legs, and soaking through her white dress. Her baby no longer lived. He died on her wedding day.

My body was shaking as I took several steps away from him. I crossed my arms over my chest, trying to breathe through what I just witnessed. It was something I could never have imagined, and now I was a witness to the most devastating event a woman had to endure.

A few feet away, Grey kept his face averted, but I knew he was crying. "She told me she wanted to name him Greyson. It was stupid. We fought about it for weeks. I told her she at least had to spell it different, or the poor kid would never forgive us. Then she sat there on that floor, screaming his name as if he could somehow hear her and come back to us. Right then, I knew he could never have had any other name. That was his. The only thing that was his."

I wanted to comfort him. Even thought of ways to do it. But I couldn't. Not yet. There was still one more thing I had to know.

"What happened between you and Spring? Why are you so angry when you hear her name?"

I pretended not to notice as he wiped his eyes on his sleeve. Then he held out a hand to me. For one second, I debated leaving well enough alone. But I had to know. The second our skin touched, the white mist rolled over my eyes.

Chapter Thirty Four

TRAPPED

Grey knocked on the open door to the hospital room. Spring never took her eyes from the window, ignoring even her mother and Summer who sat in her line of vision. Mrs. Solas was the first to notice him, and her back straightened. Her hand tightened on Summer's until the other girl took note. As one, they rose from their seats.

Taking hold of her sister's hand, Summer murmured, "We'll be back soon."

Mrs. Solas leaned down to press her lips quickly against her daughter's cheek. I knew Grey didn't miss it when she whispered, "Remember what I said. Don't be foolish."

Spring didn't react. Her mother scowled at her for a moment before turning and leaving the room. She closed *the door behind her, leaving Grey and Spring alone.*

Nervous, Grey set the vase of flowers he'd brought on a table in the corner, taking time to adjust them. Several times, I watched him open and close his mouth, as if he were talking himself out of saying anything stupid. At last, he took a breath and went to sit in one of the chairs closest to Spring. Still, she didn't react.

Grey's mask wasn't as impenetrable back then. The indecision flickered over his features, marred by his curiosity, and pain. When he spoke, his eyes were trained on the floor.

"What are you doing here, Spring? We have people at home who can heal you."

He paused and we both waited for some kind of response to that. An indignant snort, an angry retort, even a bone-weary sigh. Something.

Spring said nothing.

Releasing a sigh of his own, Grey reached out to take her hand. At once, she pulled it away. Not in a quick, instinctive fashion, but in a more deliberate rejection. I didn't have to be linked to Grey to know how much that hurt.

"You don't want to touch me." There was a raspy quality to her voice, letting us know that they were the first words she'd said in hours. All the same, there was *no inflection in them and her eyes continued to stare right through him. A shiver climbed my spine as I got a familiar taste of numbness from her.*

"Why wouldn't I want that?" he asked, laying his hand down beside her on the bed. He left his palm up in an open invitation.

A minute passed, and I kept a close watch on her features. They gave nothing away. Spring was so far gone into the numbness, it was amazing she ever got out.

"I trapped you, Grey." My heart lurched into my throat, and I knew Grey's had to be doing the same. Spring didn't even look at him as she continued, "I cast fertility spells. I charmed the watch I gave you for Yule. I did everything I could to have your baby. Because of that, he was taken from me."

I couldn't decide which was worse in that moment: her empty voice, the confession, or the look of utter horror on Grey's face. In some ways, I knew what the outcome of this discussion was. This was the betrayal Grey couldn't forgive. At only fifteen, when he was so innocent and naïve, she had gone behind his back and contrived to get pregnant. All so she could trap him into a marriage and a family before they were even adults.

Several minutes passed as Grey tried to process what she just said. Spring continued to stare off into space. As if she hadn't just crushed the last good thing she had. I knew the second that it all clicked for him; he pulled his hand off the bed and balled it into a fist over his thigh.

"Why?" I could tell he was trying to keep his temper in check, but his control was far from being perfect. "Why would you do that to me? To us?"

"I wanted you forever. I wanted to be your wife and the mother to your children. I didn't want to wait."

Grey shook his head. "No. There has to be more to it than that. We both swore that we wouldn't be like everyone else in the coven. We were going to live our lives how we wanted, instead of falling into the same old patterns. You swore that to me, Spring. What changed?"

"Nothing changed, Grey. I just lied."

Grey released my hand and I backed up several steps in order to give us breathing room. I needed it. Working some saliva back into my mouth, it was still a minute before I could speak.

"By the Gods," I murmured, dropping my

head into my hands.

"'Keep your friends close and your enemies closer.' I Ascended a year later, to the exact second that we lost him."

I swallowed hard, keeping my eyes closed. "You use 'we' when talking about him."

"It takes two to tango. There's a lot I can do to Spring, but taking him from her, even in my thoughts," he shook his head, "that's not one of them."

A thought twisted my stomach into knots. It was a horrid, awful thought, but I had to ask. I had to know.

"Do you regret losing him?"

"Every single day." The answer was hard and immediate, as if he'd had to say it too often for his liking.

His emotions, too, grew into a hard, hostile ball in his chest. Anger lashed around the edges, protecting the softer grief within. Every time I tried to pierce the shell, it snapped at me and shoved me back. Yet, I saw the heartache hidden within.

It was like nothing I had ever felt before.

Sinking to my knees, I wrapped my arms

around myself and folded over my thighs, just trying to breathe. After leaving Cedar Creek, I knew what pain was. We were on intimate terms, my grief and I. But this... More than anything else in the world, I prayed to never feel what Grey and Spring felt. It would kill me to lose a child, and I couldn't believe they were still standing.

Dropping into the grass before me, Grey let out a weary sigh. "I may not have wanted him when I first learned about him, but by the time I lost him, I wanted nothing more than to be his dad. And now I will never have that."

There was nothing I could say. There was nothing *to* say. Grey's life was easily as big a shit-fest as mine had been, and he was surviving it in the best way he knew how. What wounded creatures we were; and each one a predator in our own right.

"We were broken for a long time. I don't know that either of us will ever recover from it. Not sure I want to."

"Why wouldn't you want to?"

Then he asked, "Would you erase your scars if you could?"

My mouth grew dry. "No. They're a part of

me now."

"Exactly. It's not the good times that define you; it's the bad. Having him and losing him are both things that make me the man I am. I'll keep any part of that I have left. Even the pain."

The valerian scar seemed to grow a little warmer, reminding me of the days it stood for. There were probably more people in the world that knew what Grey meant than those that didn't. Sometimes pain was all there was to hold onto. In situations like ours, it was as much a part of us as breathing.

Breaking in on my reverie, Grey murmured, "Now you know."

I nodded. "Now I know."

"So, what will you do?"

I knew what he was asking, but I was busy tallying up the cost. He didn't have to tell me about Greyson. Nor had I the right to ask. Yet, I'd demanded this piece of him. It was time to give some of that back.

Without looking at him, I took a breath and said, "Losing your son was the worst thing that ever happened to you. I thought the worst thing that happened to me was being charged with murder when my mentor committed suicide. But what was worse than that was being taken from my home, and having to leave my best friend behind. Neither of which compare to your loss, but those are some of the things that have hurt me most in this world."

For several minutes, he couldn't feel anything but stunned. I was filled with dread. While I had dragged every last detail out of Grey, I couldn't deny that there were things I couldn't imagine telling him. Between Morgan, Nathan, and Cedar Creek, each one had the word 'pass' stamped across them in bold letters. But I had taken his worst moments from him, and he deserved something in return.

In the end, he didn't say a thing.

Rising to his feet, Grey held out his hands for mine. My eyebrows rose a little as I reached out and placed my fingertips against his palm. Even as the breath caught in my throat, Grey yanked me to my feet and dragged me up against him. Without saying another word, he placed his hands on my waist while mine went around his neck. For a long time, we swayed back and forth to the sound of our own heartbeats.

Come Tuesday morning I was informed that it was time for the official dinner with Grey's parents. In an instant, I was dreading it. Smiling, Grey had kissed my forehead, said we'd survive, told me to wear a nice dress, and he'd pick me up at six thirty.

I wasn't sure what to expect when Grey picked me up. Part of me was more or less resigned to their unequivocal disapproval.

Another part of me, however, remembered the day I first met them and Grey telling me that their opinions mattered to him. Though I knew that his defiance at homecoming was directed at them as much as it was at the rest of Crone's Crescent, there was still going to be a part of him that would be hurt by how they treated me. Which meant I wanted to make a decent enough impression to put a blockade on as many jabs and snipes as possible.

"You're nervous," Grey teased as we pulled up his driveway.

"As if you're not," I shot back, sticking out my tongue.

His grin was smug. "I hide it better."

"Whatever," I grumbled. Then I hissed in a breath of air when he reached over and took my hand in his.

"One more day of this, and then we'll have time for ourselves."

My lips pressed together and I shot him an apologetic smile. "Three more days."

If looks could kill... "What?"

I shrugged. "Cat wants our help with her Senior Project. It's going to take about two days to nail it."

"Aren't Senior Projects meant to be done by yourself?"

"Who made that stupid rule? Anyway, she needs us for modeling purposes, and I agreed. She even has Faye onboard. As soon as it's done, though, we will have you and me time."

Grey sighed, shaking his head. "Very well. I suppose it wouldn't kill me to think about my own. What are you doing for yours?"

"I already did mine." My hand traveled over the scars of my left arm. "It was about self-harm."

Nodding, Grey gave my left hand another squeeze before he shut off the car and closed the garage door. Before I could get out of the car, he twisted toward me before grabbing my chin. I thought he was going to kiss me, until his eyes traced around mine. Knowing that we both needed this, I raised my eyes to his.

Minutes passed as the air became harder to breathe. The same sparks that had plagued us in the beginning of our relationship had never ceased or diminished. Heat coated my body, almost making it uncomfortable. All the while, desire battered away at my insides and it took all I had in me not to lean forward and kiss him. When I felt I could no longer breathe, I closed my eyes.

"Let's get this over with," I said, opening the door and stepping out into the cool air of the garage.

Chapter Thirty Five

REMARKABLE
TENACITY

They rose to their feet as we entered. His father gave a solemn nod to us, keeping an impassive expression on his face, while his mother bore the same plastered-on smile that I did. All the same, I caught the suspicion in her gaze as she passed her eyes over me in a head-to-toe scan. Somehow, I figured everything had just gotten even more difficult.

"Alex, I am glad you could join us this evening," Mrs. Walker announced as she strode forward and took my hand. I was almost amazed at how well versed she was in half-truths.

In comparison, my own response seemed rehearsed. "I wouldn't miss it," I assured her.

"Would you like a drink before dinner? Anna

should be calling us in soon."

"No, thank you."

Grey led me to a couch and we sat down across from his parents, all of us letting the awkward silence fall without any idea what to say in order to catch it. Of course, when his mother did decide to continue the interrogation, I missed every second of it.

"So, Alex, tell us where you're from. Grey has mentioned that you move often."

My throat grew dry and I resisted the urge to glance at him. "For the majority of my childhood, I lived in New England. When I was a baby, my dad was stationed in North Carolina, but I don't remember it. After we left New England, we've lived on both coasts as well as Oahu for a short time. Now we're here."

"Stationed? Your father is in the military?"

"Was. He retired from the Marine Corps about a year ago."

"And your mother? Does she work?"

"Yes. She was a high school English teacher for several years. Before my dad retired, she became an interior designer. Now we travel around and flip houses."

There was a brief flash of surprise across her face and a quick look at Grey that seemed to question his sanity. A smile tugged at my lips as I felt my pride flare to life. Of course, we were both saved that confrontation by Anna's arrival and the announcement that dinner was served.

I should have known that wouldn't be the end of it, however. There were only so many questions someone my age got asked when confronted with condescending adults. Though I was prepared for the next question, I was sure they weren't.

After a few suggestive looks by his wife, Mr. Walker turned to me at last and asked, "Where do you intend to go to college, Alex?"

As casually as I could manage, I announced, "I'm not."

It looked like I'd given them both a stroke. "Is there a reason that you do not wish to further your education?" She barely kept it from being an accusation.

"There are several, but the deciding factor is the fact that I haven't decided what I want to do with my life yet."

"Well, what are your interests?" It sounded

like she wanted to cure me of my indecision then and there. I almost felt sorry for her.

"'Interests' is such a vague word. I like being outdoors. I'm good at landscaping. But what I excel in doesn't often come with a job title. My Craft has taken up the majority of my focus, and that's where I would like it to remain."

"But what will you do for an income?" his father pressed.

My eyes lowered to my water glass as I announced, "It's not something I need to worry about, actually."

"Oh." It was all Mrs. Walker could say while a new considering gleam appeared in her eyes. Then she asked, "Is it family money you will be living off of, then?"

I shook my head. "No. An inheritance."

It looked like she was going to press for more details, but Grey looked at her so expectantly that the questions died on her tongue. I shot him a grateful smile. After all, if I wasn't going to tell him, there was no way I would indulge his parents' curiosity.

Then she switched tactics. "So, Alex, is it because you move so often that you are a solitary or is that how you were trained?"

"It's how I was trained. The coven in my area had vanished long ago."

"That is unfortunate," she remarked. "We find that having a large community is truly necessary for our comfort. It is a blessing when there are others who share your ideology and priorities surrounding you. And the raising of children in such an environment is a great relief."

It sounded like she was trying to pitch coven life to me. Even had I not had my Cedar Creek Coven experiences to go off of, I'd seen enough of the coven drama in the Season Sisters to know that whatever they were doing wasn't working. I'd have been more worried about raising a child in that environment than I would ever be relieved by it.

"I'm glad you feel that way," I responded as diplomatically as possible. "To be honest, I rather like not having others around me. It makes it less of my responsibility to keep an eye on them."

"You would feel others like yourself a threat?"

It was time to tread carefully. "I would feel uncertain until I knew their intentions. As I'm sure your family must have felt about me."

Her smile was as false as my own. "Of course. Intentions that are still clouded for some."

"Then I hope you can set their minds at ease. I'm here to finish out my senior year and help my parents to flip a house. As soon as both objectives are complete, I will be moving on once more."

For the first time, I saw Mr. Walker glance at his son. There was a question in his eyes that Grey ignored. He was too busy staring at me with his own impassive expression. That didn't stop me from feeling the thread of heat that heralded his irritation along our bond. He really didn't like me announcing that I was leaving in less than a year. But it was something he had to get used to.

"Why choose a house here, may I ask?"

"It was my mother's decision. She thought it might be nice if I socialized more with those like me."

"So, she thought having a community of peers would be more beneficial than solitary practice?" The tone was a tease, but I felt the sharp sting of that barb.

"She thought that I had one year left under

her roof, and she wanted to make sure I had a full experience of options before I left it."

"And you are not at all swayed from a decision. Remarkable tenacity," she said, raising her wine glass in a salute. Another barb wrapped in the trappings of a compliment.

I chuckled. "You may as well call it stubbornness, Mrs. Walker. I know better than anyone else how deep that family trait runs."

She bowed her head and gave me her first genuine smile. "The most stubborn of creatures often make the most decisive individuals. Keep your pride in your tenacity, my dear. This world would be a lesser place if women such as us did not have that."

After dinner, we retired to the living room for tea. Grey smirked at me as I sipped at mine, glad to find something infused with flavor and carrying little bitterness. It also gave me something to be distracted by when his mother dug into yet another line of inquiry.

"So, Alex, is your name short for something?"

"Alexandria. After the city where my parents

met."

"Interesting. Have you ever been?"

"No. It was supposed to be my eighteenth birthday present. Considering the political climate in Egypt right now, however, it is on an indefinite hold. But I would like to go someday."

"Wise. Though I would have thought you'd find no risk able to match your abilities."

I shrugged, pretending to stir my tea. "Perhaps not, but I would rather not rely on them if I did not have to."

"I find that strange, considering what we've already heard of your accomplishments."

Despite myself, my head jerked up and I stared at her with wide eyes. For one, frantic moment, I thought they were talking about Cedar Creek. Then Grey spoke up.

"Alex isn't in the habit of discussing how she uses her magick. Even when her teleportation proves far more fluid than mine ever has." Then he turned a gaze on me and winked. "I had to tell them how smooth the transition was."

I forced a smile. "Well, yours feels like quicksand, so I'd rather we didn't rely on that more often than necessary."

His mother plastered on another false smile before she remarked, "You were saying that you'd rather not rely on your gifts. Why is that?"

My chest tightened as I thought of the reason for my penance. That I was even serving a penance was still a secret I was holding close. While every witch may have noticed my abstinence, there wasn't one in Grant that knew why. The longer I could keep it that way, the better.

Clearing my throat, I forced a smile of my own. "The mundane deserves as much of my attention as the magickal. I am doing my best to establish a balance."

Before she was able to say more, Grey announced, "It's time I took you home."

It was the best thing I'd heard all night.

After we said goodbye to his parents, Grey led me back to the garage. When I went to open the car door, Grey closed it quickly. Grabbing my hips, he turned me around and pressed me back against the door. I barely had time to catch a breath before his lips pressed against mine.

When he pulled away and allowed me to breathe, he murmured, "We are *never* doing this again."

There was nothing to say in response to that since I was in full agreement. Grey didn't expect a reply as he opened the car door for me. As we were pulling out of the garage, I knew better than to break the silence. Agitation was churning inside of him and I knew he would need a few minutes to calm down. Although, I did feel a little better when he reached over and took my hand.

"You don't have to be apprehensive. I'm not going to explode," he said while shooting me a wry look. "I'm sorry you had to put up with that. And I'm even more sorry that I couldn't find a way to redirect it."

"We both know there was no redirecting her. I was prepared for most of it before we even walked into that room."

Ignoring me, he promised, "I'll make it up to you."

"Oh really? Because I kind of thought this was payback for you having dinner with my family."

"Your parents didn't attack my basic ideals and values and attempt to replace them with their own. I owe you something."

"Okay, what did you have in mind?"

Grey waited until we came to a stop in front of my house before he turned to me and said, "Pick a day."

"What?"

"Pick a day. Any day. And no matter what I have planned, no matter with whom, that will be a day for you and me."

"Any day?"

"Yes."

A grin pulled at my lips and I scoffed a little, "So if I said Samhain, you'd spend it with me and no one else? No matter what?"

Grey was perfectly serious when he answered, "Yes."

I rolled my eyes before I bothered to check the link. "You can't mean that, Grey. The coven would have your head."

"Are you going to choose another day?" he asked calmly.

Shaking my head, I didn't look at him as I said, "Samhain is the most sacred day for us. It is the end of the Celtic New Year, and I would end it as I would greet it this year: with you beside me. So, if you are offering me one day to be selfish and to take you as my own, that is it, Grey. Therefore, don't make promises to me that you cannot keep."

"I will keep this one. Mark my words."

He meant it. My heart swelled as I felt his determination and certainty along our bond. Grey meant what he said; he would be with me on Samhain. It was more than I had bothered to hope for, though it also somehow seemed inevitable. What there was between Grey and I, nothing else could compete with.

Leaning over, I was surprised when Grey left a light peck on my cheek. When I gave him an incredulous expression, he grinned at me and said, "I'll walk you in."

I rolled my eyes as we got out of the car. Sure enough, Grey walked me all the way into my house. My mom was sitting in the dining room hovering over a bowl of ice cream. She smiled at us as we came in, her head tilting curiously to the side.

"Everything go well?"

Before I could answer, Grey sighed, "We're exhausted."

Her eyes darted between us for a second. "Sit

down. I'll get the ice cream."

I chuckled, "I've got it, Mom. Where's Dad?"

"Someone called about a roofing job about an hour away. He went over to give them a quote. He'll be back soon."

I nodded as I opened the freezer. "Grey, you have options. Rocky Road, chocolate swirl, or orange sherbet."

"Chocolate swirl," he answered at once.

For a while, the three of us sat around eating our ice cream in relative silence. It had a soothing effect on both of us. And when we said goodbye on the front porch later, it was with the reminder that we would be able to have one day together very soon.

Chapter Thirty Six

COMPLEMENT

Sleep was impossible to come by. Butterflies fluttered through my stomach and I waited with bated breath as the last seconds of October thirtieth began to slip away. Easing out of my tent, I paced away toward the edge of my campsite. Toward where I could feel him. The second it became the thirty-first, my eyes closed and I expelled a breath nice and slow. When I opened my eyes, I could feel him near me.

Grey approached behind me, wrapping his arms around my stomach as he pressed a kiss against my neck. "I thought you would be asleep."

Leaning back into him, I smiled. "I have one whole day that you're all mine. How could I sleep through that?"

Turning in his arms, I raised my eyes to his and held his gaze with my own. The fire flared to life, following the invisible threads of our gaze like a lit fuse. In the same instant, the pressure dropped as my lightning storm gathered. My blood began to boil while the air around us crackled with electricity. It was the first time in weeks that I'd let our eyes meet for so long.

Having become accustomed to something, it was easy to forget how extreme it was. How potent and arresting it could be. Grey and I had forgotten what it was like for fire and lightning to make love every time our eyes met. There was no better time to remind us.

It was also a first. As had happened to me the first time we touched, it was becoming too much for him. Never had I held his gaze with such intensity for such a long period of time. Long enough for the climax of this action to cause his magick to rise to the surface. With plenty of instinct wrapped in the threads, I could feel it swirling around him, ready to rescue him as mine had once rescued me.

I smiled and closed my eyes.

Grey pulled me against him as he crushed

my lips with his. Lightning laced over my skin as a familiar fire exploded within me. I ached for him in the same way that he yearned for me. For once, there was no separation of our emotions along the bond. It ran pure and undiluted with the lust thundering through us.

At last, we would sate it.

When I woke, the first thing I noticed was how sore I was. Though my body hadn't held with the stigma that virgins always bled or that it hurt the first time, it still clung to the reality that my insides would feel like a swollen bruise after the fact. Which meant, though Grey and I had enjoyed a long, passionate night, there wasn't likely to be a repeat of the event for a while.

The next thing I noticed was a little more startling. My magick fluttered out from me in lazy tendrils, moving and writhing with each pulse of my heart. More than that, it was wrapped around similar tendrils of his. And I couldn't help but admire how well they seemed to complement each other.

"So much for not sleeping today," Grey murmured, rolling over to wrap an arm around my stomach and pull me against him.

I smiled to myself as a strange giddiness assaulted my insides. Playing it off as best I could, I tried for amused and casual as I replied, "At least I'm not sleeping alone."

His lips pressed against my neck as he murmured, "Today is not about us being alone."

There wasn't an answer for that, so instead I twisted in his arms so that my lips could find his. Then I drew his attention to the magick that was still draped throughout the tent. Without thought, it fanned out around us, grazing over our bare skin and caressing our faces.

"My magick has never done that before," I murmured.

"What?"

"Lingered. It's either in me or it's being used. I've never felt it trailing around like that."

"You've never let it loose?"

I shook my head. "No. I either use it or I don't."

Grey's hand reached up and brushed against the locket resting between my breasts. "Or you put it here. Why?"

My hand reached up to cover his. "It's an heirloom. Not one I'm exactly entitled to, but it's more mine than anyone else's. This locket has held the magick of many powerful women. It's fitting that it takes from me what my penance makes available."

"Why the penance?"

My first thought was to pass. The second thought that raced through my head was that he deserved to know. Some small part, at least, he had earned from me.

Taking a breath, I said, "The penance is because of my arm. Because of the things I did when I was at my worst. After my magick was used as a weapon, it became apparent to me that I would have to go without it for a time in order to learn how to appreciate and respect it once more."

"How long have you been without it now?"

"A little over a year."

"Do you miss it?"

"Every single second of the day, and not at all," I remarked with a grin. Turning to see his confused expression, I explained, "I'm a vessel. I hold magick. It's what I do. But there's also something true about not using: there's nothing magick can offer me that I can't find a way to do without. I love having my magick, and I love using it. But it's not a requirement for me to live my day-to-day life. Not anymore."

His eyes crinkled as a tender smile spread across his face. "You amaze me."

I grinned. "You're not so bad yourself."

A mischievous grin spread across his face and he leaned down to place his lips close to my ear and whispered, "Careful, Alex, you're about to fall."

Before I could answer, his lips closed over mine in a hungry demand. Even as the lust roared through us, I barely remembered to gather some of the magick to me and send a wave of healing energy through my body. Then the storm raged to life once more.

We didn't spend *all* day in the tent. Shortly after our second savoring, we put on clothes and decided to go for a walk.

There was peace. Somehow, I hadn't realized I was missing it. Until we were gliding through the trees, hand-in-hand, I hadn't realized that the anxiousness had lifted. The weight around my shoulders and the paranoia that clung to my skin had floated away. It startled me in the same way that it seemed obvious.

I wasn't afraid of using my magick.

Still, it drifted along with Grey and I. His combining with it as often as we stopped to kiss or run our hands over each other. Like me, it was possessive in how it approached. Eager. Undaunted. Proud. The way I interacted with Grey was the way my magick cavorted with his.

I don't know when I made the decision, or if I was even the one to make it. At one point along our travels, I felt myself open to it, and it all poured into me. A pressure released and at once my body was full of purpose. My blood rushed with the heady power as each of my cells absorbed it like sunlight. It seeped into me, binding itself to everything it came into contact with. As had happened when I was a girl, I could feel that I was a vessel for the magick. This was a responsibility that was born unto me, and one I would never forsake again.

With as little call as had brought it into me, it took the barest pressure to push it back out.

To keep pushing. Stretching. Feeling every single molecule of the power that was harbored inside of me, and letting it out.

Grey stopped suddenly and turned me to face him, his hands gripping my shoulders. His eyes worked to capture mine and I allowed them to lock. Fire burst along the bond and lightning flashed fitfully through the air around us. All around, his power and my power flexed and pulsed and grew and receded with no thoughts but to stretch.

Then my eyes closed and I pushed once more. Magick poured out of me, stretching toward the sky, blasting around the trees, dropping deep into the earth, and circling back in on us in a single breath. At long last, I knew what it meant to feel invincible once more. I knew what it meant to be able to do anything. *Everything.*

When my eyes opened, a wealth of knowledge was dumped on my head. My senses were wide open and they gathered everything to them that I had been blind or deaf to for years. At once, I catalogued each creature in the surrounding area. Grey included.

He was weak. I didn't know why it shocked

me to realize that, but the moment my magick began to settle, it was all I could think. Though he was the most powerful witch in Crone's Crescent, he could reach but half of what I harbored. After all I had seen him do and what we'd already been through, I felt as if I had been duped somehow.

I had no one to blame but myself, and I couldn't even manage that. Things happened for their own reasons, and I was too tired to conjecture what they might be. Not now.

"Alex..." He couldn't finish his whisper as it trailed away with his awe.

Unable to help myself, I stepped closer and wrapped my arms around his neck. Pulling him to me, I kissed him hard. Hungry. Needy and demanding and full of the only promises I could make to him. He could be in awe of me; that was fine. But I would not allow him to realize how different we were. I wouldn't let his breeding determine rank between us. That was not for him to decide or decipher. Ever.

Later, we sat with our backs to the trees, occasionally adjusting the clothes we'd hurried to throw back on. It was almost November and the temperature had a bad habit of reflecting it. Every couple of seconds, one of us would shoot a self-satisfied smirk at the other.

With a grin, Grey reached over and gripped my chin, dragging my face to his for a far gentler kiss than the assaults I had laid on him. When he pulled away, I was surprised when his forehead lingered against mine. We took a deep breath at the same time, enjoying the sensation.

"I never expected that," he said at last.

Though I knew what he was talking about, I grinned and remarked, "Oh, I'm sure you've been sexually assaulted by plenty of women over the years."

Grey chuckled. "It's only assault if I say 'no.'"

My grin widened. "I definitely don't remember hearing that."

"Never," he promised in a moment of quiet solemnity.

The word fell like a lead weight at my feet. It was a promise I didn't want. A promise that rang with its own vehemence and foresight. Something Grey couldn't take back, even if he wanted to. *When.* When he wanted to.

"How come you never told me you could hold that much?" he asked, the awe lingering on the end of his words.

I shrugged, turning my gaze away to scan the forest. "Would you believe me if I said I forgot?"

"How?" he scoffed. Almost normal that time.

A smile pulled at my lips. "It's been a year since I've used, but my power had been held in check long before then. When I started these," I said, indicating my arm, "my magick retracted. Like it knew I would do more damage if I were given the option. It was saving me from myself. In all, it's been about three years since I could hold that much."

Grey shook his head. "I don't know how you could live without it."

"Probably because I didn't grow up with it. My gifts didn't appear until I was nine, and I had people around me to stress the importance of balance. If I'd listened a little better, maybe I'd have a few less scars."

"What do you mean by that? About balance?"

"The magickal and mundane must have some balance. It's why you drive to school, walk between classes, and do your own homework. Subconsciously, you've already drawn the lines between them, and you maintain that as well as you can. For me, there was a time where the line wasn't drawn, and even walking from room to room seemed like a chore. Absolute power corrupts absolutely. What they don't tell you is that there is always a reckoning."

"And that led to the penance."

"Yes, it did."

"But now it's over?"

I took a deep breath, feeling every ounce of my magick still spread out around us like a thunderhead. My lips pulled into a smile. "Yes, I believe it is."

Chapter Thirty Seven

DISTURBANCE

The thing about dating another magick user was that I didn't feel the need to show off everything that I could do. The thing about dating another witch was that I *did* feel the need to show off. It was a complicated frame of mind.

"What is that face for?" Grey laughed.

"I don't know. I'm just feeling restless now. Like I want to go on one long, epic magick spree. But there's nothing I want to do."

"Nothing? At all?" he scoffed.

I shrugged. "Nope."

He gave me a dramatic sigh. "All the power in the world and you don't even feel like spying on people or setting something on fire. Waste of talent."

Throwing my shoulder against his, I laughed. Then I had to do my best to smother the longing that reared up inside of me at his words. Because he was right; I had all the power in the world, and I could seek out others if I chose to. But I couldn't do that. Not again.

Forcing the thought from my head, I said, "As much as I am capable of, Grey, there's not a lot of use for it. Other than my teleportation, I don't think I've bothered with half of the things I can do. There doesn't seem to be a need."

"But what about a want?" he asked, tilting his head to the side as he studied me.

"What about it?"

"Nothing. It's just that you seem to always think in terms of needs over wants. To you, things have to be necessary in order to matter. If you don't need it, you discard it. Have you ever done one thing just because you wanted to? Not because it felt right or you thought it had to be done? One thing out of pure selfish desire?"

Only one word could answer his questions.

"You."

Neither of us was ready to say goodbye the next morning. Part of me wondered if it was because we would miss each other, or just that we didn't want to have to return to our lives and face the consequences of what we did. While we were able to forget a lot of things before, dawn had shed more than a little light on our situation.

"How upset will your parents be?" he asked as he helped me to pack up my gear.

"To be honest, I'm pretty sure my mom believes we didn't wait this long. And my dad really doesn't want to know."

He shot me a grin. "I don't know how we waited this long."

"Through your impeccable self-control. Because it sure as hell wasn't due to mine," I answered with a grin. Then I raised my eyebrows at him. "What about your parents?"

Grey pretended to think about it for a second before he said, "You may have to come and rescue me from the dungeons."

"You know, I would not be surprised if you actually had a dungeon in that house."

"Oh, we do."

Laughing, I wrapped my arms around him,

stepping into the embrace he offered. His hands trailed up and down my back and I closed my eyes as the pleasure washed through me. For several seconds, we stood there holding each other.

Then he murmured, "I have to go now."

"So do I."

"I'll see you tomorrow." With that, Grey placed a single, gentle kiss on my lips and vanished.

After he was gone, I took a few minutes to linger. My eyes traveled over the campsite, remembering each moment that we shared in the space. Though my face burned with a steady blush, I let myself go through every single second and enjoy it. Because it was nothing to be ashamed of.

At last, I got in the car and drove home.

When I arrived, the first thing I did was attempt to locate my parents. Relief flooded through me when I found that they weren't home. While my penance might have been at an end, it would take a long time before I could integrate my magick into my every day in a way that would make my dad accept it. With them gone, I didn't have to baby-step it. Instead, I gathered all of the gear up in a telekinetic bundle and allowed it to follow me from the car into the house; all the while, I had a glamour in place so as not to freak out the neighbors.

When all of the gear was stored, I went upstairs and drew myself a bath. It felt like I hadn't been in the water for five minutes when I felt the car pull up. A groan escaped my lips even as I monitored the magick that was broadcasting her approach. My head ducked beneath the water while Spring made her way up onto my porch.

Can't avoid it forever, I thought to myself. As soon as I surfaced, I released the magick into an astral projection right inside the front door. I opened it before she could knock.

"Hello, Spring."

For a second, she didn't respond. Then she straightened her spine and said, "Hello, Alex."

Silence stretched between us as I debated the merits of inviting her inside. In the end, I chose to do the hospitable thing.

"Please, come in. We can talk in the living room," I said, indicating the room off to my right.

Spring forced a smile and stepped into the room. While I was closing the door, I noticed her gaze lock on a spot on the ceiling. The awe rolling off of her was enough to rival Grey's.

"An astral?" she asked, glancing again at the ceiling.

A cocky smile pulled at my lips. "Well I wasn't getting out of the bath for your sake."

Instead of seeming offended, a wry smile spread across her face while a shade of weariness entered her eyes. "A bath sounds divine right about now. What herbs do you use?"

"Lavender for right now. But the soap is a goat milk and sage bar that I got from the renaissance festival."

"Sounds relaxing."

"It is."

Perhaps she sensed that my sharing sequence had come to an end, because her smile shifted, bearing a sarcastic twist in the corners of her lips. "Do you know why I'm here?"

I shook my head. "No idea. I thought you'd be waiting with the rest of the coven to chew Grey a new one after yesterday." From the second he left me, I could feel his agitation and frustration rise to anger before falling back into a state of indifference. It was a rollicking sea that I was glad to avoid enduring in person.

Spring shook her head as she took a seat. "There would be no point to that. Yesterday was as much a declaration of defiance as bringing you to homecoming was. I've already witnessed its effects; there was no need to experience it again."

I nodded my head, deciding not to let hospitality trample over candor. "Okay, so why are you here?"

"When last we spoke, I asked you what position you wanted in his life. You told me it was a temporary one. Reassure me of that, please."

My eyebrows rose a little. "It is temporary. I'm leaving in the spring."

"And you're sure he will not go with you?"

All at once, the air whooshed out of my lungs. My body froze in a state of petrification as a new thought occurred to me. I had never considered that Grey would come with me. Not because I questioned his desire to, but because I'd already made the decision that I didn't want him to.

I shook my head. "No, he won't. He wouldn't want to. His place is here."

A single eyebrow rose as her expression

became considering. "Who are you trying to convince, Alex? You or me?"

"Why are you asking? What does it matter?"

"It matters because we have already lost our future before. We cannot survive another blow like this. There is no one else to take Grey's place. Not without having to wade through a river of blood to reach the high ground."

We both knew she wasn't talking about herself. As far as power went, what she wielded in the coven was not due to the amount of magick she could hold. What influence she did have over them still amazed me.

"So, what does this have to do with me?"

She held her arms to the side, palms up. "You are an enigma. The Elders think you are disrupting the coven with your presence. That homecoming and Samhain prove that you are a bane to his existence. Only you and I know that you are not the reason for Grey's behavior. He would have found other ways to create his chaos."

"And have you told the Elders this?"

"Yesterday."

"Their response?"

"They sent me to you."

I should have realized she'd never come near me of her own volition. "For what purpose?"

Spring shrugged. "They want Grey here, but they want him happy. They're not fond of the discord he's stirring up. Since many do blame you for it, they want to try and bring you into the fold. I have warned them that you have no intention to stay, but they are obligated to tempt you. It is my task to convince you to meet them. In their minds, if they have Grey, the chance of having you grows; if Grey believes we have you, his chance of seeking to divide them diminishes."

My eyebrows shot up my forehead. "That is a stupid plan."

"I told them as much, but it was easier to appease them than to argue."

Tilting my head to the side a little, I remarked, "That's your role, isn't it? To appease and cajole them when things aren't going their way?"

Her head bowed a little. "Grey is the agitator and I am the peacemaker. We work well together, so long as we are on the same page. Lately, he's been getting ahead of himself and his patience is thinner than it once was. For that, I must blame you. Whatever bond you share, it is becoming more difficult for him to separate himself from it."

"But you figured it out anyway."

"Of course. Grey is devious, but rarely is he subtle. As I said: he is the agitator. His job is to rile them and force them to see that there are two sides to an issue. Then it falls to me to help them see that there is a third option they would never have noticed before. He may be a few steps ahead of me, but that makes my work that much more an art form."

"Is that why he sent you here? To help me find a third option?"

"No. He had nothing to do with this. I did."

"Why bother?"

"Because I need him. More than you ever will. And if inviting you into our world for a limited time soothes the beast in him, it is a decision I can live with."

"How? If you need him so much, how can inviting his girlfriend into the coven be a good idea?"

Her smile became patronizing. "I do not need

him because I love him, Alex. I need him because our futures depend on each other, whether he wants to believe it or not. The future of the coven depends on Grey, and I depend on the coven. It is no great mystery to think that I wouldn't do anything to ensure that future. Even accepting you."

"As long as it's temporary," I added.

"We all have our limits."

I nodded once before I asked, "When and where?"

Chapter Thirty Eight

CONTAINED

To say that Grey was not amused by the idea was less than accurate. He was pissed. I got to hear the full rant about it on the drive to school the next day, and he had let his displeasure be known for the next two days. Come Friday evening, however, he was stoic.

"So, you're actually giving me a ride to this thing?" I asked as I met him at the car.

"You will need the getaway car. Trust me."

"I can teleport."

"But you're too proud to do it. If there's going to be any escape, it'll be because I have to drag you out. For that, you'll need the car ride just to calm down."

"It's not going to be that bad."

He snorted. "Just remember that I'm not the one that agreed to this insane plan."

The car door closed before I could respond, and I figured it was best to just leave it at that. While I understood why he was upset, that didn't mean he had to make the situation bad before we even arrived. Granted, it wasn't likely to be sunshine and rainbows when we got there, but if everyone could be civil, there wouldn't be a problem.

Grey and I didn't say a word all the way to his house. The second we passed through the gate, I sucked in a breath. While I'd guessed a few times as to the population of Crone's Crescent, nothing could have prepared me for the number of magick users pulsing with power at the end of that driveway.

"A bit more than you expected?" he asked in a slight teasing tone.

"There's an army at your house."

"Not quite that many. Just a couple hundred."

"I have never even seen that many practitioners gathered in one place, much less those who can actually hold power."

For the first time in days, Grey laughed.

"Yule is really going to shock you, then."

"Why?"

"It's when many coven members return. All of the hotels and vacation homes in Grant will be bursting at the seams with all of the witches that come here."

"How many are there?"

"That'll make it home for Yule? About a thousand. Overall, somewhere near five thousand."

Holy shit. I couldn't speak; could barely think. There were almost five thousand witches just in Crone's Crescent Coven. One thousand of which would take up residence in Grant for the Yule celebrations. My head felt like it was about to explode. It was so hard to imagine.

"Where do they all live when they're not in Grant?" I asked as we came upon the house.

He shrugged. "Wherever they want, so long as they don't leave the territory."

"So, if someone got a job offer in Arizona?"

"That's Blessed Endeavors' territory and they would have to decline."

"Really?"

"Yes. Witches from other covens don't come

here, and we don't trespass on their territory."

"Not even on vacation? What if you want to go to the beach?"

"There are four out of five Great Lakes in our territory. They can pick one."

We pulled into the garage and it felt like a wall of magick smashed in on all sides surrounding the car. Almost two hundred people were pushing at my shields, trying to find a way to reach inside me and learn all that I was. My eyebrows rose as I turned to look at Grey.

"This conversation isn't over."

"We'll pick it up again later," he assured me as we stepped out of the vehicle. Before he closed the door, Grey caught my eye over the top of the Audi. After a second, I looked away and he said, "There's still time to flee. The engine's still warm."

My chin lifted and my shoulders rolled back a little. "Ryder Pride," I announced.

Releasing a sigh, Grey gave a decisive nod and headed for the door. I followed him into the hallway and was gratified when he placed his hand on the small of my back. When we reached the door to the basement room, we took a moment to brace ourselves for what would come next.

Then he opened the door and we stepped into the gathering of the coven.

A steamroller flattened my expectations for this meeting shortly after we arrived. While I was raised to perform introductions upon meeting new people, the coven didn't seem to take that sentiment to heart. In the first place, Grey and I walked into the basement room and were greeted by a heavy silence. A couple dozen witches occupied the room, gathered around the table, cluttered up to the bar, or lounging on the couch, and they'd all ceased their activities to watch our entrance. No one approached, and not one of them spoke to us as we passed through.

It was the first time I saw the glass wall retracted enough so that people flowed in and out of the house without restrictions. The patio tables were all occupied and the smell of roasting vegetables and seared meat drifted over from the grill. Again, not a sound was made as Grey and I passed through the gathering. It was awkward as hell, but I didn't dare hang my head or act like a sheepish little girl. I was there to meet the Elders, and anyone who didn't like it could take it up with them.

A strange wave of silence and whispers followed us across the lawn, as those we had just passed turned to their companions and began to circulate the rumors they'd heard. The only ones who did more than fall silent at our approach were those we saw at school each day. More than one offered me a polite nod before they drifted back into the packs of their friends and relatives.

At last, an empty expanse of grass separated Grey and I from a group of black-cloaked figures. They were standing in the middle of a circle that had been cast, but not closed. The spells around the edges were set up in layers, with each one holding a different being's magick signature, and I admired how well they weaved together and covered any gaps left behind. Yet, the most impressive was the pulsating sliver that stitched them all together into one piece of fabric. It was a powerful signature that declared in a loud voice that it was done by the hand of the High Priestess herself.

It was the very existence of the circle that

gave me pause. When Spring made her plea, she had made it seem like the Elders, alone, wanted to speak to me. She hadn't mentioned that I'd be paraded in front of every witch in Grant. Yet, the circle meant a ritual, and I was a guest either meant to witness something or be part of something without my consent. Either of which could prove harmful to everyone involved.

Grey guided me toward the opening of the circle and I felt the hairs on the back of my neck stand on end. I was powerful, no doubt, but taking on two hundred witches on their home turf was more than even I could handle. There was no way I was taking another step inside of a circle with spells that elaborate.

When I stopped, Grey stopped, too. As if he had no intention of taking another step. Together, we waited in the no man's land between the house and the circle. Either the Elders could come to us, or we could leave. I no longer cared which it was.

A mere second passed before it seemed decided. One of the black-cloaked figures raised their head away from the grouping of their comrades. Silver eyes locked on mine and a familiar dimpled smile spread across her face. While Grey had revealed that it was his aunt who led Crone's Crescent, I still wasn't prepared for the similarity. Of course, his father might have been the linking factor, except that I had not yet seen the man crack a smile. Grey's aunt, on the other hand, practically radiated spontaneous pleasure. Like Grey and Spring, she had lying down to an art form.

The Elders fell into step behind her as she moved away from the center of the circle. As she neared, I saw her cast an indulgent smirk at Grey. Stepping up to him, she placed both hands on the sides of his face, and he lowered his head so she could kiss his forehead. It seemed more ceremonial than affectionate and my wariness grew.

"You are right on time, Nephew. As usual," she remarked with pretend petulance.

"Will it begin so soon? The moon is barely above the trees and the sun won't set for another hour."

"You've learned your lunar cycle well, but you know how these things must take form when the time is right. Until it is, we prepare." Without any further explanation, the High Priestess turned to me and said, "You must be Alexandria Ryder. I am Celeste Blackwell, High Priestess of Crone's Crescent Coven."

I hated when people addressed me by name. It left me nothing to say after they finished their introduction. Instead, I forced a smile and nodded at her in acknowledgement. Then the rest of the Elders arrayed themselves on either side of her and the real introductions began. Throughout it all, I didn't say a word.

Three seconds of silence passed before the portly gentleman named Chester announced, "Look at that bearing. She is as equal to him in attitude as anyone can be."

Grey showcased a dimpled smirk. "You can say 'arrogance.' She knows."

A reluctant smile pulled at my own lips. "Better than anyone else," I assured them.

"With reason enough for it," said Gloria, Chester's wife. "Your magick has a pleasing expression about it. May I ask why it is so contained?"

As often as Grey and I tiptoed around the subject of my magick, having someone ask pointed questions set me on edge. Which showed itself plainly as I answered, "I was taught that magick is a tool, not a toy. If I've no need to use it, I don't reach for it."

"And it does not fill you of its own volition?" sneered a voice I would have rather never heard again.

Turning to Sky Solas, I felt my chin rise. "There have been a few times where my focus was otherwise occupied." Every single time was while I was in physical entanglements with Grey. As long as the magick didn't teleport me like it did the first time we touched, I couldn't give a damn if it filled me. "Other than that, the magick respects me enough to wait for my permission to act."

Beside me, Grey's spine straightened as he waited for the onslaught to come. My smile grew a little wider as my eyes traveled over each of the cloaked figures. While Grey tensed for an argument, I relaxed into it. This was my element, and they could fuss and rumble like thunder, but I would strike like lightning. All I needed was a target.

Sky Solas did not take the bait. Instead, a

smile not unlike my own pulled at her lips and her head tilted to the side in a nod of acknowledgment. Then she turned her back to me in order to face Celeste. At once, I realized it was an insult-a remark on how harmless I was-and I couldn't help the snicker that left me.

Her back straightened as she felt the sting of my disregard. Then she cleared her throat and announced, "High Priestess, it is time for the ceremony." As she spoke, some of her pride became noticeable.

Celeste nodded and looked over Sky's shoulder to me. "You are welcome to stay and observe, Alexandria Ryder. Grey, take your position."

Unease rolled through our link as the thought of being separated in hostile territory swarmed through the both of us. Then a familiar presence pushed against my shield and I whipped around to find a freckled face. Faye drifted up to my side, not bothering to hide her grin.

"Come sit with me and the younglings. We'll be out of the coven's way, and allow Grey to perform his duties."

Nodding once, I looked at Grey and let our eyes meet for a few seconds. Before anyone else could catch what was happening between us, I smiled and turned to fall into step beside the young solitary.

As we walked away, the rest of the witches filtered past us, eager to take their places. When most of them were gone, I looked at Faye and asked, "What are you doing here?"

She shrugged. "My parents are coven-bred, as is my younger brother. Since I am not of the coven and do not take part in rituals, I have proven to be their go-to babysitter for such events. The pay is good and no one harasses the girl who could walk out and leave their babes to wander into things they have no business being a part of."

"And what would they wander into tonight if you weren't here?"

Faye's expression turned hard as she looked up at me. "Summer's Ascension."

Chapter Thirty Nine

NATURE VS. NURTURE

Faye and I presided over sixteen children in the nursery, ages ranging from three months to eight years. Those in the nine to twelve categories were being watched over by the newest Initiates. They were in a pre-training stage and were all arranged on the balcony to observe the Ascension that they could not be a part of. It was such an elaborate hierarchy, that I spent at least an hour drilling Faye for details.

Four hours passed with us in that nursery. In the beginning it wasn't so bad, but after three hours surrounded by children with sparks of magick and hot tempers, playing referee over the same toy started to get old. Even Faye's patience seemed to wane, and we both made our way to the back windows more often than before.

"It should have happened by now," she murmured as we both cradled babies on our hips, staring over the lawn.

"Summer is so weak; why do they think she will Ascend tonight?"

"The Seers must have seen something. It is very rare that they are wrong. They've predicted most of our Ascensions over our cribs. Some are specific dates, like Summer's. Others are like mine and Spring's, which are riddles in themselves."

"Really?"

Faye nodded. "Supposedly, Spring won't Ascend until her firstborn takes their first breath. Rumor has it that she was pregnant when she was fifteen, but there's no baby to show for it, so it's probably a bunch of BS. And then the prediction for me says that I will Ascend the same day as the one who is my opposite."

My stomach twisted at the mention of Spring's secret, and I lunged at the opportunity to steer the subject away. "Opposite?"

"Yeah. You know, the one person who occupies the other life you could have had."

"What?"

Faye sighed and adjusted the little one on her hip. "I don't know how to explain it. In the coven, we grew up knowing that we were each one side to a coin. On the opposite side was someone else who was like us. Legend has it that this person is the one you were almost born to be. It's the other life you would have led.

"So, someone opposite to me is less independent, more family-oriented, less ambitious, more contained, and less honest. But they're also like me, because they could have been me, and I could have been them."

"I've never heard of that before."

"Most people haven't. No one knows if it's true or not, but it's kind of interesting to think that there is someone out there that you could have been. For better or worse. Sort of like a good twin and an evil one. You're enough alike to almost be the same person, but different enough to where no one can confuse you. It's sort of like a nature versus nurture argument. We go in as practically the same person, but how we turn out is a product of our environment."

"Interesting. So how do you know that about

Spring's if you were never an Initiate?"

"I was still coven-bred, Alex. The Seers keep a record of every prediction they make, and it's kept in the vault in the High Priestess's house. When I was about nine, they took us on a tour of it and they let us read the predictions. That's how I know that Grey's Ascension took place on the anniversary of his greatest heartbreak, though no one knows what that was. Autumn won't Ascend until her eighteenth birthday, and Winter is promised an early Ascension around Yule next year."

"And the Seers have never been wrong?"

"Not about us," she said with a shrug. "There are hundreds of little check marks next to past Ascensions, and even lack of Ascensions. So far, they haven't missed a single one."

As the last word left her lips, I could suddenly see that she was struggling to breathe. Faye reached out a hand, gripping the window frame. Shaking her head, she motioned for me to take the boy from her hip. I practically snatched him from her as she eased down into the window seat. A glance into the backyard told me all I needed to know.

"Kids, let's go into the other room to play," I called out, trying to grasp their attention. None of them reacted. At once, my magick pulsed out and I forced the lightning into the air and lit it up like sparklers. Arrested by the flashing pops, most of the kids followed the display into the adjoining room, while I lifted the youngest ones in a cocoon of magick and pulled them behind me. All the while, I formed a protective barrier around Faye.

It seemed like such a useless action to close the door between us, but I did it anyway. As an added precaution, I threw a barrier around the room not unlike the one Victoria had used to isolate Alyssa in the past. While I knew that my Ascension had been relatively mild compared to my Wiccaning, I wasn't about to put anything past this.

In the other room, I could hear the glass of the window shatter. The screams followed in after, and my stomach tightened. Ascensions were painful. It was the very essence of magick erupting in a body and destroying everything about a witch. Then it was repair work, after that. The remaking of the witch. What was left after it was all over was the pain and the power. Nothing else.

When I'd glanced out that window, I'd seen a wall of flame surrounding Summer. It was her element, and she would be consumed by it before she could rise from the ashes. And on the other side of that closed door, Faye was raging in a watery storm. There was no telling how long it would take before they would settle, but I wasn't looking forward to keeping almost twenty children calm while nursing Faye back into reality, either.

Along our bond, Grey's emotions grew tense and hard. Even if he couldn't feel it himself, I know that my emotions would have told him what was happening. Which was why I latched onto our bond and followed it until I reached his mind.

When it's over, you need to come here. You need to be with her, I urged.

Soon, he promised.

Five minutes later, I could feel the pressure release inside of my shield and I thinned it out enough to allow Grey entrance. He was there a second later. At once, I split myself in two and allowed an astral to take part of my mind into the other room.

Grey sat on the floor, cradling a shaking Faye in his arms. His face was pale, but hers was alabaster. My mind shot back to my own Ascension and the recovery time I'd wished for. It was damn well something Faye would get.

"Grey, send for someone to watch over the kids. I'm going to take her home with me."

"I've got the kids. You get her out of here before they figure out what just happened," he said, easing her off of him.

In the other room, I set the three-month-old into the baby rocker and opened the door. As we were trading places, Grey took one moment to place a kiss on my lips. Then I crouched beside Faye on the floor and took her in my arms as Grey had. In a blink, we left the Walker house and arrived in my living room.

"What is going on?" my mother demanded even as my dad paused the movie they were watching.

"She Ascended."

For my parents, I knew that word was going

to take them back to the night Morgan died. It didn't matter that it was doing the same to me. What mattered was that Faye wasn't going to have a similar experience.

"What do you need us to do?" my dad asked.

"Is there any food? And a blanket would be nice."

At once, my mom leapt off the couch and sprinted toward the kitchen. My dad grabbed the blanket they'd been using and helped me get Faye onto the couch and wrapped in the thin fleece. During which point, Faye remembered how to speak.

"I'm not dying," she said through a raspy voice.

"No, it just feels like you did," I said, pushing the hair out of her face.

"I was drowning," she murmured. "It was so quiet."

That had been the hair-raising part, because it had been so quiet. While Summer had screamed through the fire's torment, Faye couldn't breathe through the storm.

My mom arrived a second later with a bowl of soup and a tall glass of water. As if she wasn't weak at all, Faye shot up into a sitting position and lunged for the glass. She didn't even pause for breath as she downed it all. Then she set it back on the serving tray and shot us all a sheepish grin.

"Sorry, I just–"

"Hush. I'll get you some more water while you eat your soup."

Faye nodded as my mom left the room. Then she dragged the bowl closer to her and started inhaling the broth. On the other side of her, my dad sighed and shook his head a little.

"At least she has an appetite. I couldn't remember when you'd last eaten, and you didn't seem enticed to try anything in the days after."

I couldn't remember either. Food had been the last thing on my mind following my Ascension, but I was pretty sure no one had let me go hungry. Between Matt, Nathan, and Anne, they were fairly good about making sure I did normal things like eat and shower, so the grief couldn't take over the most basic functions of my life.

When Faye finished her soup, she downed another glass of water. Afterward, she set it aside and grinned at me. "Only time in my life I ever regretted being a water element."

"Lightning is just as bad. So is fire," I explained. "Except that it's not as quiet."

Sensing that we had nothing left to say, my father held up a hand. "I'm John Ryder, and this is my wife, Melanie."

"I'm Faye Hart," she replied, shaking his hand. "Thank you for … all of this," she added, wrinkling her nose a bit.

My mom's eyes shot to me. "Can we ask what happened? I mean, this doesn't seem to be the kind of thing that would catch you off guard."

"It wasn't supposed to," she said.

"Is it okay if I tell them?" I whispered to her and she nodded. Turning to my parents, I explained about the Seers predicting when a coven-bred child would Ascend. Then I told them the riddle behind Faye's. At that point, Faye let her head drop into her hands.

"I can't believe Summer is my opposite. I feel like I'm going to hurl."

"Actually, I'm not all that surprised," I said with a shrug.

"How?" she groaned.

"Well, she is your opposite in all the ways

that count."

Before I could elaborate, the bond between Grey and I jolted as his proximity changed. Mine and Faye's heads both snapped up a second before the doorbell rang. No one had time to move before my magick opened the door for him. It was a good thing, too, because he would have run over anyone to reach her.

Walking right past me, Grey knelt in front of the couch and took her face in both hands. "Are you okay?" he demanded, his voice low and harsh. Inside, he was seething, but the worry was also slamming itself against the inside of his skull, creating scenarios that couldn't exist in a normal reality.

"I'm fine. Calm down," she said, but she didn't push his hands away.

"What happened?" This time, the question was for both of us.

My part of the tale was simpler. "As soon as Summer began to Ascend, so did Faye. I grabbed the kids and went into another room and kept a shield around her to minimize damage."

"We'll discuss it later," Faye promised him.

Grey dropped his hands from her face and I

made room for him on the couch so he could sit next to her and wrap an arm around her shoulders. "Don't ever scare me like that again."

"It was just an Ascension."

"No, it was *your* Ascension. And I missed it because we had to have a stupid ceremony for Summer, of all people."

Faye snorted, "You can say that again."

Leaning back, Grey ran a hand over his face. "Goddess, what am I going to do with you?"

"Take me home so I can go to bed?"

Before either could answer, I said, "You're staying here. We have room, and I'm not feeding you to the sharks right after I pulled you out of the water."

Faye wasn't dumb enough to argue.

Chapter Forty

EQUAL

As it happened, my parents loved Faye. That night, we'd finished watching the movie with my parents before Grey was sent home to deal with the fallout. My parents had cleared out while Faye and I stayed up late talking.

I was still sleeping on the loveseat when I heard movement in the kitchen. Ten minutes later, it was met with voices. When the third voice was added, I knew it was time to get up. By the time I made it to the dining room, Faye was already setting the table for breakfast. With magick.

My eyes shot to my dad. His eyes followed every plate, fork, and knife as it drifted from the cupboards to the table, but he didn't appear frightened. Instead, he seemed engrossed in studying how it worked. It was more than I'd ever hoped for.

Faye didn't seem to notice, and I knew why. The magick lingering throughout the house was easily twice as much as she'd had before, and she'd carried a big enough punch then. It was so thick and enticing in the air, and she was so curious about what she could do with it, that she was going a little spell crazy.

Leaning against one of the pillars, my mom was watching her with an amused expression. "What are you doing after breakfast?"

"Cleaning up," was her immediate response and my parents chuckled.

"I meant with the rest of your day."

Faye shrugged. "Probably go to the park and see what I can do now versus what I couldn't before."

"Is that what happens when you Ascend? You are able to do new things?" my dad asked.

Faye nodded. "Yeah. I mean, when you're younger you learn a lot, but there's always a wall at the end of the tunnel. It's how they get us to focus on herbs and runes and stones. But when you Ascend, everything becomes about energy workings. Didn't you notice that with Alex?"

My parents exchanged a glance and went silent. With a sigh, I drew close enough for them to realize I was there. "No, they didn't notice. I did my best to make sure they weren't aware of my abilities."

"Oh." Faye knew better than to ask questions, but I knew she wanted to.

Clearing my throat, I said, "I couldn't teleport before my Ascension, but I could read minds. I couldn't feel every living thing within a hundred feet of me before, but I was an early empath. Before, it felt like I could do a lot. After, I knew I could do anything. Everything."

A small smile pulled at her lips. "I don't think I can teleport. Or read minds."

"There's nothing wrong with that," I assured her. Then I grinned. "Means you might get more use out of the Audi than Grey does."

"If only, if only..."

A second later, Grey appeared outside the front door. Again, I let it open before he had a chance to knock. Sensing him, Faye released a sigh.

"It figures. Any time there's food, he knows

right when to appear."

"And you always make enough for me. It's kismet," Grey announced as he joined me in the dining room.

"It's common sense," she retorted before ushering us to our seats.

Grey and I sat beside one another with Faye on the other side while my parents claimed the ends. Without any prompt other than the food appearing on the table, we all dug in. For a while, we were all too focused on our breakfast to make conversation. It didn't last forever.

"So, what happened when you left last night, Grey?" my mom asked.

He sighed, making a face at his food. Then he looked up at her and said, "Well, most everyone couldn't believe what happened, to start with. Then the drama started. Faye's mom wanted to see her, and she got upset when I wouldn't bring her here."

"I see her point," my mom muttered.

"Then Summer's family got upset because Faye's Ascension was taking away from Summer's. Since we all know the circumstances required for Faye to Ascend, that also set the Seers into an excited flurry, and they took off to go fill out their ledgers while everyone wanted them to stay and explain what just happened. All the while, the parents were upset because of the situation their kids were so close to. All in all, it was a giant mess and it was hours before we could get everyone to go home."

"Lovely. Because I so needed another reason to have Summer on my ass." As soon as she said it, she darted a quick glance to my parents. "Sorry."

"Marine," my dad said.

"Teacher," my mom added.

"Delinquent daughter," I piped in for good measure.

"Understatement," my dad muttered.

The rest of the morning faded by in the same banter. After breakfast, Grey and I chose to clean the kitchen. With a tentative flare, I began to use my magick while my parents and Faye still chatted at the dining table. My dad's back was to us, but my mom watched with a small smile. Grey, of course, took that as permission, and his reaction was far less timid.

After that, Grey said that he would go and get his car and the three of us could go out to the park and work with Faye on her new talents. When he was gone, my mother approached me with paper towels and glass cleaner.

"I have finally seen the light," she said with a grin. "Show me what you've got."

Laughing, I decided to put on a show for her. Unscrewing the lid of the cleaner, I launched it toward the windows. My mother gasped as every drop stopped in mid-air. Then I scattered the mass until every window on the first floor was targeted. I let it go all at once and several slaps were heard against the glass. A few seconds later, the paper towel was at work in the other rooms while I was quick to begin wiping up the ones in the living room.

"That's it," she declared when I'd finished, "I'm never cleaning the house again. All yours, Baby Girl."

I blamed Grey and he blamed Faye.

Saturday morning breakfasts became a regular thing. Grey would bring Faye by, and we would take turns teaching Grey how to cook. Once in a while, we'd mention a dinner dish and have to bring him back that evening to teach him something else. My parents seemed to enjoy it more and more as the weeks passed.

Alongside our Saturday breakfasts, our Friday date nights became a fast tradition. While Grey and I didn't bother to keep our hands off each other for most of the week, my dancing lessons did cut into some of our afternoons. An official date night also had the added benefit of making sure my parents didn't ask when I was coming home. Even if they didn't want to hear it, they both knew how our relationship had progressed. Plus, I gave them the small comfort that I was home at least an hour before Grey and Faye appeared.

The Friday before Yule was also the last day of school for the semester. While other schools across the state typically had their students in class until the twenty-first or twenty-second, the precedent in Grant had been in place long before public schooling was a thing. Crone's Crescent did not shirk their holidays, and they made sure the entire city was in on the festivities.

Saturnalia fell on that Saturday, so the Walkers were spending long hours in town to organize the events. Which meant that Grey and I didn't have to bother going on a real date before heading back to his house. Instead, he picked me up and drove straight there. We went from the car to his bedroom in a blink.

"Why do you always get dressed at the speed of light?" Grey asked as he stepped out of the shower, wrapping the towel around his waist.

I raised my eyebrows even as my eyes raked up and down his chest and stomach. "You have never had long hair. It is one of the most awful feelings having wet hair dripping down your bare back."

He wrapped an arm around my waist, dragging me up against him so that my back was pressed to his chest. Pressing his lips to my neck, his fingers drifted up under my shirt. I hissed as soon as they found skin.

"About as awful as having clothes between my skin and yours?" As he spoke, his hands moved farther up beneath my shirt until they splayed across my sides and stomach.

Even if I could answer that one, I wasn't

given the chance. We both jumped a little as an insistent knocking sounded on the door of the bedroom. Unwilling to let Anna know I was present, I stayed in the bathroom doorway while Grey threw on his boxers and jeans before marching across the room.

The knocking grew even more persistent with each step he took. Then, with a flash of irritation, Grey yanked the door wide open. In the single fraction of a second that he saw her, I had to steady myself against the wall as equal parts love and joy blasted along our bond.

For a moment, I could focus on nothing but that feeling. How much it transformed him or the exultation he felt upon seeing her. I would have been more amazed by it if it wasn't something I had felt once before. As I thought it, the valerian scar began to grow warm.

"Azure." His voice was soft and hesitant, as if he thought he might be dreaming.

"Grey." There was nothing in her voice to hint at her feelings for him, but there must have been a look because I could feel Grey's emotions soar along our bond.

A second later, he took a step forward and

wrapped his arms around her. Our bond became strained as his emotions knotted. With his arms around her, she was real to him. Which sent his curiosity into overdrive.

At last, Grey stepped back and motioned for her to enter. Azure shook her head. "Put on a shirt and meet me downstairs. Bring the girl."

Azure waited until she had turned her back on the door before releasing her magick.

It slammed into me with the force of a train.

I knew why she let her magick loose like that. It was the same reason I was keeping mine close. I'd known the minute that door opened just how powerful she was. Unlike Grey, she wasn't weak compared to me. In that moment, I knew that I would never find a witch more my equal than Azure Walker.

Chapter Forty One

RECKONING

"You don't have to be nervous," Grey murmured into my ear as I followed him from the room a few minutes later.

I was beyond nervous. Between the suspicion, fear, and anxiety that washed up in me, the Ryder Pride was roaring in the distance and shoving it all aside to prove that I was her equal. Which could only lead to trouble with a witch capable of smothering the ability for others to sense her magick. There should have been no way that she got into the house without Grey or I knowing within miles that she was in town.

By the time we reached the living room, I was ready to play nice. Azure was the most important person in Grey's life, and I would respect her as such. At the same time, all I could think of was Faye's declaration that everyone had an opposite out there.

When they were in the same room again, the first thing he had to do was hug her. With every fiber of my being, I understood that need, and the chasm in my chest flared to life with ghostly longing. Which was probably why Grey let her go sooner than he planned.

Then, like any good boyfriend would do, he stepped back and put a hand on my back. It was the proudest I'd ever seen him when he announced, "Azure, this is my girlfriend, Alex. Alex, this is my sister, Azure."

It was pure politeness that caused me to extend my hand to her. For the same sake, she reached across the space and took it. We were both lost in the same instant.

I was in the back parlor of the Walker house, looking out over the balcony. From there, I could barely see the circle of cedar boughs where the Walkers and Sky Solas were setting up for the handfasting. My stomach knotted as I looked to my left and found Azure's stoic expression as she studied the scene. Even though her face betrayed nothing, the fury in her eyes was barely contained.

The sounds of footsteps came from the main hall and we turned at the same time. I spotted Spring through the doorway as she paused to take a breath. A bouquet of flowers–all meant to encourage fertility and prosperity–was clenched in her hands and she took a moment to stare at them.

Beside me, Azure stepped away from the window. Spring's eyes shot up at the movement and her eyes went wide when she found its source. An instant later, all the blood drained from her face and her eyes darted to the door as if in search of an escape. Or rescue.

I had to hand it to her, she thought fast. A second later, her eyes returned to Azure and she forced a smile. "Azure. Grey will be glad you're here."

"He won't know," she promised, gliding across the floor to face her brother's betrothed.

The look on Spring's face said that she knew her death warrant was signed, but she forced that smile wider. "Don't you want to be part of our handfasting?"

Azure was close enough to touch her, and she reached a hand up and pushed dark curls from Spring's face. In a low, silken voice, she said, "There will be no *handfasting. And there will be no baby."*

Before Spring could do more than drop the flowers, Azure had her hands over Spring's womb. I didn't even feel the magick as it seeped into the pregnant witch, but I knew that it was spreading throughout her body. And I knew what it was doing.

"You're killing him!" Spring gasped.

"Yes. I am killing the child you forced into existence. Did you think there would be no reckoning for your crime? Did you think I would not interfere when you made your plans for my brother?"

"He loves me," she sobbed.

"He is obligated to you. Now I am removing that obligation. Tell him the truth, youngling, and see if his love lasts."

My mouth fell open as the blood began to seep through the dress Spring wore. It pooled on the rug, and still Azure did not remove her hands. Tears ran down Spring's face and a keening sound erupted from her throat. Her magick pushed out, trying to attack Azure, but it was swatted away like a fly.

When she could stand no longer, Spring slumped to the floor with Azure's hands still on her stomach. Her forehead broke out in a sweat and Azure leaned close to whisper, "Know that you did this, Spring. Had you not meddled, a more natural life could have come into your hands. Now, you must live with the life you have wrought."

To add insult to injury, Azure placed a kiss on Spring's forehead and vanished.

As one, we wrenched our hands away and stepped back. Azure's face took on the same emotionless expression as in the vision. I didn't bother to disguise my disgust as I backed up even farther. Never again would I let her touch me. It took all I had not to scream at her to never touch Grey again after what she did.

Yet the absolute shock radiating through our link told me that he didn't know. He never knew. Neither Azure nor Spring had told him.

Even as that thought was still reeling in my head, Grey demanded, "What was that? What just happened?"

"Visions," Azure answered, her voice cold. "Of the future."

"Of the past," I snapped back.

A single eyebrow rose in curiosity as she studied me. "Interesting talent."

I couldn't respond to that. I could barely look at her. The amount of disgust I felt for her kept rising and I wanted so badly to just announce what she did. He had a right to know. What I couldn't figure out was if I had the right to tell him. Or if he'd believe me.

Shaking my head, I turned to Grey and said, "I'm going to go."

"Alex, wait," he said even as I turned for the hallway. He followed me. "Alex, please stay?"

"I can't. You know I can't," I said, leaning my forehead against the door.

Placing a hand on my hip, Grey turned me to face him before pressing his forehead against mine. "Hey, tell me what's going on," he murmured.

Again, I shook my head. If I opened my mouth, I would tell him everything. I needed time to process it before I told him anything. Time to decide how or if I should tell him. There was so much to take in; I couldn't drop that bomb on him like it'd been dropped on me.

"What did you see, Alex? Tell me, please?"

He wasn't going to give up. If I didn't give him something, he would never let me go. My teeth pressed into my bottom lip as I worded my reply.

At last, I said, "Ask your sister what I saw. After she lies to you, ask Spring."

Chapter Forty Two

TEMPORARY AFFLICTION

I hadn't given Grey time to respond. As soon as his hands dropped off of me, I was gone. Once I was safe in my bedroom, I sat down and thought about what I had done.

If Spring hadn't told him, I had no reason to believe she wouldn't feed him the same lie that Azure did. Which meant the vision I'd had was the only proof that Azure had murdered his unborn child. Without being able to see it for himself, he would never believe me. Even if I were able to project the vision into his mind, Azure could claim it was a fabrication. And I couldn't expect him to believe me over her. It would be as impossible as me believing him over Nathan.

I didn't want to waste time pondering what to

do or why it mattered. One thought, alone, kept repeating in my mind: he deserved to know. It didn't matter that Azure was his sister or the most important person in his life. She had taken his child's life. There would be a reckoning for it, I had no doubt. All that remained to be seen was what form it would take.

When I opened my mind up to sense more than a mile around me, it was almost too easy to find all of the witches in Grant. My breath caught when I sensed far more than the two hundred that had attended Summer's Ascension. When I'd been told that Grant was Ground Zero for Crone's Crescent, I'd been woefully ignorant of what that meant.

Since the Season Sisters were so familiar to me, it was easy to lock onto Spring's magick. Somehow, I had expected her to live in a neighborhood more like Grey's, so it surprised me when I found her in one not unlike mine. That reminded me that power determined rank in the coven, and her family didn't have much of it.

Shaking away the thoughts, I let my mind drift to hers. As soon as I caught the tendrils of her thoughts, I sent my message.

I would like to meet with you.

Who is this? Her fear and awe were almost palpable in her mind.

Alex Ryder. Please, can we talk?

Why?

There were only three words I needed to guarantee her compliance. I gave her seven. *Azure is back. I know the truth.*

In an instant, she sent an image of a coffee shop to me and told me to meet her in ten minutes. I agreed and released the contact, allowing her to have a few moments to freak out. Even miles away from her, I could swear that her terror blanketed the entire city of Grant.

Neither of us bothered with small talk as Spring took the chair across from me and demanded, "What truth do you think you know?"

I constructed the silencing spell around us before I said, "I know Azure killed your son."

She looked almost ready to vomit. "How?"

"Azure has visions of the future; I have visions of the past. I saw what she did to you."

Her jaw set and she nodded to herself, her

eyes boring a hole in the table. "So, what? You know. And now you want to offer me your sympathy? I don't want it, and I don't need it."

"I'm offering you a warning. You know what is between Grey and I, so you know that I couldn't hide my reaction from him. He knows that I saw something involving Azure, and he knows it was horrific."

Her eyes shot to mine and her lips parted in horror. "But he doesn't know, right? He doesn't know what you saw?"

My jaw set. "Not yet."

Spring brought her hands up to cover her face, releasing a heavy exhale. "Damn you. Why can't you just leave it alone?"

"You know why," I snapped back. "This is not something that should be kept from him. In fact, why did you keep it from him?"

"It doesn't concern him."

"His sister murdered his son! How does that not concern him?"

"Don't you dare act all righteous. You're a temporary affliction. This is something Grey and I have been dealing with for years, and it's something that will stay between us. Azure's part in this was... Her retribution is my punishment, and I accept that. Should I ruin Grey's life even more by revealing that his favorite person in the world is the reason he could never hold our son? Hear his first laugh? Watch him take his first steps? Isn't it enough that I already have to live with that fact? Grey should have to suffer again?" Tears filled Spring's eyes, and it seemed so normal to her, that she didn't bother to fight them when they began to fall.

Leaning forward in my chair, I asked, "So he should live with that threat hanging over his head every day? Because that's what she is, Spring, and you know it. What other pieces of Grey's life will she remove because it doesn't fit her idea of what he deserves? If you don't tell Grey, then you will never break the spell she has over him. Is that what you want?"

Spring shook her head. "Have you not been paying attention? You know what she is capable of, but you don't know the extent she will go to. What do you think Azure will do to the one who reveals her true nature to her brother?"

I shook my head and said, "You know, there are a lot of witches in your coven that I pegged as cowards. You were never one of them. Against Grey, you're the only one who will stand their ground. But Azure..."

"Is not Grey. With the history Grey and I have, I know everything he is capable of. I know how he reacts when he's upset, and I know what it feels like when he is at his best. I know Grey best of all, even above Azure, and that is why I don't fear him. Azure is the unknown. Azure terrifies me, and she should terrify you."

She meant it. Deep in her soul, she meant every word she said. Where Azure was concerned, Spring knew there were consequences to standing against her.

They were consequences I had to face.

"You know, I once followed a code. It was something along the lines of me not sharing secrets I have no part in. I broke it once, and I learned something from that experience: I am not the keeper of other people's secrets. What I learn is information that belongs to me as much as it does to others. And I have the responsibility to do with that information whatever I believe to be right and fair.

"If the roles were reversed, you would want

to know. You wouldn't want to go on acting like there was nothing wrong when the person you respect most is the one who is responsible for destroying everything you held sacred. She destroyed him in much the same way that she destroyed you, Spring. The difference is: at least you know who the enemy is.

"When Azure is finished spinning her web of lies, Grey will ask you for confirmation. Do all of us the favor of not lying to him. Because he will hear the truth from me, one way or another. And if he doesn't believe me, that's fine. I won't regret telling him the truth the way you will regret telling him that lie."

Spring slowly shook her head. "You are so naïve," she remarked. "Do you think I'll regret it? Do you think I've regretted any second that I let him believe my miscarriage was natural? If you do, then you don't know what it is to love him. Not really. You see, Alex, I've already broken his heart. First by giving him a child he didn't want, then by failing to keep that child alive when I was the only one who could. On top of that, I told him the truth. My horrible little portion of it. That, I regret.

"But do you know who he turned to when he learned what I'd done? Her. Always, he turns to her. She is his world, and he is hers. What Azure did was because I was betraying him. Despise her as much as I do, that doesn't mean I don't understand her. Just as she knows why I won't tell him. Grey deserves someone who loves him without restriction. Azure is that person, and I will not be responsible for taking that from him, too.

"So, go ahead and tell him the truth. You will be the only one."

With that, Spring stood up and turned to walk away. Before she could take a step, I stated, "You may love him more than I ever will, but I respect him more than you do."

She said nothing as she left the coffee shop.

Azure took her place.

Chapter Forty Three

TITANS

She took a minute to arrange herself in the chair before she looked up at me through her eyelashes. Her voice was casual when she said, "Do you know what happens when Titans go to war? Gods rise to power."

My chin lifted a little and my voice turned cold. "And which are we? The Titans or the Gods?"

A mocking smirk pulled at her lips. "Even Titans fall when enough Gods stand against them."

I shook my head. "And you foresee a war between us, Azure?"

"I think that depends on you, Alexandria."

I wanted to ask her how she figured that one, but it wasn't worth it. Whatever she had seen to bring her here, she wasn't going to share with me.

Nor was it going to change what had to happen now. While I wasn't looking to start a war with Azure, if she pushed me into one, she would have a fight on her hands.

For a few minutes, I waited to see how she would react. With Spring departing seconds before her appearance, I knew she must have guessed what scene I'd witnessed when our hands touched. There were thousands of ways she could handle the fact that I knew, and I was just waiting to see which she would choose.

Instead, she said, "Do not fall in love with my brother, Alexandria. It will only harm you both."

"It's too late for that."

I didn't know where the words came from. Until that moment, I didn't even know it was true. Yet, as soon as I said it, I knew she was right. I loved Grey, and we would both live to regret it.

"Not all of your mistakes are made. There is still time to alter the river's course."

My eyebrows rose a little and I asked, "How would you have me do that?"

"Leave now. Sooner rather than later."

"No."

A flicker of irritation passed across her face. "Why not?"

"It's not time."

"Make it time."

"No."

Her lips pressed into a thin line. "Careful, Alexandria."

"No, Azure." My lip curled on her name. "You may have all of Crone's Crescent under your thumb, but you don't frighten me. I'm not going to walk on eggshells because your arrogance cannot comprehend reality."

"Do not underestimate me, Alexandria. It would be a grave mistake."

"Oh, I know. I saw the extent of your depravity when you murdered your brother's son."

"You don't know what you speak of."

"You have visions of the future; I have visions of the past. We are two sides to a coin."

"Yes, we are. Which is why I know you will lose. You are unwilling to do the things I will do."

"What you are willing to do and what you are capable of doing are very separate things, Azure. I have seen what you do to those you think have crossed a line. You do not know what I have done to those who have threatened me. And you don't know the cost I would face if forced to do it again. If it's a price I'm forced to pay, then you can make damn sure I will get what it's worth."

Her head tilted to the side as she studied me. "Your words ring hollow."

"What you hear is the void I've waded through to get here. It may be a chasm I return to, but I've survived it once before. Can you say the same?"

Raising her chin, she announced, "Remain in Grant and you will force my hand."

"I am already forcing your hand, but you're too timid to acknowledge it. You know what I'm aware of, and you know what I will do with that knowledge. Lie to him as much as you want, Azure, but you won't stop me from telling Grey what you did."

"Is that what you think I am here for? To stop you from tattling on me to my brother? Tsk, tsk," she said, shaking her head for effect. "No, Alexandria, I am not here to stop you from telling Grey anything. I'm here to keep you from hurting him in a far more vicious way."

My eyes closed as I took a breath. "The fact that you think there is anything more vicious than what you did to him proves that you don't know him at all."

"I know him best of all."

A smile pulled at my lips. "You know, I think every woman who loves him must believe that, because I know you're wrong. Tell me, Azure, when you warned him about falling in love with me, he also told you that it was too late, didn't he? And when you tried to force him into breaking up with me, he told you that he would do it all over again, given a second chance. You know how I know that? Because it's the same thing I'm telling you.

"It doesn't matter that we'll hurt each other. It doesn't matter how. What matters is right now. These moments. Yes, falling in love with Grey was a mistake. But it's one I would make again, because having his love is worth giving him mine."

"Spare me your poetic sentiments."

"Spare me your empty threats. Spare him your meddling. You're so certain that you know what's best for him that you don't stop to consider how it affects him."

"I will not see him live in misery," she vowed.

My chin lifted. "Then you should never have laid hands on his child, because you created his misery. You took from him that which is most sacred, and you burned it to ash. That pain defines Grey now, and he will carry it with him until the day he dies. If you think I will seal his fate, then you don't realize what you have done to him. But you will know soon enough."

"Now who makes empty threats? We both know you appealed to Spring so the burden of proof would be taken off of your hands. But she will not comply and you will take a tale to my brother of my wanton destruction of his family, and he will have to choose which of us to believe. The sister who raised him, or the lover he's had for a couple of months. Is it really such a hard choice?"

"I don't know. Why don't you ask him?"

Slowly, I placed the open cellphone on the table in front of us. Below Grey's name was a timer counting the seconds of the conversation. One glance showed her that Grey had heard everything from before she arrived. As I'd asked, he'd let me know as soon as Azure had left him, and I'd used my cell to call. He'd heard much of what Spring said as well as everything Azure had to say.

Azure's face flushed red and her eyes kept darting between the phone and my face. She was trying to determine if it was a bluff, but she didn't want to know that it could be true. At last, she worked up the nerve to ask, "Grey?"

"I'm here," he answered in a hard, angry voice. Then he said, "Don't come home." A loud beep sounded the end of the phone call.

When Azure turned her glare on me, I shrugged. "You have a wonderful respect for magick, but I wondered if you even remembered technology. I guess I have my answer."

"You bitch," she snarled.

"Yes, I am." Standing up, I nodded my head to Azure and walked out.

Chapter Forty Four

FALLOUT

I didn't have long before the fallout, I knew. Azure was going to head straight to Grey and try to work out some way to earn his forgiveness. When that failed, she would come after me. We were Titans from this point on.

"Mom? Dad?" I called as soon as I walked into the house. Given any other circumstances, I would never have done this. But this was part of our new beginning, and they deserved to know.

"Hey, Lex. Baby, what's wrong?" my mom asked as she got up from the dining table. A second later, my dad appeared at the top of the stairs, the same questioning expression on his face.

"I don't have time to explain. Faye is going to be here in about ten minutes. I need you to go with her. She'll bring you to me."

"And where are you going?" my mom asked at the same time my dad demanded, "Why can't we go with you?"

Shaking my head, I said, "Something bad is about to happen. I can't take you with me without risking your safety. Faye can protect you and she will make excellent backup. I'm sorry, but I don't have time to say more. If I don't go now, Azure may come here, and I can't risk that. I'll see you soon." With that, I kissed my mother's cheek and raised my hand to my dad before I vanished.

I reappeared at the campsite where Grey and I had spent Samhain. It didn't have the protections that my property did, but it also didn't have the potential for collateral damage. There was also the lingering feeling in the air of mine and Grey's magick. If I needed to, there was a chance I could harness it.

For once, I let my mind travel along the bond to monitor Grey's mind. Since his feelings of betrayal, fury, and heartbreak were so prevalent, I couldn't count on them to tell me when Azure had put a stop to her appeal. Five minutes later, I had a split-second warning.

My shields formed a foot-thick wall around me a heartbeat before the spell was set to hit. It collided with the shields, fracturing the two outer ones as it burst apart on my defenses. From the murderous look on her face, she didn't expect me to send it back. As it was, my spell crashed into her stomach and sent her reeling backward.

"Is that all you've got?" she sneered. The words were a diversion as another jolt of energy lanced through the air to smash against my shields. Still, nothing reached me.

At the same time she sent her spell, I also sent my own. This time, she was prepared, and had her own shields in place. Mild as my spell was, it shattered five out of the six on impact. At once, I realized that her defense wasn't as strong as her offense, while my spells weren't as powerful as hers.

Within the same breath, Azure launched two attacks. The first one punched a hole in three of my shields, with the second breaking through the next three. I didn't have time to launch a counterstrike as I mended the six outer shields and strengthened the three most vital ones.

While I did so, Azure blinked out of existence, triggering my first spell at last. Whatever spell hid Azure's magick from me, it was gone now. The virus I'd hit her with had needed only her own magick to trigger a full shutdown of her defenses. So, when she appeared behind me, I didn't even have to turn to hit her with two spells of my own.

The first one she deflected, but it disintegrated her shield. The second one hit her head on, causing her knees to buckle as the snare set in. It worked for almost thirty seconds before her own spell shredded it to pieces.

When that happened, three distinct, vicious spells sliced through my layers of protection, until the last one hit me hard. I went flying, my back slamming against a tree trunk that was almost twenty feet behind me. Dazed as I was from the impact, I was well aware that she hadn't hit me as hard as she could have.

I didn't get my shields repaired in time before three more spells slammed into me. The first made me slow to react while the second seemed to dull my magick. Her third spell stood me upright as she approached.

She thought she had me.

I let her think it.

"It did not have to be this way, Alexandria. I gave you a choice. Instead, you spit on my kindness. There are consequences for that."

Just a little closer...

"There was no choice. You knew that when you met me. Even now, you know that the future hasn't changed, and that terrifies you."

"Oh, but it will change," she promised, taking the last fateful step.

Magick blasted out of me, snapping her hold like a twig and reinforcing all nine of my shields. All while I pushed off the tree and launched myself at her. The momentum took us to the ground and I scrambled to straddle her, pulling back my right fist and slamming it forward into her face. A pleasing crunch reached my ears as her nose gave way under my fist, blood spurting from the broken appendage. Again, I pulled back my fist and hit her, this time landing on the cheek. The eye. The lip. The jaw. Knowing that I didn't have long, I got in as many hits as I could.

At last, Azure's magick pulsed up and outward, punching through my shields and sending me flying over her head. I landed hard on my back several yards away from her, and didn't dare move until I was sure my spine was intact. Then I felt her magick gathering again. This time, it felt lethal. Rolling over onto my stomach, I watched as Azure pushed herself to her feet. Blood flowed over her chin and streaked down the front of her shirt, but she didn't seem to care. When she beckoned me to stand, I knew that this was the last pass. What followed would determine our fates in a far more permanent way than we ever thought possible.

Pushing myself to my feet, I didn't gather the magick. Didn't hold it. Didn't even reach for it. Instead, I stood before her without a single shield in place. I couldn't afford it.

It all happened in a heartbeat. Azure released the last spell and I let my instincts take over. The shield was the largest and strongest I'd ever created. As fast as the spell was moving, I had to make it as big as possible to prevent any damage to myself, and it contained no less than thirteen layers. Even as it sheared through some of them, I knew it would never breach the rest.

The spell snapped against the fifth layer before it rebounded. Azure's mouth fell open, but it was the only expression she had time for. Her spell slammed into her hard enough to knock her flat onto her back. For one second, I thought she might have been knocked unconscious. Then her back arched until her head and heels were the only things touching the ground and a vicious scream erupted from her throat.

When she released the spell, I thought it was meant to kill me. As I sank to the ground a mere inch from the shield, the reality of it sank in. My entire body shook as I continued to watch in horror.

Azure hadn't been trying to kill me. She only wanted to make me wish I was dead.

Grey appeared beside me just as she caught enough breath for another violent screech. I wove a physical barrier through the shield before he could cross over it. As soon as he felt it, he rounded on me.

"What's happening to her? What have you done?" he snarled.

I wasn't in the mood to argue. I didn't want to say anything. Instead, I kept my eyes on Azure and watched as she lived through what I had experienced only once before. Even without the flames, I knew she was burning alive.

"Alex! Answer me! What is happening?" he demanded.

"She didn't do anything, Grey," Faye announced, emerging from the trees where she and my parents had been watching for the last few minutes. Thank the Gods that Azure never noticed them, or was too pissed off at me to care.

"Bullshit! Do you see what is happening to her?"

"She brought it on herself," Faye snapped back at him. "That spell was meant for Alex, but the shield rebounded it. Azure got hit with her own ill intentions, and you know it."

He looked back at his sister, his eyes growing wide. I felt it the moment he realized what was being done to her. How everything in her was dying a little bit at a time. Every organ, muscle, bone, even the very cells in her skin all perished one by one. What replaced them was something that didn't even feel alive. When the process was over, I knew Azure would wish that everything would have died at once, instead of putting up even this miniscule fight.

"That's not..." Grey whispered in horror.

"It is," Faye answered him.

"What is it?" my father asked as my parents flanked me.

"It is the unmaking of a witch," I answered. "It is losing everything that makes her who and what she is. It is death and heartbreak incarnate."

"How...?" my mother questioned, looking between the three of us.

Grey's jaw tightened and I couldn't force another word, so it was Faye who explained, "Azure sent out a spell to strip Alex of her magick. The spell rebounded and hit Azure. After our Ascensions, the magick in us is bound cell by cell. It's written into our DNA. By stripping a witch, you kill every part of them that harbors it. Everything in Azure's body is being rewritten right now, and she will never hold magick again. There's no fixing this."

Another shriek rent the air and my eyes squeezed shut as the memories of flames and smoke filled my mind. When I was burning, all I could hear were my own screams. Even over the hungry crackling of the flames, my screams drowned out everything else. For one whole minute, Azure had to live the same terrifying nightmare.

Lowering himself to my level, my dad murmured, "This is what she tried to do to you?" I nodded and his arm wrapped around me. "Then I'm glad it's her instead."

I shook my head. "It shouldn't have been either of us. If I had just stayed out of it..."

"It doesn't matter now," Grey growled.

Before I could answer, Azure collapsed and the screams ceased. I waited another heartbeat before I dropped the shield. Grey sprinted to his sister, and I watched as he kneeled by her head. It took everything I had to shut out his grief as he gently lifted her into his arms. For several minutes, he did nothing but cradle her. At last, his determination reached me and he vanished.

"Where'd he go?" my dad demanded.

"To take care of his sister."

"After what she tried to do..."

I shook my head to cut him off. Then I grabbed hold of his arm and used him to get up. "Especially after what she tried to do to me. He's spent his whole life adoring her. I'm a temporary affliction. There wasn't one second of doubt in his mind of what this outcome would be. He never thought I would triumph over her, even if he wanted me to. But this..."

There was no way to put the horror of the situation into words. No way for them to understand the kind of bone-deep terror this inspired in Grey, Faye, and myself. The fact that there was a way to strip a witch's magick was bad enough. Knowing that there were witches out there sadistic enough to do it was a whole new kind of nightmare we never imagined.

We were Titans, Azure and I. But she was right. Even Titans fall when Gods rise to power. With this spell in their hands, it would be all too easy to watch those like us topple.

This one spell could herald a war on the horizon.

Chapter Forty Five

LASTING END

Grey needed time. Even though I knew that, it didn't stop the stab of rejection I felt every day that we went without a phone call or just popping in on each other. There was a kind of wall up between us now that hadn't been there before. The worst part was knowing that Azure's name was carved in the stone.

If she hadn't come back, none of this would have happened.

If I hadn't insisted on Grey knowing the truth, none of this would have happened.

If...

If...

If...

It fixed nothing, repeating all of the things

that could have changed the outcome. Even knowing that, I knew Grey was playing the same game that I was. Both of us trying to find that one singular moment that caused it all to go to hell. Grey blamed himself because he thought it was their argument. I blamed myself because I agreed to be his girlfriend. Faye was probably the only smart one of us, because she blamed Azure for being batshit crazy.

"How long has it been?" she asked as we lingered on the front steps of the school on our first day back.

"Almost three weeks."

"Yule?" I shook my head and she released a long, low whistle. "Damn. I never thought he'd be that stupid."

"Don't. We both know how this is affecting him. He knew he'd have to grieve one of us; he just never expected it to be her."

"Do you know what happened to her?"

I shook my head as we reached my locker. "I'm not sure I want to know."

Faye shrugged and headed off to her own locker. I was glad when she was gone, since I could feel the magick pulsing out of my locker and I was eager to discover what was waiting for me. As soon as the door opened, my eyes fell on a thin white box with a blue ribbon wrapped around it. Whatever was inside of it was pulsing with his magick.

"Protection spells. Maybe a few prosperity ones woven in there," Grey remarked as he appeared beside me.

I ignored him in order to pull the ribbon off the box and open it. A charm bracelet sat on a foam pad, sparkling with aquamarine stones and silver charms arrayed around the chain. At once, my eyes recognized the ivy, oleander, valerian, oak, and apple blossom. Each one bearing the responsibility of being the most distinct scars on my arm.

"It's very detailed," I said at last.

Grey nodded to the lid. "The card is taped to the inside. Valerie is an exceptional silversmith. If you want to add any, contact her. Tell her to bill me."

I rolled my eyes. "So, if I decide I need a new charm in ten years, I should just call her up and order it?"

"And tell her to bill me. My name's on file.

As is the card. I mean it, Alex. This is my Yule present to you, and I'm okay with it being a present I make to you every year of our lives, if that's what it takes."

Again, I rolled my eyes, but picked up the bracelet and held it out to him. When he took it, I extended my right hand for him to clasp the bracelet around. Then I let my arm fall back to my side, feeling the charms drop over the back of my hand in an unfamiliar weight. Taking a breath, I raised my eyes to his for the first time in weeks.

It didn't last long. I had had enough of feeling like I was trapping him in a situation. So, I let my eyes drop after a few seconds and admired the glint of the light off my birthstones.

"Does this mean you're not mad at me anymore?"

Grey released a sigh. "Alex, I was never mad at you. I was just angry at the situation."

"If that were true, you wouldn't have ignored me for weeks."

"I didn't mean to ignore you. I got caught up in things and the days just flowed together."

"I'm almost afraid to ask."

Grey opened his mouth to answer when the first bell rang. His eyes scanned the hallway before an imperceptible shake of his head warned me what was about to happen. "I can't do this right now. Come on, we're ditching."

I didn't even say anything as I put my books back in my locker and took his hand. His magick wrapped around us and I was sucked through time and space. A second later, my mouth dropped.

"Whoa."

I spun in a slow circle, taking in the driveway that vanished into the trees, then the sharp dips and dives of the roof, before catching a glimpse of the back portion of the garden. In the distance, another tower rose from another witch's mansion. Turning again, I could see that the hills had several other manors perching amongst the trees. Though I'd always known how massive the Walker house was, being able to see for miles around somehow put it into even sharper relief; this house was most definitely created just for Crone's Crescent.

"This is where I come when I need to be away from the rest of the world," Grey remarked when

I finally turned back to him.

I smiled. "It's your sanctuary. Just like my hawthorn tree."

His lips twitched. "Yeah." Then he sighed and turned to survey his surroundings. "I've spent hours up here every day since it happened, thinking about all that needs to happen now."

Taking a step closer to him, I asked, "And what do you think that is?"

He raised his eyes to mine and I let them linger for almost a minute before I broke contact. After taking a steadying breath, he said, "You know about the five major covens in the U.S. What you don't know is our history. There are feuds, land disputes, rogue witches, asylum, and a dozen other forms of chaos involved. Killing each other used to be common, a few generations back. But with a spell like this..."

"They wouldn't need to kill each other; they'd just kill off what makes them a threat."

"Exactly. What's worse is wondering if this is the tip of the iceberg."

"What do you mean?"

"I mean: Azure was a powerful, gifted, infamous witch. For her to create a spell that damaging, I have to wonder if she created others. If she did, then whose hands are they in now? Did she even write them down? What if she didn't work alone? Is there someone else out there that I have to beware of? And how easy would it be for other witches to replicate what she's done to herself?"

"That's a lot of questions."

"Yeah, and I have no way to get the answers, because Azure is completely out of her mind right now and she can't focus enough to tell me. Not that she'd want to. I'm the reason she's like this."

It wasn't even worth it to try to assuage his guilt. Instead, I asked, "So how do you plan on getting the answers? You can't give up."

"No, I'm not giving up. My plan is simple: find where Azure has been, and go and search for clues. But to know where she's been, I'll need your help."

My stomach twisted into a vicious knot. "What kind of help?"

"You're psychometric and retrocognitive. If I can give you her clothes, do you think you can figure out where they've been last? Or would it be more effective for you to touch Azure again?"

At once, I lashed out, "You can't ask that of her or me. She may be the one without her magick, Grey, but that spell was intended for me. If I never set eyes on her again, it'll be too soon."

"Okay, okay," he said, holding up his hands in surrender. "It was just a thought. Forget I mentioned it."

I took a deep breath before I let it out slowly. "Have you tried scrying?" Scrying could be done a number of different ways, but almost any witch had the power to do it.

"She's made it impossible to scry with her things." Not every witch had the power to do that.

"Damn it." After another deep breath, I asked, "What do you have of hers that she wouldn't take off? I'll see if I can get something off that."

Grey snorted. "I'm sure you can. This thing's been in the family for generations. It follows the females of our blood. Thought I would have to cut it off her finger, but she threw it at me in a rage, screaming that she was unworthy of it now."

As he spoke, Grey held out a hand to me. The small object dropped into my palm, almost burning me on contact. I had barely enough time to register the bulbous ring with the garnet stone protecting the poison chamber before the white mist crept across my vision.

The woman who slid from the saddle looked slightly familiar, but I couldn't place her. Not that she gave me time to study her features as she stepped away from the beast and brushed the pale wisps of hair out of her face. Then she turned to examine her comrades.

There were thirteen in all. Each looked haggard, exhausted, and scared to death. They took turns looking over their shoulders as if expecting a pursuit. Others eyed the trees, wondering if an ambush was set for them.

"Francesca, we cannot go much farther," a man grumbled as he approached. "This is wild country. If the Indians find us trespassing..."

"They are open to being reasoned with, Benjamin."

"You are so certain that you will risk our lives?"

"What risk? Thirteen of us there are. None of us without the use of magic. If they come for us, we will be able to defend ourselves."

"What if your sister follows us?" demanded another woman.

"She will not. She is too busy trying to banish the infamy surrounding our name."

Benjamin smiled. "Is that not why we have all come with you? To banish what ill words are spoken of us?"

Turning to the group, Francesca smiled. "It is. As such, I think it time we declare ourselves free of our past. Let us choose new names for our new home. What say you?"

There were a few moments of general muttering before Benjamin stepped forward. "Blackwell. From this day forth I am Benjamin Blackwell."

At once, the others began to step forward and declare their names. When they were all finished, there was but one name left to be spoken. My blood ran cold when the declaration came.

Staring at her hands, she twisted a poison ring around her finger. "I am a Vaile no longer. Now, I am Francesca Walker. And so my children will be Walkers until our line comes to a lasting end."

Then she looked at her companions and said, "This will be our home, and may our descendants know what we have done for them by creating this community." That was when she glanced at the horizon and a smile pulled at her lips. The Crone's crescent was a sliver in the sky.

Chapter Forty Six

WRITTEN IN BLOOD

"Alex? What did you see?" Grey murmured.

I shook my head and made to pass the ring back to him. When his skin brushed against mine, it sent a jolt through me, helping to clear the vision. Then I looked at him and said, "I saw the beginning of your line. The beginning of Crone's Crescent Coven."

Grey's eyes widened before his gaze dropped to the ring in his palm. "It goes back that far?"

"Mid-to-late 1600s I'd guess."

At once, he shook his head. "No. Our histories... We couldn't have been here that long."

"You were. Thirteen witches took on a country they barely knew and set up camp right here, in spite of the dangers. They risked everything to escape what was left behind, and they chose new names the same day that they decreed Grant their home."

"Wow," he murmured, still staring at the ring.

Already, he seemed to have forgotten its purpose. I hadn't. "Give me a few minutes to breathe and I'll seek out the next one."

"Next one?"

A smile tugged at my lips. "It's been around for centuries. Do you think it has only one memory to share?"

Grey shrugged. "I don't know. I've never had visions, so I don't know how they work."

It was another poignant difference that separated Gods from Titans, it seemed. "I'm not sure anyone knows how they work, but we do get some sense of what will trigger them. It also takes a great deal of energy, so after about three visions, I will need to eat something and rest for a while."

His head cocked to the side. "You've done this before."

I didn't try to hide my reality from him. "Yes, I have done this before. Now give me back the ring."

Grey didn't hesitate as he stepped forward and dropped the accessory into my open palm. My fingers closed over it as my mind drifted away.

What was more maddening than the ring's insistence that it show me everything in chronological order was its limit. Two visions a day. No matter how I coaxed, pleaded, or attempted to force it, I was getting nothing else.

Ten days after the first two visions, Grey was more anxious than ever. The longer we went without finding where she was living, the harder it would become to track her belongings. More than anything, her Grimoire was the key to knowing her secrets. If we couldn't find it and someone else did...

"We're getting closer," I told Grey as we walked into the basement. He nodded, but didn't seem convinced. Then he turned around and held the ring out to me. With a sigh, I took it from him and allowed my mind to drift.

It was jarring to see Mrs. Walker standing in front of a mirror. Her hands traced over her extended stomach, a frown twisting her lips. Then she reached over to her vanity and removed a glass vial. She was just about to pour some essential oil mixture into her palm when she suddenly stopped.

A piercing cry sounded from the room across the hall, and I suddenly understood why she was having such a hard time with her figure. I followed her across the hall as she made a beeline for her child. When I entered the lavish nursery and found the blonde baby in the crib, I wasn't all that surprised.

Azure couldn't have been more than a month old. She was still tiny and awkward, without muscles strong enough to support herself. Though she seemed far more aware than other babies might have been. The way her wide, blue eyes sought out her mother seemed almost too knowing. Then they latched onto me for a second and I couldn't be sure that Azure wasn't seeing me in that moment in the same way I was seeing her.

Then the child looked away and I could breathe once more. Her mother made quick work of changing her diaper before they settled into the rocking chair in the corner. Then she started to croon a mangled lullaby to the infant.

Before I could do more than cringe away from her lack of a singing voice, the infant made a noise that served to shut her up right quick. When she looked down at her chest, she saw that Azure's tiny fingers were clutching at the ring her mother wore on a chain around her neck.

"Ah, yes," Mrs. Walker murmured. "It will be yours one day. Either you will be able to wear it, or it will remain nearest your heart on this chain. And when you have a daughter of your own, it will be to her that you pass it. When she is ready. Only when she is ready."

A shiver crawled up my spine as Grey took the ring from me. He didn't even ask what I saw. Instead, he poured me a glass of water while I sat at the table. After a few sips, I told him everything I'd seen and heard. I was surprised by his laugh when I mentioned that his mom couldn't sing three notes.

He was staring at his own glass of whiskey, chuckling as he remarked, "Neither can Azure. Worst punishment in the world was the two of them trying to sing a duet."

"Well, even that young, Azure seemed to think it a punishment as well. I couldn't even tell what she was trying to sing."

He shrugged. "Probably our old family lullaby. I was so glad when my dad learned it and started singing it to us instead."

"Your dad sang you lullabies?"

Grey grinned. "You never would have guessed, would you?"

"Not at all."

For a while, he seemed caught in the memories as he turned the ring over and over in his fingertips. Then he murmured, "She gave this to Azure before I was born. Probably the same day that Azure announced my birthday."

My eyes flew wide. "She did what?"

He didn't look at me as he said, "When she was just turning three, she looked at my parents and told them that on November nineteenth, she was going to have a baby brother."

I had nothing to say to that, so I reached my hand across the table to take his. On accident, my thumb brushed against the ring and the white mist rose up over my eyes.

A chalk circle was marked into the floorboards of a bedroom. Azure's, I assumed, since she was sitting cross-legged in the center. Colored candles marked the five elements, illuminating the open book, athame, chalice, and quill arrayed in front of her. Without opening her eyes, the young witch murmured the indecipherable words of a spell.

All of a sudden, she thrust her arm out over the chalice and made one sharp slash across her forearm. The blood flowed from the cut, dropping into the chalice with a crimson splash. I stared in astonishment as she allowed the cup to fill halfway before she twisted her arm and shook it. When she lowered it back to her side, there was no evidence that a cut had been made. No streaks of blood, no careless drops, and certainly no scar.

As if I couldn't be any more astonished, I then watched the young teen pick up the quill pen and dip it into her blood. She began writing in the book.

I took a step back as every tiny hair on my body rose. Bodily fluids were one of the major cornerstones of witchcraft. Things like blood, urine, and semen were used for powerful rituals and bound people in the most primitive of ways. By using her own blood to write in *her Grimoire, Azure had bound herself to that book in formidable ways. It assured its absolute obedience to her.*

Even without her magick, that book would answer to no other.

"Damn it," I hissed as Grey pulled the ring out of my grasp. Leaning forward, I let my head land on my arm and released a heavy sigh.

"What did you see?"

"Her Grimoire," I snarled.

At once, he was excited. "You saw it? Did you see where it was?"

I shook my head and felt all of his anticipation drowned out by his disappointment. "I saw it when she first began to create it. Grey, it's written in blood."

His mouth dropped. "What?"

"Azure wrote it in her own blood. Even if we find it, there's no chance any of us can read it, if we can even open it."

"Without her magick–"

"It's her blood on those pages, not her magick. Without her, the book is useless."

"What about me? We share DNA."

I shook my head. "Unless she factored you into it, then there's no hope even for you."

"What would she need to do that?"

"Blood. Once it was written in blood, there's no writing it in ink or anything else."

All at once, his eyes narrowed, "How do you know that?"

A weary smile pulled at my lips. "I could have been her, you know. If your story of opposites is true, then she is mine. In some other reality, she is me and I am her. Yet, in all realities, our books bleed with us."

Chapter Forty Seven

ASSASSIN

That ring bonded with Azure more than with anyone else. It had memories upon memories of time spent with her. So much so that it was almost the end of January before I finally saw what we were after this whole time. When I realized it, I came out of the vision and laughed so hard that tears were coursing down my face.

"What? What is it? Alex, tell me," Grey urged as it became harder to breathe.

In fragments, I was able to gasp, "It's … in her … room."

He rolled his eyes. "And where is that? In a house in Portland, or Salem, or Dallas? Where is it, Alex?"

Tears rolled down my face as I finally managed to spit out, "Upstairs."

His face turned to stone. "Upstairs?"

I nodded as I wiped the tears from my eyes. Grey didn't wait for me as he twisted around and strode toward the bar. He pressed a button that revealed the hidden staircase and charged up it. Leaping to my feet, I darted after him.

Grey took the steps two at a time all the way up to the third floor. When we burst into the hallway, one of the maids nearly jumped out of her skin. I shot a quick apology at her as his long legs carried him toward the family bedrooms. As he reached the door next to his, he came to a sudden halt. Stopping beside him, we both waited with bated breath.

At last, Grey turned the handle and pushed the door wide. Without another pause, he stepped into the room. Even though I knew he needed me to know where the Grimoire was hidden, I waited a moment. I'd seen enough of the things Azure had done in this room, and I wasn't thrilled to have to physically enter her space.

Taking a breath, I stepped into the room and reached out to close the door behind me. A gasp escaped me a second before the mist obscured my vision.

I couldn't stay long. The situation within Sacred Summit was precarious, and I had to get back before I was missed. While Ivan would never question my actions, I didn't need him getting curious. He was one being that never understood that curiosity would get him killed, and there would be no satisfaction to bring him back.

As usual, my adolescent bedroom appeared untouched. A mark of my mother's care, undoubtedly. She would allow no other into the room, and she wouldn't dare to touch anything herself. I'd trained her well.

Reaching behind me, I attempted to turn the doorknob, pleased to find it locked. Then I stepped farther into the room, seeking out the bookshelf that was built into the corner. I was halfway to it when I heard the laugh.

At once, my eyes closed and I stopped to listen. She yelled his name in a chiding manner with no force behind it. Then the laugh again. He was tickling her.

"Ow! That hurt," *I heard him scold.*

"You were warned," *she answered.*

A smile pulled at my lips as I unconsciously moved

closer to the wall. They continued to bicker, but I knew where this was heading. Running my fingers across the wall, I disabled the spell that allowed me to eavesdrop on my brother. Still, I was smiling.

He was fond of this one. There had been others over the years, but after the catastrophe that was Spring Solas, he hadn't bothered to become attached to any. This one, however, made him laugh. Made him joyous with her, and anxious without her. It made me want to grab the girl by the shoulders and shake her until she understood how lucky she was. And to make sure she didn't ruin it. Grey deserved happiness.

Another smile pulled at my lips as I took a moment to glance around the room. It had been a while since my last visit. I could wrap up things with Ivan and Sacred Summit before Yule. Then I could spare a few weeks of vacation. I could visit them all, and he could introduce me to the girl. He would like that.

Shaking my head, I dispelled of the nostalgia and headed toward the bookcase.

"Alex? What is it?"

I shook my head, feeling tainted from head to toe. In all of my visions, I hadn't been stuck in someone else's mind since Freyja. The last thing I had expected was to get stuck living through Azure's assessment. What was worse was knowing that, in that moment, Azure had wanted to meet me. She thought I was good for him.

"Alex? Talk to me," Grey urged, his hands resting on my shoulders.

Shaking my head, I let our eyes meet for a second. Then I looked at his lips and announced, "She came back often. One time, she heard us in your bedroom. That was when she decided to visit for Yule." Before he could get caught up in that, I plunged on with, "And she kept thinking about some guy named Ivan who, I believe, was part of Sacred Summit. There was something about a situation she needed to resolve, but I don't know anything else."

"Ivan? The name was Ivan?" His face had turned white.

"Yes. Why?"

"Ivan is the husband of Marlena, the heir of Sacred Summit. When her mother steps down, Ivan will be married to their High Priestess."

My eyebrows rose. "How do you know that? I thought the covens didn't interact?"

"No, we just don't allow our own to trespass, except in special circumstances. That doesn't mean that we never see one another, or that our Priests and Priestesses don't meet on occasion to discuss things."

"Where do you usually meet?"

He shrugged, "We prefer neutral locations, so we often meet in New England. It was at one such meeting that I met Marlena and Ivan."

"Well, if I were you, I'd figure out what happened with them. From how she sounded, Azure was about to tie up loose ends."

His eyes grew wide. "You don't think..."

"I don't know what to think. I don't know what we walked into. But I can tell you that her Grimoire is hidden in a compartment behind the third shelf down on that bookcase."

There was no need to tell him that the wards around the book were strong enough to kill. He could feel that himself. Which was why he didn't have to worry about it, because Azure had woven him into the spells. I no longer had any doubt that when he opened that book, he would find his name scrawled in his own blood. Grey was the most important person in Azure's life, and she had wanted to share everything with him. Even this.

Once Grey had retrieved the book, he walked slowly back toward me, his eyes never leaving the ebony leather. We both knew he was afraid to open it and find the truth. At the same time, we both knew that every second spent without knowing was eating him alive.

"Come on. Let's go somewhere more comfortable," he suggested in a low voice.

I nodded and let him pull me toward the door. Glancing askance at the wall between their bedrooms, the hair on the back of my neck rose suddenly. As the prickling feeling grew stronger, I pulled my hand from his and turned to place my palm against the wall. The spell was still there, albeit dormant.

The magick filled me in an instant and I began to craft it into something similar to the spell that had dismantled the cloak Azure had placed on her magick. Instead of acting as a virus, however, I welded it into a sledgehammer. This wasn't a spell that required subtlety and finesse. It was meant to destroy.

In the second I unleashed it, I knew it would

be successful. My spell slammed into hers, displaying veins of magick like an electric web across the entire wall. Then it all vanished, leaving no trace of mine or Azure's magick. Taking a breath, I turned to see Grey staring at me with his mouth agape.

I didn't give him a chance to question. Instead, I placed my hand in his and repeated his suggestion to find somewhere more fitting for this conversation. When we left, the door was still unlocked.

As I'd warned Grey, I couldn't read the Grimoire. As he'd assured me, he could. I don't know when Azure added Grey's name to the book, but it was written in his blood, right beneath hers on the inside cover. When he suggested that he write it all out for me in a separate notebook, I refused. That book was the closest Grey would ever get to knowing his sister. For good or ill. And I knew all of Azure that I'd ever wanted to.

It also meant that the fallout over Ivan and Sacred Summit was his to deal with. Considering I'd given him an approximate timeline for

Azure's movements, it shouldn't have been hard to discover what happened. But Grey couldn't flip to a page and decide to read it. As desperate as he was to know who his sister really was, there was no rushing him.

Around the beginning of March, I was surprised when he asked Spring and I to meet him at his house after school. By the time I arrived, they were both sitting at the table in the basement. I walked in on them both throwing back a shot of whiskey.

"What did I miss?"

"Nothing yet," Grey answered.

"Just prepping for the worst," Spring grumbled as she poured herself another shot. Then she raised it up to Grey and said, "She's here now. Want to tell me why I needed this?"

He waited until I took a seat before he opened the briefcase sitting on the table. One by one, he set seventeen manila envelopes in front of us. Before we could even reach for them, he pulled out Azure's Grimoire and laid them across the files.

At once, Spring's face lost all color and she laid her shaking palms flat overtop the glass surface. After taking a few deep breaths, she glared up at Grey. "What is going on?"

Without looking at us, Grey trailed his fingertips over the folders. He paused on the one nearest me and I couldn't ignore the name labeling the folder. His voice sounded rehearsed when he announced, "Seventeen cases of madness. Four early cases of individuals being institutionalized. Then seventeen prompt suicides."

"Azure's victims," I murmured.

He nodded once.

"Victims? What does that mean?" Spring demanded, her eyes growing wide.

Grey's eyes raised to hers and the words fell. "Azure is an assassin."

Chapter Forty Eight

POWERLESS

Spring looked as if she were about to vomit. Just as she was turning away, Grey reached across the table and took her hand. At once, we all froze.

She was the first to recover as her eyes darted to me and back to him. "She told you." He nodded. "And you believed her?" Tears began to form in her eyes and I could almost hear her pulse pounding.

His jaw set a second before he said, "I believed Azure. She admitted what she'd done."

Spring shook her head. Violently. "No. She would never."

"I tricked it out of her," I admitted. Then I took a breath and added, "The same way I tricked it out of you. Grey heard you both."

Her eyes narrowed into a glare. "You bitch."

"So I've been called," I said.

Slowly, Grey released her. "Relax, Spring. You don't have anything to fear from Azure. Not anymore."

She raised her chin even as her lip curled. "You just told me she's an assassin, Grey. Forgive me if I don't believe you."

Instead of answering, Grey looked to me. "Tell her."

There were so many layers to that statement, an onion would have cried over them. As it was, I took a breath and met Spring's expectant gaze. Then I told her everything that had occurred between Azure and myself from the moment Spring left me in that café. When I told her how Azure's magick was stripped from her, she waved me to a stop.

"Is this true?" she breathed, her eyes boring into Grey's. "Is her magick gone?"

He nodded. "It's true. Azure is powerless."

Tears sprang to her eyes and she relaxed her fists so that her fingers splayed across the table-top. Bowing her head, it sounded like she was laughing and crying at the same time. It might have been a good thing if the laugh didn't sound so sarcastic.

"Powerless? Azure?" she muttered, raising her tear-streaked face. "No. No, she may be without her magick, but she is anything but powerless. Magick or no magick, we will all feel her wrath."

"If she recovers her sanity," Grey announced, bringing our attention back to the files.

"What do you mean?" Spring demanded.

"Her first four victims were experiments. They survived several years in padded cells after she stripped their magick. In all those years, not one of them showed any sign of improvement. And when given the opportunity, all four lunged at the chance to take their own lives. Who's to say Azure will ever recover from this?"

Shaking her head, Spring announced, "She will. If anyone is capable of it, Azure is. Then she will finish what she started, if she has to do so with her bare hands."

He shook his head. "She won't hurt you anymore, Spring. That I can promise."

There was something in the way he said it. Something that told me there was more to the story. He was holding back, and I was desperate to know why.

"What aren't you telling us?" I asked, my eyes taking a moment to clash off of his.

In that brief second that we were bound, he said one word, "Pass."

As had happened once before, the word hit me like a physical blow. In months, neither of us had needed to use it. Bit by careful bit, we had exposed ourselves to the other. Now, with something as important as his homicidal sister, he chose to invoke his last pass.

While I was stunned, Spring was not. "Pass? Are you serious? Why can't you just tell us?"

Guilt lanced across our link as Grey's eyes lowered to the table. "Not 'us.' Just her," he admitted with a heavy sigh.

Wow.

Up until that very second, I had forgotten my place. Forgotten hers. His. I'd let myself forget that I was temporary, he was permanent, and Spring was stationary. And I was upset because he was treating us accordingly?

Even when there was bad blood between them, Grey and Spring were a team. She mended the rifts he created, and he secured her place in the coven. They relied on what each other brought to their community, and they pushed one another to do better. Despite their betrayals, they still had each other's backs.

And I was a temporary affliction.

Without another word to either of them, I rose to my feet and walked out the door. I arrived in my bedroom in the same step and curled up on my bed to let the heartache have me. Just for a little while. Just long enough for me to stop recognizing that Spring was the most stable thing in Grey's life. Long enough to stop remembering that Nathan was the most stable thing in mine.

Grey and I tried to ignore it. Neither of us wanted to ruin what time we had left; especially since it seemed like it was slipping through our hands like sand. So, I tried not to dwell on this new secret that was drawing him and Spring closer together. I tried not to dwell on the jealousy that gnawed on my heart every time I saw them together. And I tried like hell to pretend that I was jealous over how close they were becoming, instead of the fact that I wished my best friend was there by my side in the way she was at his.

I wasn't good at pretending.

I was even worse at lying.

The morning of my eighteenth birthday, I woke up and tears sprang immediately to my eyes. They weren't happy tears. Instead, they were the grief-stricken kind as some inner promise of my own snapped in half. From the day I left Cedar Creek, part of me always believed I would return on my eighteenth birthday. Yet, when I opened my eyes, I realized that it wasn't meant to be. I had to finish what I'd started.

It surprised me to find that Grey understood.

After breakfast, my parents and I all dressed up and went to a portrait studio in town to fulfill one more tradition. Ever since I was born, a professional portrait was taken of me and my family on my birthday. Even the years of burning had not interfered.

When we got back, it was to find Grey and Faye swaying lazily on a new porch swing. As soon as they saw me, they smiled. Faye's was full of excitement. Grey's was more timid than that. And when we all entered the house and Faye went into the kitchen to help my dad with lunch, he held me close for a minute and whispered into my ear, "It's okay for you to hate me. At least for today."

For that one day, I did. When it passed, however, I came to the realization that there was a shift. A turning of the hourglass. Other than the strengthening bond, there was little left between Grey and I. And as April passed, yet one more of the ties that bind fell away.

The house was finished.

It was time to move on.

On April twenty-fourth, a couple with two boys and a golden retriever put in an offer on the house. On the twenty-sixth, my parents flew out to Colorado for a week in search of their next project. They left me behind to begin packing. It was the first step in separating our lives.

Beltane dawned over the world with a joyous sunrise and drifted into a warm, bright day. The sun was so blinding, colors began to run together, and anything on the edge of my vision turned white. It seemed so perfect as I delved into my sanctuary and picked the early flowers of the hawthorn tree and began to weave them into a flower crown.

I felt him arrive a few moments later. Then his exaggerated sigh reached me as he climbed beneath the overhanging branches that I refused to trim. "No candles or incense. Not a single sign of respect to the God and Goddess on this day especially. You really are terrible at rituals," he pretended to chide as he sat beside me.

I made a point to place the crown on my head, giving him an impish look. "Didn't I tell you once before that I'd rather not waste a ritual on pleasuring myself?"

A roguish grin spread across his face as he placed a hand on my waist and pulled me toward him. "Pleasure is what this day is all about," he whispered in my ear before nipping at my neck. Then he kissed me and I relearned what the word pleasure meant.

Fire was borne on his lips, and I gave him some of my electricity in turn. Even while my body suffused with heat, the nerves jumped and snapped as the static ran through them. Grey's hands traveled over me, with the thin dress I wore serving as no barrier to the sensations his skin ignited. At last, the desire coursing through me reached a peak.

Minutes melted away into hours as our storm ebbed and swelled. At last, the wildfires were buried and thunder rolled as the last of the lightning faded into the night. Together, Grey and I drifted to sleep.

And for the first time since the coma, I dreamed.

Chapter Forty Nine

LET GO

I stood in a sea of hawthorn flowers beneath a brilliant blue sky. The white petals reached up to my waist and their bitter scent flooded my nose. It all seemed so bright that I could almost see a halo of fairy dust giving everything a distinct sparkle.

In a blink, a wind kicked up and all the flowers blew into the air. My vision was clouded with pink and white blossoms as they flew past. As the last began to vanish, their scent was replaced by the enticing smell of apple blossoms, and the fluttering oak leaves seemed to sound a 'welcome home' march.

Tears filled my eyes as I looked down Old Grove Road. At first, it was just as I remembered. When the tears began to fall, however, I realized there was someone standing in-between the bicycle tracks pushed into the dirt.

An older Faye smiled at me and nodded her head in acknowledgement. "We will meet again," she assured me. Then she turned toward the woods and vanished between two of the towering oak trees.

I started after her, but stopped when I felt a tiny hand pulling on mine. Shocked, I looked down into familiar silver irises set in a face that looked much like mine. My mouth fell open as I slowly kneeled in the dirt. Taking both of her hands in mine, I turned her toward me, so that I could see every part of us in her face. And as I held her there, my lungs constricted when she smiled and two large dimples appeared in her cheeks.

"You're staring, Mommy. It's not polite to stare."

"No," I assured her, "it's not." But I couldn't stop myself. There was but one thing I wanted to do more than look at her, and that was to hold her.

As if she could read my thoughts, the little girl pushed herself forward and wrapped her arms around me, nuzzling her forehead into the crook of my neck. For a moment, I was too choked up to react. Then my arms wrapped around her and I hugged her as tightly as I dared.

Something wasn't right. It was off somehow.

Though I was almost crushing her to me, she seemed less solid. At the same time, where she rested against my body began to grow warm. I couldn't understand what it was until I opened my eyes and realized that she was fading away. By increments, the child in my arms was seeping into my body. Into my womb.

It didn't stop with her. When all of her was harbored inside of me, it seemed like the rest of my world meant to follow her. All around me, Old Grove Road began to seep into my body, following after my daughter, and leaving only the blackness in its wake.

Fear thundered through my body as I turned, and turned, and turned, and found nothing but the blackness. The darkness was absolute, without a single light to guide me. My chest tightened and I tried to think, but the panic froze my mind and I couldn't breathe.

Then a voice called out, "Lex!"

I spun in place, flinging myself into his arms. At once, I felt home. In that moment, nothing else existed but the two of us. Nothing else mattered but what his presence promised me. With him, I was where I belonged.

"Come home, Lex. Come home."

At once, I nodded, pulling back a little so he could see the promise on my face. The last thing I saw before

I awoke was not the empty blackness, but a pair of
beautiful emerald eyes.

I realized two things when my eyes snapped
open: I was alone, and I was still beneath the
hawthorn tree. Dawn had passed by some time
ago, because the day was bright outside of my
shelter. Grey had been gone awhile, but had seen
fit to retrieve a blanket for me before he'd left.
Not that it mattered. Something in me felt ...
hollow.

Contrary to what some distant portion of my
brain willed me to do, I stayed there. Stretched
out beneath the boughs, I stared up at clumps of
flowers as they took over so much of the tree that
I could not see any leaves. Their white petals re-
flected every scrap of sunlight, almost flashing
as the breeze tossed them about. Beneath their
cavorting, my mind studied the significance of
a dream.

Having never seen a fairy, I hadn't thought
sleeping beneath a hawthorn on Beltane night
would set up the risk that I'd be carried off to the
land of the Fey. As it happened, I'd discounted

much more than that concerning the tree. Not the least of which was its use in many common fertility rites. Given that Beltane was the only pagan holiday that encouraged love making for the entire purpose of procreation, I almost couldn't believe my own stupidity. No better recipe existed. Grey and I were practically begging for it.

As the thoughts filtered through my brain, they were forced to skirt the hollowness that existed there. In an effort to make it easier, I focused on the puzzle that was losing so much of my mind. It was harder to force a cognitive response than it should have been and I fell back on a self-awareness I hadn't accessed since my Ascension.

At once, a full mental calculation took place. The answer it gave back to me was as astounding as it was unsettling.

I can't feel Grey!

Even thinking the words felt like being electrocuted. At once, it felt like my thoughts fell over the edge of a cliff into the hole where his emotions had once been. Part of me let them linger there, wondering what could have happened to cause us to disconnect in that way. Another part began the search for something else. Which it found.

Yes, the awareness I had of Grey was gone. A new awareness took its place.

In the pit of my stomach, where everything that made me a woman was centered, I could feel the gentle pulse of something greater than myself. It was like the fluttering of fairy wings, that life was so small. Tiny. Delicate. So easy to miss. But I didn't. I couldn't miss *this*.

Morgan had once told me that having a child meant that they would become a part of their mother. Well, she was right. That fluttering, tiny, fragile little awareness made me all too knowledgeable about what was happening now. What had happened last night. What would happen in the months to come. I would know every breath of this child's life just as I had been able to know her father's only a few short hours ago.

At that point, my brain short-circuited. For a minute, I thought I would cry. I wanted to cry. It seemed the most appropriate time in my life to sit there and bawl my eyes out. But I couldn't make the tears come. Or the indignation, or sadness, or self-loathing. In my mind's perfect sense of self-preservation, it had dropped me into the numbness and it wouldn't let me resurface.

That numbness caused me to push myself to my feet. I gathered up the blanket and my dress and flashed into my bedroom. Then I grabbed clothes and took a shower, all while on autopilot. Even when I went downstairs to make myself breakfast, I thought it was a state I could continue to survive in. At least for a while.

Then Grey appeared in my kitchen looking white as a sheet. I didn't even have it in me to be shocked. Not even when he grabbed my arms and dragged me into a hug so tight, I thought he might crack a rib.

"Oh, thank Goddess!" His hands moved to either side of my face and he leaned his forehead against mine. "I thought something had happened to you."

The numbness was fading. Fast. In its absence, everything I couldn't say got lodged in my throat.

"What's going on, Alex? I ... I can't feel you anymore."

In my head, I'd been able to ignore it. Despite

my thoughts darting around the space he once occupied in my mind, I was able to keep moving forward without thinking about it. Now that he said it, however, it hit me just as hard as it had the first time.

It was worse when I raised my eyes to meet his. For the first time since we met, nothing happened. Not a spark or a rise in temperature. There was no smoke. No fire. No thunder or lightning. The air didn't become charged and the oxygen level didn't drop. This once, we were just two people who had the option of walking away.

"I can't feel you, either," I admitted, surprised by how little heartbreak marred my calm façade.

"Why?" he murmured, more to himself than to me. "What could have happened between yesterday and today?"

At once, I fought the urge to bark a sarcastic laugh. What hadn't happened? Of all days to lose absolute control over ourselves, we chose to do so on Beltane beneath a hawthorn tree. The fact that we hadn't expected anything to happen was a form of irony that was not lost on me.

"Alex? Do you know what happened?"

It wasn't until he asked the question that I

realized a sneer had curled my lip. Shaking my head, I tried to clear my expression. Grey was having none of it.

"You know what happened, don't you? Damn it, Alex, I'm freaking out here. Tell me what you know. Please?"

As he'd done a thousand times before, Grey took a step toward me. If I let him, he would take me in his arms and do his best to comfort me. He would kiss my lips and promise to figure it out. And the second his skin touched mine, I would be forced to admit that he felt foreign to me.

I took two steps back, holding up a hand to stop him. "Don't touch me, Grey. Please. Just don't touch me."

He looked as if I'd shoved a stake through his heart. It was the first time I had ever seen him so exposed. Vulnerable. At once, I was touched that I was the one he felt he didn't have to conceal things from. Then I realized that the reason was because he was used to not being able to conceal things from me. That would soon change.

"I don't understand, Alex. What did I do? What's wrong?" he murmured.

It's now or never, Lex.

Taking a deep breath, I looked him in the eyes and announced, "I'm pregnant, Grey."

After the words left my mouth, I didn't know which of us needed to sit down more. Grey sank onto the stool by the island and I leaned back against the counter as I tried to get my quaking knees under control. All the while, I had to focus everything I had on breathing.

It was bad enough knowing, but I hadn't even dared to think the words in my own head. Now that I'd said them, it felt like my world was performing a tailspin. Of all the complications I didn't need...

Silence reigned for at least twenty minutes between us. It was so hard to wrap our minds around that asking us to converse was too great a task. At last, Grey raised his eyes to mine and I sighed.

"How could we let this happen?"

I shrugged. "I think I'm kind of impressed that it didn't happen sooner, to be honest. You and I weren't exactly the pinnacle of safe sex couples."

His head dropped into his hands. "When did it happen?" he groaned.

"Last night."

Grey's entire body jerked before he turned an accusing glare on me. "That's not possible," he growled.

My spine straightened and my teeth ground together. "You know it is."

"You can't know this soon," he argued.

"Really? Why do you think I can't feel you, Grey? It's because I can feel someone else instead." As I said it, I lowered a hand to my stomach, where the barest spark of life was flickering deep inside of me.

I had never in my life seen a man look as haunted as Grey did in that moment. It was the look of a man who'd stood on this particular cliff before, and had suffered the worst kind of fall. The question was written all over his face as he debated what to do now, and which fate he would force upon us.

At last, his eyes seemed to come back from the edge and really look at me. The longer he stared, the more determined he appeared. At last, he pushed up off the stool and loomed over me.

"Leave, Alex."

My mouth dropped. "What?"

"Leave. Today. Now," he urged.

"Why?"

"Go home, Lex. You take that baby and you get as far from my family and my coven as you can. Do you understand me?" There was nothing but pure desperation in his eyes, and I suddenly understood all too well.

I nodded as tears filled my eyes. "What are you going to do?"

Grey closed his eyes and drew in a deep, lasting breath. When he released it, he opened his eyes and I could see the tears gathered in them. Then he reached out and used one hand to tilt my head back a little.

Pressing a kiss to my forehead, he whispered, "I'm going to learn to let go."

When I opened my eyes, he was gone.

I was alone again.

Chapter Fifty

HOME

So, this is how it was supposed to end, I thought to myself as I sank down onto the stool Grey had vacated less than a minute ago.

Despite the urgency of his words, I couldn't move as the seconds ate away at several minutes. Some dim portion of my brain screamed at me to go. It wanted me to pack up all of my things, empty my bank account, and vanish without a thought. If I really needed time to think, I could always take a plane. Something. Anything, so long as I was on the move. So long as I escaped. And still I could not move.

The more active part of me still couldn't believe it was happening. My reality had been turned on its head, and I almost couldn't get my brain to accept it. I was just glad that there would be no fight on my hands. Grey had given me the greatest gift by telling me to go, and I couldn't wait another minute.

They said that the first step was always the hardest. If it wasn't, I wouldn't have been able to take that second step once I was off the stool. A second later, it all fell into place.

Splitting myself in two, I left the astral projection to oversee packing and preparation while the more physical part of me took my mom's car to the bank. It took at least twenty minutes to convince the tellers and managers that I was serious about wanting to close my account. At last, I was able to get what belonged to me. Then I called the airport.

Ever since Samhain, I knew that I no longer had limitations on my magick. If I wanted to see the boys at any time, all I had to do was will it into existence. Same with an astral projection or teleporting. My magick usage was back at full strength and that meant that I could do *everything* once again. That didn't mean I was ready for everything all at once.

When I got back to the house, all of my

belongings were in boxes gathered in the living room. It was amazing how little I was taking with me. Or how the past four years of my life could be reduced to six boxes of clothes, books, and ritual supplies.

Taking a deep breath, I pictured the cottage as I had last seen it. Complete with the thrift store loveseat Nathan had somehow managed to fit through the door. Once I had a complete picture in my mind, I let the magick gather around the boxes, and I transferred them from one location to another. As soon as it was done, I sagged against the couch as the energy flew out of me.

A sarcastic smile twisted my lips as I felt my pulse grow stronger beneath the hourglass inside my wrist. It was as if it were telling me that everyone has their limits. Even when they can do everything.

With that done, and still an hour before I had to be at the airport, it was time to do the hard thing. While I wasn't about to pick up the phone and call my parents, I couldn't let them come home to an empty house without some idea of what had happened. My dad, especially, wouldn't be able to understand why I left a mere two days before they returned, and that wasn't a conversation I was ready to have.

Running up to the office, I grabbed a single sheet of stationery and cut it into three pieces. The first one was the easiest to write. It was for Faye and simply said, *We will meet again.* I knew she would pass on my regards to Delaire and Catori. Of everyone I was leaving behind, I knew those three would accept it best, and lament it least.

When I picked up the pen to write a note to Grey, I already knew what needed to be written. Out of all the time we spent together and the things we shared, there were few things that went unsaid between us. We had come to a point where we knew each other so well, that words sometimes weren't needed. This, however, had to be said at least once, and this was my last chance. For Grey, two words sufficed.

Thank you.

By the time I finished my parents' letter and placed them all in envelopes, I was surprised at the amount of time that had passed. Taking them to the kitchen, I fanned them out on the island, knowing my mother would be diligent in delivering them to their intended recipients. Then I took the cell phone and house keys out of my pocket and spread them out beside the envelopes. At last, I was ready. As I turned to leave my parents' house for the last time, the words I'd written for them rang in my ears as if spoken in prophecy.

I'm going home.
Love, Lex

Dusk had descended by the time the taxi pulled up to the corner. Before the driver could ask me a thing, I handed him more than enough to cover my fare and stepped out into the cool night air. A gasp escaped me as soon as my foot hit the dirt that made up Old Grove Road.

For a moment, I could only stand there. Before me stretched a dark strip of cold ground, framed in by a tunnel of trees and the low spring growth coming up between them. As the wind stirred, the branches seemed to wave to me in welcome, beckoning me home.

Home.

Just thinking the single word caused my heart to swell and I knew that with each step I took, the longing I had carried with me every day since leaving here would fall away. So, I took the first step.

My pulse was so loud and quick in my ears, I could have danced to it. I almost did. If I didn't want to treasure every moment of the long walk home, I would have laughed and spun about in the middle of the road. As it was, I still had to stop myself from sprinting straight to the cottage. To see for myself that it was still there and everything I knew and loved and had waited for was once more within arm's reach.

As I walked, I couldn't help but remember the last time I traversed this road. Back then, I'd been escorted by the other two Musketeers, fighting the urge to cry. My memories of them had been buried inside of a glass vial; it was my buried treasure.

Different tears threatened my vision now. In my mind, I pulled that vial out from behind the black wall I'd been forced to banish it to. The cork guarding my ocean sand twisted away and everything came flooding back. A second later, the last of the longing melted away. I didn't have to miss anything anymore.

Stopping before the gate, I could feel my chest constrict. All at once, it looked as if nothing had changed, and everything was different. The garden was more overgrown and wilder than it had been before my departure, the fence had been mended in several locations, and a new roof had been put the cottage a few years ago. At the same time, the gargoyles continued to keep watch from their posts on either side of the gate. A fight had been put up to keep the bench from vanishing within the garden's plot to take over the lawn. And a fresh salt line marked the boundary between the world outside my protection, and the world that was all mine.

Except that it wasn't just mine anymore. The biggest change that I became aware of wasn't something to be seen, but felt. My hand closed over the locket around my neck as I realized that the cottage belonged to Nathan, too.

I wasn't in this alone.

With that thought in mind, I patted the gargoyles on the head and pushed open the gate. At long last, I was home.

ACKNOWLEDGEMENTS

When it comes to making a book, it is impossible to do it yourself and have it turn out well. I am so lucky that I don't have to do that. Throughout this entire series, there are several people who have been integral to this adventure, and I would like to thank them all for being a part of my life and this story.

First of all, I have to thank my best friend, Chrissy. She is the most talented person I know. Besides writing her own books, she takes time out of her busy schedule to help me piece together my own manuscripts and turn them into works of art. Cover design, interior galley, and chapter graphics are just a few of the incredible things she does for me, and I could not be more grateful. You deserve all the credit and praise for the things you create, Chrissy. Thank you so much for everything.

Next, I would like to thank my sister, Mariah, for always being there for me. When Lex's story was first written way back when I was nineteen, she was the one person who was in constant demand for updates. We've bonded over this series in ways that most would probably consider unhealthy. We don't get to have a lot of adventures together, sister dear, but I'm glad we can share in this one.

A small shout-out to my niece, Aurora. She is the main reason I keep doing what I'm doing. Even though we're so far away, this is a part of my life that I get to share with her. That means something to me. Love you, Beasty.

My Nana and Papa always make the acknowledgments and that is for one simple reason: I couldn't have done any of this without them. Their support and encouragement has kept me going more than anything else could have. They've always pushed me to follow the weird little trains of thought that my mind follows, and I've always been given the opportunity to express them. Growing up with these two people in my life has made all the difference, and I have nothing to repay them with but my love and gratitude.

When it comes to accepting me as I am, no one does it better than my significant other. Like Lex and Grey, I know the worst parts of myself, and therefore they cannot be used against me. That doesn't mean they're easy to live with, and I'm amazed Christopher is still putting up with my nonsense, if I'm being honest. As different as we are, there's still so much love and respect there, and I cannot imagine my life with anyone else. I'm all yours, Honey. I love you.

Last of all, I have to thank my Big Dude. You're the most important person in my life. I will be able to say that for the rest of my life. Even when I drive you crazy, you love and support me in every way possible, and you are the greatest mother in the world for it. Thank you for believing in me and loving me like you do. You go above and beyond every day, and I love you more and more for it.

ABOUT THE AUTHOR

Hollow Ryan is a Michigan native with thirty years spent too much in her own head, and twenty years putting it all on paper. This obsession with the written word has led her to publish the five-book paranormal series, *The Prideful Magick Collection*. It has also started her on a journey full of *Demon Kin*.

When not working on her ever-expanding Work List, Hollow is dealing with the three most spoiled fur-children to be found in Northeastern Michigan. (Her spouse is absolutely to blame for that.)

For more information, please visit:
www.hollowryan.com

Chapter One

REUNITED

I'd forgotten what it was to feel so alive. The second I stepped into the circle, I remembered.

All around me, an electric pulse shot through the barrier, awakening every tiny aspect of the dormant spells. For a moment, I was overwhelmed by the information that swirled around me. Pieces of the past drifted through me, leaving imprints in my skin. As each memory seeped into me, I could feel the weight of responsibility settle into my bones. Upon my return, I took up my duties to this place, and now I could never take them back.

Taking a deep breath, I stepped farther into the fold. Like a rubber band, everything snapped back into focus. Moonlight bathed the circle in a pale glow, lingering over the smaller circle in the center. A brisk, cool wind pushed through the barrier and swirled around me before slipping out again. For that one brief moment, I could almost hear a whispered *"Alexandria"* in its gentle embrace. Fighting tears, I took my place in the center.

It was harder to breathe once inside of it. There was so much history buried in that soil, and much of it was mine. My past life of Mary Sullivan was burned at the stake in this place. I'd found that out during my Wiccaning at the age of nine. On the night of my Ascension, I was witness to my mentor's suicide. Yet another blessing met by a curse. That was the balance of being a witch.

Standing in the midst of the memories, I started to pull back. If I lost myself in them now, I would never find my way out.

With another deep breath, I raised my face to the moon and closed my eyes. I let the power fill me. There was so much of it. More than I had ever needed. Now I had a use for it, and I would make it count.

I let the magick fill me until I could hold no more, then I pushed it out. A dome of it formed around me that slowly grew outward. Farther and farther I pushed it, cataloging every single flicker of life as it encompassed them. As it began to inch over the entirety of Cedar Creek, I felt at peace. All of this was mine, and I intended to claim it.

When the entire town was within my grasp, I sank a pulse into every life-force.

The Witch of Old Grove Road had returned, and now all of Cedar Creek knew it.

When I had first returned to the cottage, I let the nostalgia have me. In the dim light by the fire, I relived every memory, and cried every tear. There was a cost to being home, just as there was the promise of it. Within the shadows, I let the memories have me. Come dawn, I remembered what it was to live for the moment.

Daylight brought responsibility. So, I put on my grungy, paint-stained overalls and a tank top and set to work with a dust rag. Keeping a notepad and a pen in my back pocket, I began to jot down everything I thought I would need. It didn't take me long to realize that there was a whole lot more to be done than my little dust rag and some water could handle.

With a sigh, I finished off the grocery list before I headed out to the garden. As soon as I was amongst the wilderness that had once been a forest of organized chaos, a pang shot through my heart. Not only were the non-native species nothing but compost now, but the carefully trimmed weeds had exploded and choked out many of their brethren over the years. Making the list of what needed to be replaced was difficult enough, but what was worse was knowing how much time it would take to restore it to the glory of before.

For a moment, my mind stalled on that word. *Before.* As if there were stages of my life that were encompassed in simple words like *before, after,* and *now.* Before I left Cedar Creek. After I left. Now that I've returned. The history of Cedar Creek from before was something I didn't need repeated. The after, however, would have to be broken down for me, and the list of people I trusted for that conversation was short.

Shaking the thoughts off, I went inside and grabbed my wallet. Shoving that in my pocket with the grocery list, I started the long walk to the store. It wasn't so bad at first, but a quarter of a mile down Norfolk Street I was wishing I had a bike. One more thing to add to the list.

As I was getting to the business quarter, I was gratified to find that a few new ventures had filled some of the spaces in the older buildings. There was even a café that looked promising. A fact that seemed reinforced by my sudden change of direction once the doors opened and I caught the scent beyond. My stomach growled in pleasant anticipation as I entered the quaint establishment.

It didn't occur to me what kind of reception I could expect. Even though my announcement had hit every living creature in Cedar Creek, it had somehow escaped my notice how it might affect them. As soon as I walked in, however, I was treated to several people performing a double-take. Conversations faltered as I walked past, and I felt my spine straighten in response. Only the barista who took my order seemed ignorant as to who I was.

I had just finished paying her when a bell above the door jangled in announcement of two new arrivals. All at once, my chest tightened and I couldn't catch my breath fast enough. Bracing my hands against the counter, I closed my eyes and let myself get lost in the feeling of security that enveloped me.

The pair stopped almost right inside the door, and I could feel his gaze boring into my back. For several seconds, he neither moved, nor spoke. My brain was short-circuiting and I couldn't figure out what to say or do. Not when the moment I had waited almost four years for was finally before me.

At last, I heard him clear his throat and I raised my head a little. Then a warm, rich voice forced out in a casual tone, "Only one girl I know would wear those overalls in public."

A wide smile spread across my face as I stared at the wall behind the counter. After clearing my throat, I remarked, "Only one girl you know has enough pride not to care what anyone else thinks." When I'd finished speaking, I turned slowly in place. The second my eyes met his, everything in the world felt right.

There was another moment of silence as we smiled at each other. Even that seemed right. Just like old times. Then our eyes broke apart and we scanned one another, noting all of the changes and taking stock of what the years had stolen from our sights.

It looked like he'd finally stopped growing, though not before he reached six foot one. His brown hair was cut shorter than the last time I'd seen it, and no longer fell into his emerald eyes. What little baby fat had clung to his face when we were fourteen was gone now, leaving his features in sharp relief. Opposite of this occurrence, the rest of his body had filled out with the ropy muscle common to teenage boys. In four years, the gangly teenager had vanished and a man had replaced him.

"You're home," he mused.

"I'm home."

Nathan wasted only a second before taking three long strides toward me and I rushed to meet him. I threw my arms around his neck in the same instant that his arms wrapped around my waist, pulling me off the ground in a crushing hug. Both of us laughed like giddy children, unaware or just unable to care about the people watching us. My hold tightened as he swung me around and I squeezed my eyes shut in order to absorb the feel of him. As had happened with Matt, every memory of my time with him came flooding back.

There was my first day of school when we were introduced. The day I first traveled down Old Grove Road and passed through the gate into Morgan's garden. I could almost feel the ghost of his hand on my arm from when he'd dragged me out. All at once, countless memories of bus rides, shared classes, and shopping trips fluttered through my head like the pages of a book. Those images blurred together, adding up to the time where we barely spoke, but kept each other's secrets.

Then the memories hit a speed bump on the day I'd met Matt, and they trickled into the strange phase our friendship had taken prior to Morgan's suicide. At last, I was forced to relive every second of our time together following my Ascension. Tears filled my eyes as I found myself remembering the last time Nathan's arms were around me. The hourglass scar inside of my wrist throbbed as I was forced to relive the moment we had said goodbye.

Before I could stop myself, my body spasmed with a small sob and I felt Nathan easing me back to the ground. As soon as my toes touched the tile floor, I loosened my arms and brought my right hand up to scrub away at the tears trying to make an escape. This was neither the time nor place to be crying.

As my left arm was slipping down his shoulder to rest on his forearm, Nathan released a choking sound. Before I had time to wonder what that was about, he grabbed my hand and straightened out my arm, examining it in the light. Unable to look at the scars magickally burned into my skin, I watched his features instead. Remorse was written across his face, but I couldn't bear to ask him about it. There would be time for that later.

"Oh, Lex," Nathan whispered in a voice low enough that only I could hear it.

Working to catch his eyes with mine, I forced a sarcastic grin into place. "It's not as bad as it looks. Not anymore."

"Uh, Nathan, I'm just gonna-" Mark took a step back toward the door before I ever realized he was there.

Nathan turned toward him, but didn't release my hand. "Sorry, man. Get yourself something to eat. I'll drive you back once lunch is over."

Mark looked between us for a long moment. Then he offered me a timid smile and said, "It's good to have you back, Alex."

Before I could reply, I heard the barista calling out my order. For the third time. All at once, the world seemed to snap back into place and the present popped the bubble that had surrounded us. Forcing a smile, I shot Nathan a look that said 'give me a minute' before my hand slipped out of his.

Once I'd picked up my order, I motioned to a table and Nathan was quick to follow. The second he dropped into the seat beside me, all else was forgotten. All that mattered was that we were together again.

There were so many things to say. So much that I needed him to know. More than what I'd been through or the things I'd done, I wanted Nathan to know that I essentially hadn't changed. I was still the proud, stubborn, smartass little witch he'd always known. I was still his best friend.

And of all the things I wanted to say ... I didn't say a word.

Neither did he.

We reveled in that. The old camaraderie where we could sit side by side and not speak a word. Not about our pasts or presents. Not even about how dreamlike this all still felt. No questions. No answers. No words. Just us.

Staring into his emerald eyes, it was all I could do to stay in the moment. There was time for the heavy, and we had it now. All of it. For the rest of our lives, Nathan and I could deal with having lost each other. That didn't have to start the second we were reunited.

A smile pulled at his lips and I knew we were thinking the same thing. Even so, there was one memory neither of us could ignore. The one that meant the most to both of us. When the world was black and I was in his arms as he asked me to come home. Finally, I had listened.

Because of Nathan, I had returned to Cedar Creek.